P9-CQB-938

ALSO BY

SARAH BLAKLEY-CARTWRIGHT

Red Riding Hood

ALICE SADIE CELINE

SARAH BLAKLEY-CARTWRIGHT

SIMON & SCHUSTER

New York London Toronto Sydney New Delhi

Simon & Schuster
1230 Avenue of the Americas
New York, NY 10020

This book is a work of fiction. Any references to historical events, real people, or real places are used fictitiously. Other names, characters, places, and events are products of the author's imagination, and any resemblance to actual events or places or persons, living or dead, is entirely coincidental.

First Simon & Schuster hardcover edition November 2023

Interior design by Wendy Blum

Manufactured in the United States of America

10 9 8 7 6 5 4 3 2 1

Library of Congress Cataloging-in-Publication Data

Names: Blakley-Cartwright, Sarah, author.
Title: Alice Sadie Celine / Sarah Blakley-Cartwright.
Description: First Simon & Schuster hardcover edition 2023 |
New York : Simon & Schuster, 2023. |
Identifiers: LCCN 2023000517 | ISBN 9781668021590 (hardcover) |
ISBN 9781668021613 (ebook)
Classification: LCC PS3602.L34983 A45 2023 | DDC [Fic]—dc23
LC record available at https://lccn.loc.gov/2023000517

ISBN 978-1-6680-2159-0
ISBN 978-1-6680-2161-3 (ebook)

For Carroll

I lived like an angry guest.

—Anne Sexton

FIRST WEEK OF JUNE

Chapter One

ALICE

FRIDAY

Opening night and, as soon as they could get Leontes's detachable sleeves Velcroed on—the adhesive tape was moist and mucky in the record June heat, not sticking to the tunic—the show would begin. The sun had risen each day that week angry and blinking, baking the asphalt. Alice, sweltering, was tucked away backstage, hidden in the narrow wings.

Sadie had once observed that Alice's favorite part of acting was disappearing. Alice couldn't deny this was true. This may have been *why* she loved coming in with clean hair and knowing someone else would take care of the rest. She would be provided the exact words to speak, down to the punctuation, and directed where to stand. Told which shoes to wear to become queen of Sicily. Alice liked to place herself in others' hands. She liked how easy it was to slip into another life.

And slip into another life she had. A year and a half ago, ditching the Bay Area—and her family, and her best friend—for Hollywood, to pursue stardust dreams she was scarcely sure she had.

It had all started in second grade, when Alice had auditioned for the school play, *Under the Sea*, and landed a role! She'd played a cold-water sea urchin who lived in the Shallows, the underworld of King Neptune's marvelous kingdom. It was considered an undesireable bit part. Alice couldn't sit down or pee. All the classmates, mermaids and starfish, shunned the monstrous urchin. Alice had one line she did not understand, about being turned into uni. Still, having been *cast*, in a *role*, to her, life could not be improved upon.

Now, in L.A., things were more complicated. Staring down the nothing, the zero, the black hole, the unmanifest, the 100-percent-pure potential, the no-thing. Submitting headshots online, not even landing auditions.

But Alice's mind was peaceful. She was inclined toward the world, and liked participating with it, even if that meant auditioning for a role and being rejected. She had what she realized so many actors lacked. She believed she had a right to be in the room.

Evenings, she worked at the lustrous lobby restaurant of a radiantly white beachside luxury hotel, where $500 a night meant rattan everything, soft-grid cotton blankets in organic shades, and buckets of seashells under museum lighting.

She worked downstairs, in the more casual, beach-level dining hall—Pico Boulevard sloped as it dropped to the shore. Elevators opened straight onto the dining room, out of which merry children poured with harassed nannies. The skinny silver flower vases were always tipping over, the paper teapot handle covers always slipping off. But the job supplied Alice with a chance to be her most refined self. She switched on the waitress role, maintaining a straight face as she logged infants' orders for Pellegrino, circling back to inquire apologetically whether Perrier would suffice. The nannies nodded, catching her eye. She was glad they did not know she, too, came from a modest dynasty.

Though she didn't need to, Alice always had a job, whether or not she was suited for them. During school, she had worked retail, at a boutique first, then a cruelty-free "skin hair and body formulations" shop, but had been rightly suspected by the manager of extending most patrons her employee discount after failing to ring up every fourth item. What could Alice say? She was a giver. It was just her nature.

And last month, she had put her waitress role on hold to return to the sweltering East Bay for rehearsals and for the show tonight—to the Brackendale, a pocket-sized community playhouse. The theater was in the basement of a large, underused movieplex—the kind that were vanishing everywhere, with the advent of streaming, on their last legs—elaborate with elevators. Audience members occasionally overheard a burst of volume, the action upstairs, giving the quieter live plays downstairs the feeling of a second-tier show.

The theater was located, providentially, not ten minutes from the childhood home of her best friend, Sadie. And yet, stunningly, Sadie had bailed on attending, with the excuse of a prebooked trip with her boyfriend. Alice felt sure she was being punished. Sadie had never forgiven Alice for moving to L.A. "Doesn't it bother you, to be a make-believe person?" she had inquired when Alice planned to pursue acting. Los Angeles was a place where Sadie, with all her managing, counseling, and advocating, wasn't. A place where Alice could reinvent herself. Not that she would. Just that she . . . could.

Perhaps for the best Sadie wasn't here. Tonight's show was off to an unsound start—Archidamus's microphone level was set to a higher input than Camillo's, so his voice thundered and boomed. Alice was aware of the sound operator taking penitent notes beside her; he'd have to recalibrate the mics' volumes.

Rehearsals were one thing, but it was different tonight, the proceedings activated by the presence of the audience. There were particulars Alice hadn't noticed before. The curtains were cheaply made: by no means velvet, not even velour. The sound operator had been munching Pringles before showtime and the can stood upright on the audio monitor beneath the call-board. His breath smelled of sour cream and onion. It was so hot the windows of the theater could fold and melt. Pity the audience. Alice hoped they'd be able to forgive it.

"Pardon," a stagehand tech whispered, scooting past with a rack of polyester-fleece prop sheep.

Every mistake that night counted; any extension of the show's three-week run would be provisional. Truth be told, there were still eight or ten lines in the play that Alice did not understand. She did not have the Folger edition many of her castmates had fluffed up with sticky tags. The edition gave a synopsis of every scene. Alice did not want to look as if she needed footnotes to digest something so handily absorbed that the entire audience broke into merriment before Leontes was even through with the line.

Why Alice didn't just SparkNotes them she could not say. Hermione's lines of dialogue were straightforward enough. That was the benefit of playing an openhanded character. No machinations, no dissembling wordplay, no complex, conflicting motivations.

Goodness was clear. Decency made sense.

Alice readied herself, positioning her velvet bodice with voluminous sleeves tight over her jeans. If the small details were sound, the rest would follow. She tried to summon regality. At her cue, she took a steadying breath and her place at center stage, beside her wrathful, insecure, and tyrannical husband. Hot, hot, the lights were. She felt her freckles flush. Her face, really: every inch was blanketed with them. Back one middle-school summer, at Fernwood summer camp, a hardy, indelicate girl—probably sensing the effect Alice had already even then over the male gender in general and specifically the one male she coveted—had accosted Alice in the dining hall, waving a napkin: "Oops. I thought you had mud on your face. I guess it's just your freckles." Mean, mean, girls were mean.

As a teenager Alice's face had resolved into beauty—like a camera brought into focus. And Alice's fate was set. Her fate: to be exquisite. Alice knew it, couldn't help knowing—even as she knew it would have benefited her not to know. An innocence impossible to retain when she saw the facts plastered across the face of every person whose eyes she met.

A handful of lines later, Alice moved downstage left, to lay her hand on Polixenes's elegant, ornamented arm, radiating heat under the embellishments. She squinted out at the shifting audience—only forty people, though it looked like an ocean. She was scanning for her best friend's mother, who had come in her stead. Or who was supposed to have—though Alice had comped her ticket, she knew she was liable not to show.

As a renowned feminist, Celine was a woman who defined what women were. Gender was a construct, she alleged, smiling lopsidedly, daring someone to hold her to account. Bio-sex meant nothing. Simple as that.

Alice was surprised that someone who wrote about women's solidarity could have such a complicated relationship with her own daughter. Sadie had shrugged when first introducing Alice to her mother. "Sometimes moms have charisma and sometimes they don't." Alice hadn't known they could.

Tonight, Alice knew Celine would report back to Sadie. Sanford Meisner could be there, and his opinion would matter less.

Alice stammered, "I had thought, sir, to have held my peace . . ." But before her character could even get through her line, she was being hauled off for sins she had not committed. The play was a tragicomedy and Alice felt unsteadied by the shifts in tone, finding them difficult to track.

"Away with her!" Leontes shouted, in the low growl he had cultivated over the prior week of rehearsals. He paused for audience reaction. The king, undone by his mania, exiles his one true ally: "To prison! He who shall speak for her is afar off guilty but that he speaks." This spoken more limply than in the prior four days of rehearsals, when he had still been full of freshly cast bravado, and before the heat wave had hit like an anvil.

Alice was always surprised at the ease with which acting came to her. She did not want to be a movie star. Really, she didn't. She just wanted to stretch her sense of self. She wanted to get to know other people, within the comfort of her own person. The only hiccup was that, as Alice understood it, genuine artistic expression required suffering. "Raise the stakes," Alice's teacher had advised. This, Alice was not sure how to do. She had never, as a rule, sought out suffering, never been attracted to it.

"You gods," Alice pleaded, as Hermione. Pregnant and powerless, she is imprisoned for a crime she has not committed. Another actress might lose patience with the character's abiding, saintlike composure.

Before Alice knew it, her character had died of grief, then revived, and reunited with her daughter, her husband's allegations having been proven unfounded. Alice wondered if, out in the audience, Celine was thinking of Sadie. Alice hurtled through the final scene, then the stage lights bumped off, a zero-count fade to black. Then the lights were up again for curtain call.

Bowing blindly, Alice's eyes swept over the audience. There she was. Once you caught sight of her, it was hard to see anyone else. That slow, rebel grin, lopsided, kind of cowboy. Her effortless lean, inclining from her waist, still slender at forty-seven, her hair tightly curled and slightly ragged. Scowling and alone, she remained seated. In an unfriendly mood, then. Celine.

She was a big-league lesbian, a patron saint of the case for social construction. Celine was as close as a sex critic came to a household name. Rumor had it that she had once been piloting a one-seater plane when it crashed into Buchanan Field, and waltzed away from the wreckage without a scratch.

As a child, Alice's favorite cartoon character was the Brain, a mouse scientist with a bulbous noggin to accommodate his outsized brain. That was what she thought smart looked like. Now she thought it looked like Celine. Celine looked like she had spent time at distant, clandestine coral-sand beaches, like she had just sauntered in from a day in the sun. She made it appear effortless, to change the world.

In the theater lobby, the king was encircled and laureled. Alice struggled through the clamorous crowd, in heat so sultry it could burst a ripe fruit. The air wavered. There was the stage manager, Darius, who during rehearsals had begun steering Alice, only Alice, into position onstage with his arm encircling her waist. She knew he wanted something from her. If she had not relocated down to Los Angeles, she might have tried to figure out what.

Alice's eye found her. Celine loitered in the dim light of a portico under the exit sign, her hair aflame, perfectly backlit by the white LED signage. She was leaning casually against a column, her set brow keenly directed at the greenroom outlet, not knowing that Alice would come out the opposite side. Celine was leggy, five-eleven, with well-built shoulders. She struck Alice as solid, durable as a mountain. Mother and daughter bore little resemblance, except when they crossed swords. In those moments, you could mistake one voice for the other.

Alice waved like a windshield wiper, but Celine didn't see. Alice shouldered through the crowd, sidestepping a few well-wishers.

She cleared her throat to attract Celine's attention. She wiped her forehead.

Celine turned left, straightened, and patted her pockets. She had a particularly masculine way of inhabiting a space. A demonic, flaring hank of orange hair tumbled over her forehead.

Her words cut through the thickness of the air: "There you are, hey-hi." Her voice was scratchy over the rising noise and she smelled spicy, like men's red deodorant. Just like Sadie's, her skin glowed, lunar. "Didn't see you come out."

They moved together toward the dormant concession area. It smelled of the coffee that had been poured out after intermission.

"You lived."

"What?"

That askew mouth, tilting when Celine smiled. "In Shakespeare, the women reliably—" And she made a casual noose gesture over her neck.

A dark and glossy bouquet of exotic flowers, tied oddly with a raggedy ribbon, hung limp at her side, as though she were trying to keep it from Alice's line of sight. *Here's flowers for you* was a line in the play. *Hot lavender, mints, savory, marjoram, the marigold.* What was hot lavender? Alice liked the sound of it. Celine tucked the bouquet behind her further. "Sadie insisted I come." The words seemed prickly on her tongue.

Alice would not let this get to her. This was no slap in the face. It was just Celine, waiting for this little ceremony to run its course. Alice was habituated to Celine's oddity of manner. And yet, for her uniform lack of social grace, Celine felt uncomplicated to Alice. She was just the way she was. Alice vowed not to let this diminish her.

As a teenager, Alice had come across a feature spread promoting self-confidence in a monthly magazine. A sunny-haired girl perched on the front stoop of a brownstone, smiling hugely with her teeth.

So unlike the mean models you usually saw, with drawn faces and drained bodies.

Alice had decided, in that moment, that happy people were beautiful. Much of her fate seemed to have been decided just then. She was grateful to have come across that photo, on what must have been an impressionable day.

"Rude of her not to come, you must be thinking," Celine said, with deadly accuracy.

"That's not true."

What eyes Celine had. The better to eat you with. Celine's tank top was road sign orange. *Caution*, her jacket said. *Warning. Detour.*

"I'm sorry, have I said too much? I have a terrible habit of that."

Alice searched Celine's eyes to gauge which Alice she would prefer: the devotee or the disinterested. Alice suspected that her customary persona around Celine—quiet ghost gone unseen, veering clear of the friction between mother and daughter; occasionally trying to curry favor with household deeds, scouring the cast-iron pot and toting in the grocery haul—would not suit the occasion, that in this escalation of their proximity, something more was required of her.

"No, I'm glad you're here."

Celine's eyes froze. Wrong, all wrong. In that family, they addressed one another with coolness and irony. "But I'm sorry if you had other things to do tonight—I mean, I'm sure you did."

A little under two years prior, Alice had audited Celine's Cal Berkeley class alongside Sadie—after a persistent campaign, she had talked her friend into it; convinced her that someday she'd regret not having seen what was said to be her mother's best quality.

In the library, Alice had plucked Celine's book of lesbian-feminist theory off the shelf. Sadie had been righteously indignant: "No big deal, just some casual reading by your best friend's sworn enemy."

Alice had smiled to herself: Sadie and her mother shared a sense of drama. Sadie dismissed the major feminist text summarily: "It's guerilla scholarship, derivative Paglia." Once, while Celine and Sadie were squabbling in the kitchen, Alice had peeked into Celine's office to admire the stack of pages on her desk, scrawled with handwriting black and perilous.

It made Alice sad, how unconscious Sadie was of her mother's wonderful qualities of perception. Alice had been intoxicated by the book—Celine coming across, as Alice devoured the stream of saturated prose, like a friend Alice wished she had, an antidote to Sadie, the friend she did. The only way she could describe it was that she wanted to turn the text on its side, fry the text up, and eat it like a hamburger patty. The chapter on mother-love, "Nurturance and Tyranny," was unapologetically about Sadie and managed to be, by turns, both razor-sharp and heartfelt.

The archaic myth of sexuality, Celine had written, *is not just a façade but an overprotective armor against emancipation. A hard outer shell so that we feel the cold and the wind only in our private ocean, inside the conch shell in which we can hear the remote whisper of the self.*

Alice should not have pointed out to her friend, the subject of the chapter, that it was like nothing else she had ever read. Sadie would not engage with the grist of the content, retorting only that Alice was impressed purely because it was the *only* book Alice had read that school year, focusing instead on having fun. It was not precisely true that Alice did not read. It was that she read the same books over the years, for comfort. She had an inclination for nice stories with nice endings. Pretty books with good morals: Louisa May Alcott and Laura Ingalls Wilder; stories of women facing a certain hardship and pulling through with aplomb. Each time she revisited, she saw something new.

Sadie read biographies and was interested in life in its most material terms.

Celine had come from Ohio, from nothing, her appetites propelling her like an engine. She was a hip, interesting person who had made her own way. Alice's family was nothing like this. For the millionth time, Alice was struck by the dissimilitude. Alice had grown up in the upscale valley town of Moraga, where corn grew bearded with long blue silk. Though it was only twenty minutes by car, it was a different world. Alice felt a cramp of guilt at the thought. She had never been nearby without telling her mother, Hadley.

Seeming to decide something, Celine thrust her flowers at Alice, gripping the stalk far south, like the hilt of a sword. "Here."

Alice presumed she was meant to take them.

"These are from Sadie. Anthuriums. You're supposed to snip the stems." Celine rubbed the scar on her inner forearm. Alice nodded gamely. The flowers were scary: black-brown, plasticky vinyl, rubbery, with assaulting stamens. "Otherwise, they won't drink."

Darius's eyes rippled in their direction, through the congested lobby, from the nucleus of his crowded circle. Alice knew he was holding out hope, one of these days, either during rehearsal or the run, for her to consent to an after-show drink. For once, she wished he would come over, spread his entourage's chatter, and relieve Celine of her. If he'd asked for a drink right then, Alice would have said yes.

"That was nice of her." Alice was a sucker for flowers. She had grown up with them. They did not seem frivolous to her, but essential. She breathed in deeply, the bloomy scent hitting deep in her belly. They probably *were* from Sadie. That would be like her, to go to the shop, select the flowers, wrap them, tie the ribbon, and drop them at Celine's.

"Is your mother here?" Celine asked, a little sour. She had always been suspicious of Alice's mother, mistrustful of Sadie's open interest in her. Alice had vowed to invite her mother next week when the show's kinks were ironed out. She suspected that Hadley thought, behind her façade, that her daughter was a nonstarter, like bread that wouldn't rise. Not that Hadley, brisk and clarifying as sea air, inevitably halfway out the door before Alice could get a word in, would be idling, awaiting an invitation. She was used to hearing little from Alice.

"She doesn't leave the house in this heat." Alice tidied the scruffy ribbon on the bouquet. "It would be a whole situation."

They stood there. Celine's smell had softened. It was nice, actually, like spiced cloves mixed with sunny morning. When she still lived at home, Sadie had always hung both their sets of washed clothing outside to dry. She said it made the clothes last longer and made them smell of sunshine.

The bright light radiated from the popcorn vitrine and, in the clotted room, their two shadows merged into one. Alice was just wondering how to resuscitate the conversation when Celine shifted foot-to-foot. "You were really good."

Alice gloated. She didn't like approval. She loved it. She couldn't live without it. It was why she lived.

Sidelong, Celine seemed to suppress something. "I mean that." Her voice was shaky, not unkind.

"There was a prop flop. Did you notice?" Celine stared at Alice so that she had no recourse but to keep talking. "When the goatherd tripped on the tablecloth? And the whole feast came crashing down and Perdita stepped on a prop chicken, and it squeaked because it was a dog toy?"

"Fine, just a hiccup."

"Was it all right, really?"

Together, they were gaining no ground, spinning wheels in gravel.

"I already said it was." Celine hooked her jacket on her finger.

"Sayonara." And then, inexplicably, she paused, as if there were something more she wanted. She even leaned in for a brief, exhilarating moment before seeming to conclude the space between them was a gulf she would not breach. And then she turned heel, not offering so much as a handshake.

SATURDAY

Entering the relative cool of the theater the next afternoon, Alice could not help thinking about Celine's awkward departure of the preceding night, and what it might mean. It drew Alice's uneasy attention to the thing she hated most: upsetting others.

It was impossible to find a moment to call Sadie. Alice ducked into the scene dock, where the theater group kept set pieces—the cardboard pillars of the Sicilian court and the stuffed "exit-pursued-by-a-bear" bear—to call Sadie and ascertain how dismal Celine's report had been. But as soon as she had settled in among the oversized chicken-wire-and-spray-foam enchanted oaks that signified pastoral Bohemia, she was called to makeup, where soft hands would layer foundation over the existing foundation Alice had not succeeded in removing the night before, and then Darius called her to the stage to rework a flawed bit of blocking.

The two best friends had not spoken since the week before, when Sadie had phoned just as Alice was leaving rehearsal, enlivened by an eccentric prospect. "Get ready for this," Alice had said. "Someone in the show has a contact at Anaheim Disney. They're casting for a new Cinderella. I'd ride in the parade, stroll around Fantasyland in PVC slippers, and sit at a banquet at the Royal Table. I don't know if they actually serve dinner. What if it was actually fun, meeting kids and blowing kisses and strutting around in a sparkly hoop dress?"

Sadie was deadpan. "Cinderella's a blonde."

"She wears a wig."

"Get real, Alice. These are the things that ruin a career."

Sadie saw the world with unclouded eyes, joyless but calm and cool as a lake.

"Natalie Portman was discovered at a pizza joint!"

"Stop shouting." Alice could feel Sadie's smile of veiled knowing, of always knowing better. "Don't delude yourself. This is where your career and your substance of character go to die."

Alice groaned inwardly. Anything less than Euripides or Ibsen was, according to both Sadie and Alice's mothers, beneath a person of substance.

Sadie spoke drily. "Brain scans show actors have decreased brain activity in the regions that form a sense of self."

"What is it about my acting that grates on you?" Alice asked, clicking her key fob and settling into her hatchback's driver's seat. Though her two-hour parking was up, she did not insert the key into the ignition. "You're very hard on me."

Alice tapped the steering wheel, ostensibly to the beat of the bubblegum pop song playing over her car stereo but really, she knew, to fill the silence. To the question *What do you want to do?* Alice had always wanted to reply, *Can't I just be?*

"Listen." Sadie sighed, softening slightly. "I think you'd make a great Cinderella. You're so good with kids, you're patient, and you're beautiful, and it would be very like you to fall out of a shoe and leave it at an epic party. But not at a theme park. You're better than that."

The truth of Sadie's tough counsel surfaced. She had softened, so Alice could, too. "You're right. It would probably be depressing, and career suicide. How's it going with Cormac?"

"Oh, god, horrible. I mean, *he's* great. But I'm a nightmare."

"Clamshelling again? We should talk about why. Why you can't be open with him."

"No mystery there. It's Mama's prurient interest. PTSD much?"

Alice made a noise of acknowledgment. "You know, we did emotional recall in rehearsal today—dredging up our own pain to access a character's."

"Dig up any bodies?"

"Maybe."

Maybe was an understatement. Once Alice started on her insecurities it was like *Night of the Living Dead.*

Exhumed: Alice's feeling that she was blank and passive, bare and undeveloped.

Disinterred: Alice was a shadow person, a raw hunk of clay waiting to be shaped, a canvas on which others could express themselves, a coloring-book page.

Resurrected: Alice was a perfectly acceptable outline who required another person—whoever she happened to come across—to add the substance.

"Has anyone studied the psychological effects of all this?" Sadie asked.

Maybe this was why Alice allowed so many men access to her. Each one, substituting the prior, represented a chance at self-actualization, of shading her into completion. No wonder Celine had balked the night before.

These thoughts consumed Alice, back in the playhouse, and before she knew it, the show was on, and soon enough Camillo was saying, "Come, sir, away." Lights out on Act II, ushering in the forty-minute stretch she was offstage, "imprisoned" by Leontes, possessed of a jealous rage, then dead.

Like a lizard into a wall, Alice slipped into the wings. Concealed for sixteen stage-years, Alice vowed to stay in character. She watched the mechanisms of the scene changes without seeing them, as if with a glass eye. Raise the front cloth, lower the tab. She peeked out at the blue-lit house.

Startled, she checked again.

Celine was in a similar seat as last night, if not the same one, shifting her weight in the cushioned folding chair, even wearing the same clothes, rumpled like she'd never gone home the night before. One could only imagine.

Alice hurtled through her performance, eyes fixed on Celine, herself transfixed among the assembled crowd. All the light was strange under the blue-white gels. Finally, Alice, as Hermione's stock-still statue, thoroughly vindicated after enduring wrongful accusal, blinked into waking life, and the second act was concluded. Applause at curtain rolled over Alice like a wave. She raced offstage and bustled out of her costume, snagging it sidewise onto the hanger.

Turning from the rack, she saw that Darius had followed her into the clogged dressing room and was gawking, looking appalled as she swiped off her lashes. "I thought those were real!" He seemed wounded, as if she had deliberately misled him.

The costume designer snorted in Alice's direction. "Isn't that just like men?"

Alice, who did not like to generalize, swept around, gathering her belongings. Darius cornered her near the whirring fan. "Who was that woman last night?" he asked, bemused voice chirred by the blades. "My brother was seated next to her. He said she was rustling around the whole time, making noise fidgeting and slurping a soda."

Alice had the sudden thought that perhaps Celine had come again because she felt bad about being rude the night before.

"I'm sorry." Alice did not bother to remove her makeup. Her face, still contoured for the stage, was tight with a batter of foundation. She patted Darius's arm on the way out. "Promise I'll tell you later."

Alice twitched. She had been watched, again, by Celine. She thought of texting Sadie to tell her that Celine came twice. Instead, she chased through the swarm of the exiting audience. Around her, the lobby erupted, but Celine wasn't there.

SUNDAY

By the third night, Alice knew where to direct her attention. She fastened hot, agitated, steady eyes on Celine, who was present in the audience just the same as before, rooted in the same seat. From Alice's marble pedestal, still as stone, something stirred inside her.

She focused on Celine the concentration of her performance. It was surely ill-considered and irresponsible. Celine had every right to rubberneck Alice—she was paying audience—but what right had Alice to return the thrill? Though she did not understand it, the charge of electricity was already ignited and, like a current, traveling a wire.

Around Alice, the stage lights deepened. She offered her performance to one single person. She even directed a condemnatory finger at Celine at, "Not guilty." Alice's costar, the king of the stage, attempted to regain her attention with an emphatic, effectless wheeze. No: tonight, the self-denying Hermione had a new focal point. Tonight, Hermione was having her fun.

After the bow, before house lights had a chance to rise and before Alice could wonder what she had done, she flew past her cast members, following the weak glow tape offstage into the wings.

The heat had risen, making Friday's low nineties seem moderate in comparison.

The nominal back changing room was hot, despite the time-worn AC unit, and heavy with the scent of pickles and onions. "That was a penetrating performance," a stagehand remarked, a little fearful. Alice felt a pinch in her stomach. "Anyone have a Tylenol?" No one did.

Her ardent performance had to have disconcerted the audience.

The heavy-chested costume designer was installed at the vanity mirror, at work on the hoagie sandwich she opened toward the conclusion of every performance. "This is delicious," she said over the wax paper, "and profoundly hard to eat."

Alice could not listen, kindled with the current that for the moment had no outlet. Her adhesive mink eyelashes stuck to her fingers. She wrangled with them, finally managing to flick them onto the vanity counter, coiled like dying caterpillars, rather than into their diminutive plastic case. The falsity of them dogged Alice suddenly, arousing in her a scorching antipathy. Why the ruse? Celine would never allow anyone to amend her. Why should Alice? Feeling emboldened, she flung her costume headlong over the hanging rack.

The costume designer swallowed hard. "Really?" She set down her sandwich. "You're not going to hang that up?"

"I'm sorry." Alice stepped into her street clothes, a fragile vintage housedress the color of a pale winter peach. Sadie said that Alice's clothes always looked like they were about to fall off her body. Her heart sped along as she zipped up the side of the brittle, delicate dress. "In a rush." She scooped up the mink lashes with a swipe of her finger and scraped them straight into the costume designer's vinegary hands. Alice had taken such good care of them so far. She had been so meticulous. The costume designer looked up at her, aghast. Alice wished fleetingly that there were two of her. Sadie called it the Disease to Please; Alice hated to disappoint people.

Alice emerged into the still, languid heat and found Celine waiting at the front of the playhouse. She looked uncharacteristically small in her oversized white T-shirt, her button-down balled up in her hand. She leaned to one side, her smile wonky. She was wearing an edgy pair of high-top sneakers this time, kumquat and lime. She was lit by the adjacent street-level storefront, the crowd dispersing around her. Greeting Alice, Celine tugged at her earlobe. She mumbled something inaudible. Alice noticed her small breasts, all but nothing really, curved against her T-shirt.

"Some people are going out," Alice said, her breath thin.

A car honked from the street, a ride anticipating its rider. Alice felt the world of concessions, the smells of coffee and popcorn, the anxieties of the play she was not sure she understood, fade.

Alice had begun to sweat. She pressed her fingers to her hot, doughy cheeks. Celine's olive-colored eyes watched Alice's fingers imprint her flushed skin.

"Don't go," Celine said, her smile off-center. Her eyes met Alice's with a look that brought a warmth to the base of her stomach, a trailing, emptying feeling, like a drain. Alice felt something shift within her, substantial as Earth's plates.

"All right." Two words, easy enough to say. Then two more: "I won't."

Celine's eyes brightened, lifted, then lowered with a forbidding finality. There seemed to be something they each wanted to say. The urge whispered through Alice. The lobby air was stifling, hot as a furnace. Five-blade ceiling fans spun pointlessly, far away at the room's upper limits.

"Your place or mine," Celine blurted out. It wasn't a question; it was a certainty. The words evidently shocked Celine as she spoke them, the pull of a gun's trigger disarming its operator.

Beneath Alice, the sun-warmed concrete seemed to slant upward. Sadie did not live, anymore, with Celine. Nonetheless, the place would be full of her. The answer came to Alice crisply. It was easy enough. Her Airbnb—attached to nothing, familiar to no one—was the only option. The street rippled. Feverish heat lifted from the asphalt. A police siren blipped, turning a corner.

"Mine."

Not half an hour later, cramming tightly together, Alice and Celine stepped into the single-occupancy Tower C elevator. The rasping elevator carriage smelled stale and rattled slightly. Celine stood close enough, a mere few inches away, that Alice could feel her adrenaline. Even here, the heat was inching in.

"I might have half a bottle of wine I brought up from L.A.," Alice began, "but I'm not sure and it might be vinegar by now."

Alice parted her lips to say more, but Celine put a finger to them. She squeezed closer in the elevator compartment, compressing Alice, shutting her up. The vintage slip dress Alice had selected so deliberately, only hours ago, in this very same multistory edifice, was swiftly hiked up around her waist. Alice felt the elevator winches shudder as Celine's strong fingers slipped under the thin strap of Alice's G-string, then inside her. There was a callus on Celine's thumb, the skin rough as a guitarist's. Craggy from what? From work? Flattened, Alice ebbed from her body. She could not begin to think.

Chapter Two

CELINE

FRIDAY

It was a practice of Celine's to steer clear of the folksy playhouse on Claremont's main drag, a few short blocks that served the neighborhood. The community theater was tucked into the basement of the local cineplex, some oddity of leasing, possibly a tax incentive. The company's motto was "simple storytelling at the forefront," which was code for "no production budget." Its only redeeming quality was that at least tickets were priced accordingly. It cost Celine enough dignity to attend—it need not also bankrupt her.

Tonight—feeling like Big Bird, as she often did, feeling eight-foot-two, ungainly, and bright yellow with tufty hair, a slender neck, and sleepy eyes—Celine approached the creeping box office kiosk line, flowers in hand. They were wilting; even the pockets of shade were hot.

Celine had puttered in from her perch up Telegraph Canyon, in the Oakland-Berkeley suburbs, where she had resided since having relocated from the city center back in 2002. Rich in wildlife, quiet streets, easy parking, well-lit sidewalks she could amble alone at night. So what if it wasn't Upper Rockridge, with its winding footpaths, or the sweeping view from the hill covering Lyon Street to Divisadero?

Celine had sought to escape the fray, to venture outside the nucleus. She wanted to ease off the pressure to *participate*. She had never wanted to speak for the world. But this relocation to the suburbs had gradually stoked in Celine the spark of her greatest fear: that she was becoming conventional. But she loved her scraggly little misshapen cottage, something out of a fairy tale, with its tunnel-like proportions, its mismatched styles, rustic then Bohemian, asymmetrical, wearing an unbalanced hat of a chimney. Even the floors were uneven.

Around Celine now, a clump of grad students Sadie's age milled about. They looked spirited and intelligent, Millennials maturing. She knew their type (they took her class). Drinking cans of something called Yesfolk and reading magazines called *Kinfolk* and banking with Everence and buying loafers from Everlane. Carrying unmarked leather tote bags in neutral tones, unmarked, unbranded. Sometimes Celine wondered, what *did* they stand for?

She was grateful for students—even if whenever she thought of her own, she felt a low-level sense of duties left undone. Things had changed around Berkeley. Celine had arrived in 1992, when Berkeley's Naked Guy was still wandering campus in the buff (but for shoes and his house key hung around his neck), and staging nude sit-ins. Celine didn't participate, nor did she mind. But by the following year, he had been expelled after a handful of female students alleged this amounted to sexual harassment. He'd killed himself in 2006 in the Santa Clarita jail, awaiting trial on charges of battery and assault.

Picketers across the street from the theater were chanting in protest of the FEMA-funded clearing of eucalyptus trees in Claremont Canyon. These days, what *wasn't* endangered?

Community action in Berkeley was so passionately and earnestly undertaken that activists had a tendency to lose perspective and position the prosperity or decline of native plants—or whether the Thomas and Louise Hicks House should get historic designation—on the same level of importance as the city's rampant homelessness. Everyone always wanted Celine to be an activist. She refused to be so reduced. This made people mad.

At the box office, the young kiosk staffer, a cute girl with thumb-printed eyeglasses, seemed to recognize Celine. "Celine McKeogh. Your ticket is comped."

Celine ran a hand through her static hair, wavy and woolly as a poodle's. Even twenty years on, it was still a boon to be recognized.

From behind the glassed-in desk, the girl tapped the sealed envelope: rat-a-tat. "You wrote *The Body Borne*."

All day, Celine fell in love with women. The girl was cute, no doubt about it. But too young, a student, a child. Celine prided herself on never having been pinioned into the bait-and-lure trap of such a multitude of mediocre men before her—Humbert Humbert's trip of the tongue as he savored his young lover's name. Still, she would have stayed and flirted, if not for fear that there would be hell to pay with Sadie. Sadie came first.

Celine pushed open the heavy entrance door. She looked longingly at the latest Fast and the Furious film, wishing she could pick up some popcorn and jujubes and settle in for a real show. No such luck.

Due to maintenance, escalators were not running. Celine—trapped behind a slow-moving old lady in a hemp scarf and chiropractic-support Mary Janes—was routed upstairs and down, and down a second set of stairs to a shrunken theater in the deep basement.

The show had not begun. Celine shimmied down the aisle, stepping over a few handbag straps and displacing someone's aluminum water bottle, which clacked down two sloping ramps and had to be passed back by a pickled old codger. "Scuse me kindly," Celine said to assuage him, peeling off layers of clothing as she went. Her uniform: a tank top under a T-shirt under a button-down. High-top sneakers. She never deviated. It was part indecision and part unwillingness to consult the daily weather forecast. It was more than halfway unreliable anyway, in the Bay.

She located her seat and concealed the tasteful bouquet beneath. Sadie had brought the flowers by that afternoon, rushing off toward her mysterious destination. Sadie had summoned Celine to the theater but would not reveal a thing about where *she* was going. Sadie did not explain herself. That was not her way.

At the last moment, pleased with herself, struck by a stroke of inspiration, Celine remembered a shopping bag she had been saving, with ribbon handles, and tied one on. Then she'd gotten ready, slashing at her stupid hair with a comb. Her hair was a preoccupation. It never sat right.

It had been nice to see Sadie, even for all of forty-five seconds. She had looked like a bisque porcelain doll—her skin always took on a silky luster in the heat. Celine felt Sadie, flesh of her flesh, like something amputated. She always had, since the separation of birth, as something severed from her body. A part of her. When Sadie had moved out of the house and across town, Celine had tangled with awareness of the proximity. A mother could feel her baby in the next room.

Sadie was Celine's anchor. She made Celine feel happy, weighted with history. To Celine, Sadie was home.

Were flowers for *closing* night? Maybe they were bad luck, an extension of the dramaturge's omen that "Good luck" would yield its opposite. "Break a leg" meant you wouldn't.

Good, then. Celine would keep the bouquet for herself. It was a nice bouquet her daughter had put together.

The truth was Celine was baffled by her daughter and a little afraid of her. Sadie put the fear of God in Celine—no one else did. Celine was proud to have raised a strong woman. Nevertheless, it could make life difficult. Sadie could be temperamental, flaring up, then with a superior pivot—a pirouette on the head of a dime—default back to implacable serenity. As a child, Sadie had micromanaged her ant farm.

Tonight's request had taken audacity. Sadie could effortlessly have attended the play. North Berkeley not so far, a fifteen-minute jaunt if you drove. And less than thirty by public transport. Why, then, send Celine? It became apparent that Sadie was withholding regarding her romantic life. That much Celine knew. The only thing she did not know was why. Sadie got like this, hermetic. She had allowed only, "It's important that I spend this weekend with Cormac. I can't explain why."

Cormac was an okay guy, decent, Celine thought, adding to herself cynically: if your standards were low. Sadie said he was a beekeeper and a bicycle repairman and knew about computers. Celine herself, as his professor, had seen him twice a week for months. He was tall as a pine and dressed like a *Jeopardy!* contestant. He was like plankton, she had told Sadie, overstating the case to see if she would defend him. He wasn't hurting anybody. All to say, he did not deserve Sadie.

Shortly after Celine had given Sadie the green light earlier that afternoon, a bright text had appeared from an unknown number.

Dear lovely Celine, I'm so glad you're coming to the show tonight!

Words candied with affection. The text closed with more Xs than Celine cared to count. Sadie had shared her number. Celine had closed her phone without responding to Alice.

She had known Alice what, now? Say eight years? Since she was a young teenager, flat-ironed and velour-clad, legs studded with bug bites from summer camp, and yet also anatomically faultless, as young girls tended to be. A tawny brunette with a foggy beauty that had gradually rolled sharply into focus. Those freckles all over her face like a painter's final flourish, a flamboyant finishing touch. And her eyes: huge discs, precisely circular with smooth edges, saucers that seemed to engulf anything they set upon.

Alice flopped casually around the house (though Celine had noticed she always tidied herself and straightened when Celine came into the room)—nothing like Sadie, with her majestic composure. Sadie was imperiously beautiful in a way that someone uninspired would consider plain or unremarkable. Sadie's hair had a metallic sheen, the color of terra-cotta. Cheekbones so defined that Celine had always wondered if they hurt. She favored a high waist, even occasionally empire, whether it was skinny jeans or a bikini bottom. Alice's presence, and attire, were softer, looser. She was to everyone's taste.

Sadie was so discriminating in all things that for years Celine had searched to perceive what was unparalleled in Alice. She hadn't found it yet; besides that she had stayed bonded to Sadie with an almost duty-bound sense, Celine detected a certain slavish quality in Alice that she did not think was healthy for her daughter. Alice was from an utterly banal, tedious, salmon-pink East Coast background, her family among the enduring 1 percent.

The only thing Celine *did* welcome: Alice had consumed Celine's book, which her own hypercritical daughter hadn't. Thank God there was someone around the house who appreciated her.

"How about the pages on rape and infantilization, Alice?" Celine had asked once, meeting the girl in the hallway on her way to the kitchen. Celine had recently been criticized by some starchy blog. It was a minefield if one wasn't current on that week's values. Like the Soviet purge trials, one week someone like Celine was a hero in the court of Literary Twitter, the next a traitor. The internet was where the active mind went to die. "Do you think that disaggregating the clusters by gender was incautious?"

Alice had blushed, a pretty hint of pink. "Can you give me twenty-four hours on that?"

This made Celine laugh. And she was touched when, amid her morass of misunderstanding, Alice had even picked up on Celine's adoption of certain words for her own use in a chapter on the semantic derogation in Jacobean-era texts. This happened to be one of the author's personal favorite subtleties. Not unintelligent, then. No one had ever pointed that out before. Occasionally, Celine had probably teased Alice a little. Celine couldn't quite remember, but then she must have, as was her habit with pretty girls.

There was a bleary sound, now, as a mousy house manager tapped the microphone. "Good evening, ladies and gentlemen." Celine waited. The mic squealed like a piglet, then quieted. "Welcome to the Brackendale production of *The Winter's Tale*. Thank you for your patience. The show will begin shortly. This would be a good time to silence your cell phones."

Celine turned *on* her phone to check the time. Late.

She was ravenous. Celine was an impatient chef, slicing when she was supposed to chop, chopping when she was supposed to mince. For this reason, she lived on sashimi from Quan Sushi. Uni, downed with an ungodly heap of wasabi, was her lifeblood. Kept her young. Before the show, she had called down to Quan. They were used to her order: five pieces uni, seven servings wasabi. But, annoyingly, they were closed tonight for renovations.

She had barely had a hot meal since Sadie had lived at home. Sadie had used to prepare bone broth and poke, nourishments labeled biodiverse and biodynamic, that Celine was happy to eat but did not understand. If Alice was over, Sadie would double the portions and disappear down the hall with her pretty friend and two thirds of the meal. They came out in pajamas, with their hair freshly and intricately braided, eerily silent as they rinsed their empty plates.

"How's it going?" Celine might ask, hands jammed in pockets.

"Fine," Sadie would say, the ash-gray cat fastened to her side, Alice just smiling, a ballerina bun at the tip-top of her head—as if responsible for keeping the whole thing upright, imparting the sense that without it she would lose her equilibrium.

Celine wondered if Alice, so quiet but with that sway in her step, judged their humble home. The moment Celine turned her back, they would explode into laughter, giggles hitched to no intelligible joke. Those two always seemed to conspire, sharing some covert secret they were shutting Celine out of. Probably Sadie had told Alice the same thing: "It would mean a lot to my mother to go." Celine loved being Sadie's mother but hated being someone's doting *mom*.

The show had not begun. The teenager to Celine's left slouched halfway over the armrest. Celine's sense of indignation pulsed. Only because she was a woman. He wouldn't do that to a man. Just when Celine was thinking she might even leave, to hell with it—she was impatient, despite being herself often late—the room dimmed. Stage lights rose.

The production had taken liberties. The fable-like tale of sixteen years of family tragedy, jealous patriarchal delusions, and deceitful accusal—with a superficial and abrupt tacked-on *happy* ending—had been transposed to an unspecified metallic future, Bohemia dropped onto New York City's silvery, geometric boroughs. The first lines were pronounced, the show promising to be the slog Celine imagined it would, and then it was time for Hermione's entrance.

Alice strutted out, taking her place under the set's starry glow. Celine had never been able to see Alice before. Standing hip-to-hip with Sadie, as they always were, they were like one unit, inseparable into parts. Alice was a silver-lined silhouette in dust-blue jeans that hugged her close. Celine leaned forward in her seat. Immediately, a hazardous feeling. Deep in her blood, she felt something stir, almost like dirt.

"I do feel it gone but know not how it went." Alice's lips landed together after she spoke, like butterfly wings.

Those dust-colored jeans were evocative for Celine. They were Jordache, were Sergio Valente's longhorn label, the iconic H.I.S. jeans ad. Were the model in heeled boots, with her leg hiked up onto a bistro chair, the brand's lettermark embroidered onto the back pocket. They were Nastassja Kinski and Monica Bellucci. Now were Alice. It was as though Celine had never laid eyes on her.

"I never wished to see you sorry," Hermione says. The words rang out like vengeance, despite only being the bare fact of premonition. "Now I trust I shall."

So this was what Sadie had been hiding, stashed in her room.

At Intermission, Celine paced like a wildcat. She could not get those crisp jeans out of her head, dusty blue. The image stuck like a burr, like a fishbone. Semiconsciously, she ordered a bottom-shelf whiskey with ice from the concession stand and was met with impediment.

"Sorry, no liquor license. We've tried. Blame the universe."

Celine could almost taste what those provocative jeans were: *something* from her past. What was it? The concession stand was not even set up to serve lemonade, so Celine settled for a stale cookie, three quarters of which she scrapped into the lobby bin when the lights flashed.

Celine reached her seat. The teenager slid in beside her, hunched like a hyena, apologizing for his existence.

With that silt still buried in Celine's veins, she watched Hermione, the long-suffering Sicilian queen, die of a wrecked heart. But in the play's final, astonishing act, Hermione rises resurrected. Alice returned to the stage, eyelashes candied with mascara. Her lips were pink as if she had been sucking on watermelon candy. Celine remembered what it was: those jeans. There it was, the missing piece: Cassie, her first lover, in stonewashed jeans with light pink pinstripes. Celine's body flooded hot, almost like she was afraid.

SATURDAY

The next night, feeling unhealthy, Celine slipped her fingers inside the thin flap of the envelope handed her by the box office, exposing her own name. She could hardly bear to think about the night before. She had thrust out the flowers and, as soon as humanly possible, sought out the exit, feeling she had dodged something terrible.

And yet here she was again. Doing something she knew she shouldn't.

But then, why *shouldn't* she? After all, she had been rude the night before. Maybe she was here to make amends. She would find Alice afterward, apologize for being so uncomfortable and tongue-tied.

The same employee greeted her approvingly. "Cashing in on that university-affiliation discount." Her mouth ticked up and the smudged eyeglasses with it. "You can't keep away!"

And what *was* Celine's thinking, with this apology? She needn't bother Alice with that.

"I'm just going to see the beginning and then leave," she said, nauseated and smiling.

What was she doing there? She had only come to see what all this was about.

Finally reaching the theater, having conquered the expiring

movieplex's byzantine halls, Celine sank into her comfortable seat. Furtively, she sipped the Dr Pepper she had smuggled in, stashed in her bag, weeping condensation onto her students' papers. She took a long glug. Staying hydrated in the heat.

The show's opening scenes were a desert without water and Celine's head lolled. She knew it: Waste of energy to have come. Nothing for her here. But when Hermione entered, a sudden twist in her low belly, a suggestion.

"There some ill planet reigns," Alice's lips forecast.

Like something hunted, flooded with adrenaline, Celine felt she had to keep alert. Her senses sharpened. She felt skinless, flayed. Sometimes, infatuation just transpired this way. Instantaneously, with no warning. A kind of alchemy: the spark bright as a candle. It seemed implausible that you couldn't see it in the air.

"O, she's warm!" Leontes murmured onstage, beholding Alice. "If this be magic, let it be an art lawful as eating."

Celine closed her eyes. Blissful dark. Stay there. Seen enough.

"I have drunk," Leontes recited, "and seen the spider."

My god. What was Celine thinking? What was going on in her crooked mind? This was a girl she had watched grow up—even if distractedly—from an unformed teenager, underdone. When the lights went down, before curtain call, Celine scuttled out of the theater, slamming out the exit door, coming to her senses to the fading sound of applause.

SUNDAY

The third night, Celine went because—drawn like a magnet to its opposite beckoning pole, as if led by an invisible hand—she could not keep away.

Chapter Three

ALICE

MONDAY

The morning after the weekend's final show, heavy-lidded, Alice blinked awake to the foreign click of the Airbnb's Timex wall clock. She felt remarkably free of concern and despite the heat, extraordinarily rested. It was not until she rolled over, the lumpy futon unforgiving beneath her, that Celine was live and robust beside her.

"Hello." Celine's lizard-wide eyes were right there, unblinking, looking straight into hers.

Alice's blurry mind jolted, her organs radiated, thinking back to the night before. They had made it to the bed before abandoning it for the shower's cool running water, then for the chair in front of the rotating fan, then for the chilly kitchen floor, then for the refreshing marble kitchen countertop.

"My God." Alice clapped her hand over her mouth. She toppled back against the pillows. She slid down onto the mattress and stared feebly at the ceiling.

"Hi."

Alice thrust out her shaky, uncertain hand, wondering if her charm could possibly smooth an iota of the regret Celine must be feeling. "Who are you again?" she asked, parodying confusion. "Hi, I'm Alice."

Celine grinned like a demon at the gag. What could they possibly do but laugh? As she accepted Alice's hand, Alice felt she was signing a dangerous pact.

Celine looked at her squarely. "Are you okay?"

Alice blinked. "No."

It was strange. Alice felt not so much regret, her own, as a cringing feeling that *Celine* must be feeling a gut-wrenching remorse.

"It's going to be painful for a minute."

"Okay."

There was something disconcerting in the way Celine would not avert her eyes.

"One, two, three, four . . ." Celine counted to sixty. It took a long, long time. "Are we better?"

"No," Alice said, but like a bizarre miracle, she was. She steadied herself by looking out at the bay, at the row of bridges shrouded in morning mist. Celine murmured how, as the day's temperature rose, the tidal waters, essentially, cooked. It seemed such a sensible thing to say. Alice found herself enjoying Celine's quiet company. She had never seen Celine be quiet before.

The two women stayed moored in the queen-sized bed. Alice, keyed into Celine, could tell she preferred not to break the spell. When Celine asked if she should go, Alice said, "Not yet." She felt she was on a ship, afloat at extremity, far from everyone she knew.

"Trick question. I was hoping you'd say that."

Eventually they did make it out of bed. Alice slipped on her vintage housedress, which Celine said was "a little *Rosemary's Baby*." They emptied half a tray of ice cubes into their palms. Celine poured the other half into a bucket and made Alice a clacking foot bath. They groaned. "How can it be this *hot* at eight in the morning?"

They did not plug in the toaster. As if hungover, they devoured cold bagels and mulchy bananas left as a courtesy by the Airbnb host. They remarked on how the bananas felt velvety on the tongue. Celine counted Alice's freckles, losing track every thirty or so and starting again. Everything was new as a baby. The sunlight flooded in. A flock of starlings murmured, showing off their trim shipshape, tidy as Navy Blue Angels. Alice kept waiting for things to feel weird. They didn't. Was *that* weird?

While Celine tended to her Monday morning emails and brewed a fresh pot of coffee, Alice slipped into the shower. She turned tightly in the narrow stall, encased in steaming hot, soaping herself under the prickling water, aiming the nozzle, adjusting the setting to a consistent high pressure. It was her first moment alone and she tried to collect herself. She scrubbed, trying to wash something off. Trying to wash off Celine? No, trying to wash off Sadie.

Sadie, who had been so elusive in the first place. She had been a mystery on their high school campus, invisible at the lunch break, not deigning to arrive until thirty seconds before class began, slipping down the aisle in Bio II like a celebrity shy of exposure, just as Mr. Cady had begun distributing brick-sized fetal pigs from bags of formaldehyde (How had they died? Had they been bred for the piteous purpose?) with a gigantic pair of steel tongs. Though Sadie could easily have landed among them, with one hand tied behind her back, she was not one of the campus's commonplace "cool kids," which made her cooler.

Alice and Sadie met already bonded, exchanging a small, lopsided smile after both nearly missed the shuttle for the Food Waste Tour, a high-school-wide field trip, in which they learned to spawn mushrooms in coffee ground waste. Missing the bus would require a Herculean journey by public transport.

Both girls, late, dashed and made it, tumbling onto the chartered bus just as it shuddered into jerky action. The happenstance meeting was a rare time Sadie was caught off guard, teetering off-balance as the tired coach bus bumped into action over the Caltrain railway tracks.

Moving swiftly, Sadie had commented on (was it a compliment?) Alice's Fugazi sweatshirt, the moth-eaten collar crenellated with wear. To this day, Alice had never confessed she had only borrowed it from a guy, though she did—sensing that Sadie was someone worth impressing—go home and study *Repeater* that night, trying to decode its cacophony. And then Alice concurred when Sadie complained about the shuttle, stopping off at the Banway Building rather than cutting straight to Kittridge parking, grumbling about its inefficiency.

On the Food Waste Tour, Sadie listened to the volunteer docents with her head poised at a slight three-quarter angle, Alice thought, like the patron sitter in a Flemish portrait. "So elegant," Alice said, seeing Sadie unsheathe a skinny gold retractable pencil from a velvet-lined case.

Sadie sized Alice up, looking her over to ascertain whether she would actually be interested. She was conspiratorial, handing Alice the pencil. "It's the Smythson Viceroy wafer."

Alice admired it. "My mother uses Blackwings."

"Go ahead," Sadie said. "Try it."

"That is fantastic," Alice said, trying out a spiral and her own name, then Sadie's. "Better than a Caran d'Ache. Smoother."

Sadie positively radiated. And after that they were friends, consecrated, without any throat-clearing. They skipped all the clamor of straining to establish that they *wanted* to be friends. They just were. They wandered the warehouse together, noses pinched, Sadie mostly stone-faced but laughing sometimes. Fallen in with each other over a precocious connoisseurship about pencils.

The friendship was all-encompassing and, without even realizing it was happening, Alice gradually withdrew from her former friends. Plain, plumb forgot until she ran into one or another outside the science lab or the Monterey Bay Aquarium and faced a chilly reception. Until Teague called out, "Dumpling-shaped ho!" and slid diagonally, sharklike, toward her across the math building hallway. Alice could not help but admire this insult. Heart pumping, smiling just a little, safe in her new and superior friendship, she had ducked into a classroom.

When Alice saw Teague's posts now, they were of weekend parties in the desert. Itchy, sun-withered blankets, dry heat, bodies on the floor, drugs. Alice felt she had dodged a bullet.

Everyone was constantly falling in fervent love with Alice—even people who shouldn't. In elementary school, two girls played tug-of-war with her on the schoolyard, to determine who she would sit with at lunch. Literally grabbed her by her arms and yanked. But Sadie wasn't one of her annoyingly easy hangers-on.

Alice still wasn't sure how she had been selected for the privilege of Sadie's friendship, admitted to the most exclusive club of one. She loved Sadie's looks, her long nose and sharp jaw. She had none of the asymmetry that characterized Celine's face. She was rumored to be judgmental and standoffish. All the other kids were intimidated by Sadie, with her imposing bearing, ramrod posture, and composure of a sphinx.

With a patrician air, Sadie's every gesture was eloquent. Different from Alice, who conserved no energies, gesticulating widely. The funny thing was that their great-grandparents could have met. Both families had traced their lines to Ohio, Alice's paternal side bearing early industrialists, processing tobacco in the 1810s, and Sadie's, more loosely, as Irish migrants working the meatpacking floors. "My great-grandmother could have scrubbed yours's boots," Sadie said.

Celine had come from nothing, really. To Alice's mind, it rendered her doubly impressive. In childhood photos, Alice smiled, cradling her stuffed bunny, Felty, with their family's tartan ribbons looped into her hair, procured during a recent trip to Scotland. Sadie was severe, dressed in gray tones, with what was now called a power part slicing a vertical line from her crown to her hairline. But something about the contrast clicked.

Alice had never been in love with a friend before. She and Sadie grew so close that they shared everything, so close that it felt perfectly natural that even their birthdays fell one single day apart, so close—a hair's breadth apart, the narrowest margin of difference, which both believed nothing on earth could ever breach.

Unlike Celine, always leaving the house for one of her vigorous outdoor walks, Sadie was an indoor person, coccooned in her inner circle. She could be clannish. Alice occasionally yearned to branch out. She didn't like to sit sequestered at home, her charms going to waste. She liked to be out in the world where she could buy things, anything she wanted.

Alice recalled the first time she had been to the house and met Sadie's mother, who, she pieced together later, had written a landmark text and was, actually, famous. Of course, Sadie had said nothing about it.

The day Alice first met Celine, she was at the bottom of the curved driveway washing her car, in cut-off shorts and a moth-eaten Herizons T-shirt, blasting Bikini Kill. Alice prepared to offer her hand in greeting, but instead Celine turned, grinned wickedly, and doused the two girls with the hose, set to full blast. Cackling like a goose, with a crazed gleam in her eyes, she waved it over her head like a lasso. When Sadie went running for cover, Celine lobbed the soap-soaked sponge at her back.

"She can be such a bitch," Sadie had muttered, wringing out her hair. Was that what it was? Later, dazzled by Celine's repute, Alice remembered this. She did not know what she had imagined a public intellectual, a decorated feminist participating honorably in the high-minded affairs of society, would be like, but this wasn't it.

Alice had grown up in a large, cold house, cold for being large. Her mother, Hadley, did not like to host guests. Perhaps more to the point, did not have guests to host, having left them all back east, and most rooms in the house spent the better part of the year unlit.

Hadley fixated on what was in front of her: striding up and down the shambly stairs to tend to the dowdy heirlooms of her antecedents, which she refused to replace because they had been the best in the world *once*. Anything she had was the time-tested best of everything; anything new was dubious and unproven. Somehow, all her efforts never added up—the curtains always due for a wash just when she got the sills scrubbed down—and there was a general sense of shabby neglect among the grandeur, of inaction amid the ceremony.

Alice had grown up with the best the world had to offer and all she wanted was to walk away. She felt the house like a snake feels the fraying skin—shiny scales gone lusterless, old iridescence—that it is past time to molt.

When it was time to apply for college, both girls knew what they wanted. Sadie's immovable timeline stipulated she stay in California, taking advantage of in-state tuition to bank money for her imminent future. Grudgingly, given its indissoluble connection to Celine, she would apply early decision to UC Berkeley—it was the best school for the price—and stay local. Alice preferred an intimate school, one that was prestigious for Hadley, but laid-back for Alice, with a homey atmosphere. She applied early to Oberlin. This was met with little resistance from Sadie, who was focused on assembling her own application materials and, Alice suspected, enjoyed the prospect of attending college alone.

Alice was a little wounded, but she understood. "Choosing a college because your best friend is going there is a do-not-do."

"I guess we're supposed to spread our wings," Sadie said, sounding unexpectedly glum. "Embrace change. Make new friends. They sound overrated already."

But gradually it became clear that, actually, Sadie wouldn't mind if Alice joined her. "Apply," Sadie said, "and you can decide later." But over the weeks, her early-decision acceptance and Alice's early-action wait-list at Oberlin, Sadie began to worry. "Do I like premature entrepreneurs? I hate computer science, economics, engineering. I'm going to hate everyone." Though it was last-minute, only six short days until regular-decision applications were due, she began to insist, even require, that Alice apply to Berkeley.

Alice protested that she did not fit the profile. "Plus, there's no way I'd get it in, with my scores." Alice had not condescended to accept her mother's offer of a SAT-prep tutor, on grounds of inequitable privilege.

"Just write the essay."

The essay: In 7,000 characters or less, describe one of the communities to which you belong. How did being a member of this community contribute to your personal growth?

Alice essayed, in the French sense. She spent a weekend penning a j'accuse about growing up in a knot of privilege. Alice tried to convey a sense, as someone wealthy and fortunate, of her insecurities, of feeling she was not substantial, of feeling that *real* life was somewhere else. Wealth, like anything else, fell on a continuum. It wasn't like Alice was among the 0.5 percent. And yet her maternal grandmother's pool garden had resembled a private sculpture park. Her maternal grandfather had owned a share in a private jet but didn't tell anyone. It was just a Cirrus SF50, anyway. It wasn't like it could make a cross-continental trip.

Sadie, who had already submitted her own to *The New York Times*'s college essay open call—she hated that it was about Celine, but then, Celine was a name, and no one could ever accuse Sadie of not using every lead to her advantage—demanded that Alice share her essay, ostensibly for proofreading purposes.

When Alice walked into the editing session, Sadie was at the kitchen table with her laptop open to a bright white Word document, cursor blinking. She had a Moleskine notebook, and her Viceroy pencil, loaded to a point, with two tubes of 90-count refillable lead beside it. Alice handed over the printed pages.

Sadie swirled her hair up into a twisted bun in order to read closely.

"*Hawaï* with a diaresis," she said. "How very *New Yorker* style guide of you." She plowed twice through, before looking up. Her long lashes made her eyes look dark. "So, the community to which you belong is the wealthy class?"

It sounded stupid when Sadie put it that way.

"You're critiquing your own milieu? That's the essay's conceit?"

"It's awful." Alice knew it was. "You hate it."

"I don't like it," Sadie said. "It's not worthy of you. I know you can do better." She thought a moment, tapping her pencil. "Where's the adversity? What are your extracurriculars? Did you ever serve

Thanksgiving dinner at a drug treatment center? Or spend the summer assisting victims of the Valley Fires? There were like *ten.* You never bothered?"

"Did you?"

"Not the point."

Alice scoffed. "I spent my summer at the San Francisco Ballet Academy. We slept in Frette sheets and ate quinoa bowls. On Thursdays, we had massages in the health-care suite."

"Slow down," Sadie said, scribbling with her Viceroy.

"Good luck adversifying that."

Sadie frowned. "How often were you dancing?"

"It was an intensive. Six days a week."

"Strenuous," Sadie said, approving. She scribbled faster. "What was it like? Details."

"We had to wear leotards."

Sadie tucked her elegant pencil behind her ear and switched to typing. "Go on."

"And really itchy tights."

"You felt exposed."

"Maybe kind of?"

"Did you have a cruel and demanding instructor?"

Alice had always liked and admired Madame Tara. Tara treated her with dignity, like an adult. Alice said as much.

"Standard," Sadie said. "AKA average. AKA not Berkeley material."

Alice racked her brain. "She once said I needed to work hard if I wanted to succeed."

"I knew it!" Sadie returned hungrily to the document. "She said you were at risk of failing. As the microfailures added up, the stress mounted. You cried after every class."

Alice began feeling nervous.

"The pursuit of perfection had you spinning like a ballerina in a jewelry box. Your self-esteem was completely dismantled. You were voiceless, a spinning doll."

"But that's not true." Alice could not sit still.

"How will they ever know?" Sadie's eyes tunneled into the document. "Your body was a burden. Tara called you flabby and you began starving yourself. She told you you could only eat hard-boiled egg whites."

"But it's slander!"

"So we give her another name."

Alice blushed. "These are potentially serious allegations." She began pacing. "What if somebody knows her? What if they call the school?"

"We're just embellishing minor details," Sadie said, then conceded: "I'll delete SFBA. 'At *a prestigious summer ballet program.*' And I'll change Madame Tara's name. Happy?" She looked up. "What's your favorite fruit?"

Alice considered this. "Mango?"

"You lived on slices of dried mango. You would suck on them. You wouldn't even swallow. You were rewarded and began to advance. You fell deeper and deeper under Madame Oksana's spell."

"Oksana? Sounds like a fortune teller."

"You found her authority intoxicating. Your eyes spiraled like a cartoon, wee-oo, wee-oo. You *liked* to be dominated."

"Why would I like it?"

"Because your ballet improved. And your character and your buttocks firmed up under her influence. She had her claws in you. Long fingernails," Sadie embroidered. "In fact, I think you became bulimic?"

"No," Alice interjected. "Too much."

"Fine, I guess one adversity fewer won't hurt." Sadie frowned. "You liked the grotesqueness of your new body. You got a chilling thrill every time you looked in the mirror and saw your bones."

This was all a bit much for Alice. "Are you sure we haven't gotten away from the topic?"

Sadie reread what she had written. "It's perfect. Final paragraph will be about how the whole experience instilled in you a terrifying confidence. You learned grit and perseverance. You learned to cope under extremism."

"Why not just make me an ISIS fighter?" Alice sighed, admitting defeat. "Well, it will certainly be distinctive."

"They'll never have read anything like it. They'll be so afraid of you they won't know what to do but accept."

Together, they edited a bit more—Alice managed to prevent Sadie from inserting a reliance on ephedrine pills—and then Sadie pronounced the essay complete. Alice dutifully attached it to her e-app and, with a once-over to confirm the autofilled contact fields, clicked SUBMIT.

When Alice's acceptance letter came, slipped inside a thick FedEx package alongside the formidable Cal Berkeley course catalog, Sadie danced around the room, glorying in her triumph. "What did I tell you?"

From the shower, in her Airbnb, for the second time that day, Alice scrubbed and scrubbed, scouring until her skin turned a bright carnation pink.

Chapter Four

SADIE

FRIDAY

Sadie had to call her mother.

Last she had seen her: Cormac had suggested they share a bottle of wine with Celine over a game of Monopoly at her place. What could go wrong? Celine had lost the rule book. And the two women were so competitive that the evening dissolved into a bitter, tearful dispute over whether a player—Celine—could or could not collect rent while in jail.

Sadie reminded herself that she was in control, ensuring that the weekend, a celebration of her and Cormac's one-year anniversary, went off without a hitch. It was the first vacation she had ever booked on her own, and the occasion on which she would lose her well-kept virginity—twenty-three *years* kept, though who was counting?

Sadie and Cormac had done a lot of kissing. Most teenagers lost their virginity at prom, in formless, strapless satin and needlessly extravagant updos. Or folded like origami into backseats of Subarus at make-out points. But Sadie puzzled over the mechanics. Would every male organ slide snugly into any female, like a pen in a cap? Such synchronicity seemed less than likely. Sadie had seen Cormac's private parts, of course. But had not managed to measure them against her hand for later assessment.

But this time, she was committed. Every detail had been pre-arranged. Sadie had chosen the guy. She had strategized every feature. It was in her schedule. And damnit, it was too bad that Alice had accepted a role in a rinky-dink little play that weekend, but there was nothing to be done. It necessitated, of course, in the ghastly final facet: the execution of Sadie's deflowering, horribly, would require her mother's collaboration.

Not that Celine had not had her hand in this. As a child, Sadie used to open Celine's bedside drawer and study the toys that she instinctively knew not to inquire about. They were toys Sadie understood she would not have known how to play with. Sleek, the colors not quite childlike. Something about their shape and placement marked them as Celine's, not for sharing.

"Do you know how difficult it is to have a sex-positive parent?" Sadie had asked Cormac once.

Celine had a word for Sadie's fears in her book: *coitophobia*. Sadie had waded through Celine's book on the sly. But when Celine accused her of being unsupportive for never having done so, she kept quiet. She did not want Celine knowing she had ingested her hubristic pages, reveling in her own carnal pyrotechnics, in orifices and bodily fluids—leaving little to the imagination. Sadie even wondered, privately, if she had a dishonorable microdose of homophobia in her. She had noticed that lesbians made her nervous.

Therapy? Sadie had tried it. Healing? No dice.

Despite Sadie's diligence, her well-*laid* plans seemed determined to go awry. The weather was slated gray and Sadie had thought she would buckle and reschedule her and Cormac's trip. But Friday morning, the fog burned off, the skies had cleared, and pale sun marked every spot. No mind that it was swelteringly, blisteringly, climate-change-affirmingly hot. Cormac said that was what the ocean was for.

"We're going," he said, waking in his shared apartment. He knew how hard she had worked to put the trip together.

Sadie hoped the cabin she had booked was the "right" sort of place. She had phoned a number of times to confirm details—which bedroom afforded which view, whether the fireplace was merely decorative, whether nonallergenic pillows were provided, whether they had starter logs and how many and did extras come at a cost—so that the owner now answered the phone, "Yes, Sadie?"

Cancelation at this point was out of the question.

Curious whether the cottage owner had returned her inquiry as to whether the slow-baked bread promised in the listing online would be white, wheat, or sourdough, Sadie tapped her phone awake. She saw that there was a harried voice mail from Celine. Just as Sadie had been about to call her. It often worked that way with them: they both needed something.

Sadie had enabled visual voice mail expressly for this reason. Celine unleashed tsunamis of grousing first thing in the morning. Sadie had vowed not to tolerate her mother's microaggressions anymore—least of all before she had begun her day. What Sadie was supposed to do, instead, was have a glass of hot water with lemon and meditate. No time for that today. No time most days.

"Mayday," the voice mail transcription read, and already Sadie chafed. "Of course, when I'm having a good writing day, the computer goes out. A person could even start to feel like it's a plot! Call me back immediately, if not sooner."

Celine raged and cajoled, evaded and pushed; she drove Sadie to run-on sentences. This rapacious narcissism did not only cause superficial damage. It was the reason Sadie had no father. It was all there, in the exploitative chapter on Sadie in *The Body Borne*. As a little girl, Sadie had considered faking suicide in a stab at attention. She wondered if, at her funeral, Celine would finally be quiet. Probably not. Her sobs would probably echo through the chapel.

There was no getting away from Celine. She was in Sadie's bones. Sadie had a full day of work ahead of her, from which Cormac, after his biocomputation class—he was almost done with his Masters in Comp-Sci at Berkeley—planned to pick her up at closing. He told her he hoped to work in the Valley of Industry, doing important, influential, invisible things. He hoped to launch what he billed as the Uber of collaborative consulting, the Airbnb of intellectual capital. It might even be possible, Sadie thought. In the Bay Area, things started up, sprouted swiftly, and fattened to abundant size.

Sadie had accepted, now, that she was not, in the end, a sociologist. She was not even sure she liked people all that much. Growing up, she had wanted to be like Amy Goodman, who Celine listened to on *Democracy Now!* while she had her morning smoke just far enough outside the kitchen door that all the smoke blew back in. Sadie wanted to be authoritative, like Amy, to relay facts and the correct way to feel about them.

But she began to notice, by balancing against Alice—months ago, back when the two friends were together twelve hours of any given twenty-four—that where Alice saw the big picture, Sadie saw details. She found herself arranging her bookshelves by color. Confoundingly, one afternoon, it was nearly dark before she realized she had squandered four hours researching sconces for her first apartment. Alice would have sorted by rating and clicked BUY NOW on the first sconce within her price range, not getting hung up on whether the flush mount had a hinge or a pivot. Sadie admired that.

Alice's indifference to tastefulness stemmed from an infuriating sense of innate aesthetic superiority. She had the comfort of being able to reject *good taste*, because she was already a member in good standing. "Taste" had been spoon-fed to her from the start—she was sated and had no further need of it.

Not that Sadie *wanted* to be interested in interiors. She found most decoration more distracting than comforting, like frosting when you only wanted bread. She considered decoration insufficiently serious. But Alice had made it better, pointing out that even the Stoics were not above a fair appreciation of beauty's harmony. Sadie had accepted her fate. Beauty was artifice, but artifice was powerful. Wasn't Alice walking proof, with her freckled adornment?

With a feather-light senior schedule, Sadie had applied for part-time jobs that could springboard into careers. On the strength of her portfolio and a gushing letter from her former boss at the campus café, Sadie had secured an entry-level station at Blackbird, a micro-batch wallpapers-and-textile firm committed to "positive impact through human-centered design."

Sadie initially responded to a hiring call for a designer, admittedly a reach, but had been offered a decidedly less distinguished role doing secretarial legwork. She maintained the print-to-order catalogue and the office library, prepared spec sheets, and placed vendor orders. The higher-ups quickly recognized that she was attentive, organized, motivated, and that she had impeccable taste. She was off to a strong start there, and she didn't hate it. Still, the most they had let her design, so far, was packaging and insert cards.

Cormac rolled over toward her side of the bed. "Sure you don't want a ride to work?"

"Very much so." Sadie climbed over him. "Stop asking."

He stuck with her; on what grounds she did not know. It could not be her glowing personality.

"Sorry," she said. "I'm crabby. I have to call my *mother.* Am I the worst, missing Alice's show?" Sadie was Alice's best friend. Of course, she was expecting her.

"You're never the worst," Cormac said. "You're the best."

Cormac was utterly convinced of Sadie. Trouble was, she was not utterly convinced of herself, which left him looking like a poor fool who had drunk the Kool-Aid.

It was a precisely technical undertaking, Sadie thought, falling in love. Making someone fall in love with you. Something she seemed to know that the wider world didn't: It was procedural. First the intrigue. Then the deliberate withholding of oneself, the coy cat-and-mouse dodge. Intermittently seizing sensual and prolonged eye contact. The olfactory element: easy on the deodorant; a human's response to the bid of pheromones was no more developed than a mangy stray dog's.

All that strategizing, then comes marriage, then comes baby in a baby carriage.

The call would require some negotiation.

"Fucking shit" was Celine's greeting when Sadie returned the call from her seat on the Caltrain, which she disliked taking. She preferred to pilot herself. She liked to get herself places. She didn't like to be driven in Los Angeles, or to take a taxicab in New York City. She liked to drive herself, or to walk. In all things—in her work, in relationships—she preferred to steer. "Another hellish day."

Celine had a remarkable ability to sniff out happiness and stifle it like a fire extinguisher. She was disruptive, a destabilizing agent. This weekend, Sadie would refuse to fall prey to her bulldozer energy. This weekend, stability was precious to Sadie.

"But I'm happy to hear from *you*," Celine said, changing tone falsely, Sadie felt.

"I'm not sure I have the bandwidth for this call." It was 96 degrees. Sadie had applied sunscreen assiduously every day since she was twelve, onto every exposed inch of her body, except one. What she did not know and could not find an earthly answer to was whether one needed to apply it on one's eyelids. Dermatologists shrugged. "Of course, one should . . ." was all they would say. Why was no one precise?

"I'll stop," Celine said, her paroxysm subsiding. "Your sweet voice always makes me feel better."

When Sadie was young, Celine had taken her to see a therapist with a trim goatee. He always seemed about to cry, a dull twinkle in his eye. *What did that feel like,* he had asked, about Sadie's permissive upbringing. *To be so loved?*

So loved? How about so emotionally manipulated? When Sadie told Celine she wanted to contact her father, whom she had withheld "for Sadie's own good," Celine glowered, then wept, then finally threatened suicide. *Well, not in so many words. She had said she didn't think she could survive it.*

But Celine was writing the therapist's paychecks and in recompense, he wrote off her behavior. That was when Sadie wrote off therapy.

"You were saying?" Sadie said, flat as a rug.

"Yours is the most sonorous voice I've ever heard," Celine expounded, choosing to overlook Sadie's reticence. "I've always told you that."

Celine was fire and Sadie was ice. Celine had to be mitigated. She was always trying to get too close. Sadie stood to cede her seat to an elderly woman. A courtesy she had learned as an adult; as a child, Sadie had never been taught how to behave. Imagine, having to teach yourself.

"What's your emergency?" Sadie asked her mother, as if she were a 911 operator. All her life, Sadie had looked after her mother's impracticalities. Celine was always in a tangle of living and it was Sadie's job to unravel the knots.

Celine murmured assent. “They delayed my pub date *again*.”

Sadie got off the BART and decided to take the long way, to avoid Jones Street. Sadie liked things old and worn, with a patina. She hated the bright millennial style that characterized the “eclectic” luxury shops in Nob Hill. “Could that possibly be because you haven’t handed in the manuscript?” she said into the phone.

On the heels of the second wave of feminist thought and arguably the third, Celine had made a name for herself with a rousing treatise proposing a redress of covert binaries in language and thought. Her second book had been well received but had not been greeted with fireworks. The third: there had been some complaints. And since then, she had been working on the fourth. The more she worked over the manuscript, she felt it getting worse and worse, its power weakening.

Celine was prickly. “Probably because they paid some astronomical advance to some overhyped pop psychology distillation everyone will buy, including me and you, by Kathleen Hanna or the pretty one from Pussy Riot.”

“Nadezhda.” Sadie pushed her oversized sunglasses up the bridge of her nose, feeling haunted by the infallibly refined spirits of Joan Didion and Anna Wintour. She knew she was not wearing them with the appropriate dose of je ne sais quoi. “Do you have your book backed up?”

“I think so, but I don’t know what that is.”

“Your laptop is ancient.” Sadie knew, because she had taken Celine to buy it. Because she was the competent one. “The processor is out of date. Technology has a life span.”

Celine muttered, “I give all my money to Apple.”

“You don’t *give* it to them.” Celine played fast and loose with language. Sadie felt it essential to assign the right word to the proper article.

"Thousands of dollars," she said fiercely, trampling on. "They're running a good hustle."

"It's not a *hustle* for a retailer to sell you something." Sadie felt her temperature rise, like an egg about to crack. "*You* want what *they* have and you're either willing to pay for it or not."

Now she was sinking to Celine's level. The trick to sustaining equilibrium, the umbrella against the rain of madness, was to disengage.

"They sell me something," Celine cut in. She loved to argue in the morning. It was her cup of coffee. "And when they want me to buy a new one it miraculously stops working. It's called planned obsolescence."

Sadie waited out this circular logic. She reminded herself that this morning, Celine held the cards. Sadie would have to go through the motions, do the hokey-pokey.

Celine began to bluster. "Concerns me that you'd take the side of a trillion-dollar corporation over your own mother." She sniffed. "Loyalty, it appears, is one of my better qualities, which you were not lucky enough to inherit."

Sadie considered offering to lend Celine her creaky old MacBook. It was woefully outdated, but it still worked. Anything lent to Celine would be wrecked upon return. She would read a book in the rain, muddle a silk scarf with sauces leaked from takeout containers in the bottom of her handbag. She would insist, despite your protestations, on providing you a replacement. She never would.

"I gave birth to you," Celine said. "Don't forget."

Celine's approach was to self-deprecate so as to get ahead of any critique that anyone might reasonably level: yes, she was selfish. Of course she was egoistic. Had she denied it?

At this cue, Sadie flattened her voice to explain the thrust of the call: she had a favor to ask. "Go on," Celine said.

Sadie had always taken a secret comfort in their spats. She liked how they could recover, the pressure between them a balloon they could blow up and puncture endlessly. Soft-pedaling, she introduced her request and steeled herself for opposition. "Can you go to Alice's show for me?"

Celine laughed aggressively. "Sounds like you don't want to go yourself."

"I have to be out of town."

"Interesting. Tell me why."

Sadie could not tell Celine that her hang-up had to do with mechanics. She had studied up. She understood that a flaccid penis became erect when the erectile tissue filled with blood, the direct consequence of arousal; she could even see how lubrication facilitated; but the part she couldn't see was actually pushing the penis into the vagina. "Did you ever have any . . . problems?" she had asked Alice.

"I once met a needledick!" Alice said, cackling. "We had to resort to other measures." Sadie, dismayed, could not find it in her to laugh. She could not erase the image of Alice having some undefined form of alternate sex with a human male with a 1:300-scale needle adrift in his broad crotch-field.

"I would if I could." Sadie refused to confide in her mother. She so rarely did—such confidences were the currency of their relationship and were not freely given. "Yes or no?" she pressed.

Celine was quick with her answer. "No."

"Great," Sadie said drily. "Thanks for your help. I'll tell Alice that you couldn't be bothered."

"Can't be bothered? This is *your* best friend. You're accusing me?"

Sadie sighed. Celine had pegged her. "Can you do this for me? I really can't make it."

Celine was churlish. “I bet you could if you wanted to.”

What Sadie could not tell Celine was that losing her virginity was predicated on this trip. Sadie had been dieting for three weeks in anticipation. She did not understand how such an onslaught of babies were born every day. She thought that sex required perfection; if a female was not utterly desirable, with no caveats, why bother to have it?

Sadie blamed the cyst; back when Sadie was sixteen it appeared cruelly and abruptly on her inner labia. Without telling Celine or Alice, she went to the gynecologist. There was no problem, apparently, it would take care of itself. At home, when Sadie applied pressure, the ruby gem gave way to bursting, a gushing geyser, leaving an abscess. Squeamish, she had decided then that her vagina was a kind of mysterious grotto with its own sickening geology. Best left alone, not tinkered with.

“This would be a huge help, Mom. Please.”

Celine asked, with an air of deep-wounded dignity, “Is the play one of these dystopic retellings where woodland fairies are contemporized into space invaders, and sprites are astroninjas, and the parade of the dead in *Richard the Third* is a horde of zombies?”

“Don’t think so.” Sadie had not read the play, had not read Shakespeare, had huge gaps. As an adolescent, she had relinquished intellectual pursuits. Despite everything, she admired her mother’s rebelliousness so much, and her mother so applauded dissent that she thought there could be no better way to earn Celine’s endorsement than to reject those very things she held most dear. This had pained Celine, as expected. Whether it had the desired effect of making her more respectful of her daughter was indecipherable. The trouble was: Celine had *always* esteemed Sadie; in this arena, there was little room for growth or development.

"I wouldn't go *out of my way*," Celine granted, drawing boundaries like a line in the sand, "but I suppose I could stop off on my way home from the hardware store."

The hardware store was on Highland, next to the cosmetics kiosk that sold makeup for men and gender-free fragrance. It could not be denied that Celine's assault on gender had become ubiquitous, ushering in a new era. Her male students wore skirts, not out of any ideology but because they liked how it looked and felt. If culture had shifted, it was in part because Celine had nudged it.

"I do pass by the theater," Celine said. She seemed not to be in the mood for one of their legendary spats. "I can't really *avoid* it. Because, as I said, I'm going to the hardware store. Because the, um, kitchen water filter is broken."

"You didn't mention that." Almost against her will, Sadie felt the relief of being reconciled with her mother—they seemed to have decided together that they would not self-implode this time.

"I don't tell you everything," Celine snapped.

Sadie brightened, participating in the charade. "If you're passing the front door, you might as well stop in."

Celine clucked her tongue. She would never admit it, but she preferred to be tasked with an activity. Otherwise, she dragged out nights, tackling social theory at all hours in scant light, amassing additions to the extant seven years' worth of writings she had compiled on no discernible topic. Gender was about society was about cultural presuppositions was about *everything*.

"You'll owe me," Celine said, on impulse. "And you'll have to book my ticket. You know I don't like to input my card number into those—"

"Entry fields?"

Celine grunted.

"I'll order it with my card," Sadie bargained. "My treat."

Celine lit upon this. "It is big of me. I won't let you forget it."

"No, you wouldn't."

"I think this calls for a trip to the diner." Celine switched gears, began her usual pitch, sounding victorious now. "Of course, it gives you the double reward of my favor and my company, but I suppose that's fine. Why don't you treat us to Sunday brunch? I can tell you about the show. You can have your signature—"

"Mickey Mouse pancakes," Sadie cut in, nicking off the end of her mother's sentence. "I couldn't go, even if I wanted to. I'm away this weekend, remember? Hence this call?"

"*Next* Sunday."

Sadie yawned, to show how little the proposition appealed. "Probably not. Work, et cetera."

"You don't want to see me." Sadie could sense Celine's disappointment through the receiver, her proud voice slackening. "You think I can't read between the lines?"

Sadie kept her cool. She had learned self-control in the face of a lifetime of her mother's provocations—and sharpened it like a switchblade anytime Celine flew into a rage. "You promise you'll show up tonight? I can count on you?"

Celine assented haughtily. "*If* you think it would mean that much to her."

"It would."

"I'm not wasting my evening," she countercharged, "if your friend doesn't care."

"She does."

Sadie thought of something. "Say you liked it, even if you don't."

"I will do no such thing." Celine's voice was haughty. "I probably won't," she added, "like it."

"Alice is sensitive right now. She's grasping at straws and I'm asking you to extend her the slightest courtesy."

"The courtesy will be my attendance. It'll have to suffice."

Reaching Rincon Park, Sadie shaded her eyes. Overhead, the sky was smooth and blue, the sun shining bright as a lamp. An early butterfly sunned on a patch of long grass. The weather had cooperated. "I bet they all go for a drink after," Sadie embellished, feeling generous. "Ask if you can come along. Alice won't be put off. She loves you."

This seemed to pacify Celine. She responded more baldly to flattery than anyone Sadie had ever met. "We'll send you a selfie." Celine's titanic voice sounded depleted. "Is it called a selfie if there are two people in the picture?"

Chapter Five

CELINE AND SADIE

When Celine was a girl, she had taped two ends of a length of thread to either wall flanking the top of the stairs, hoping to trip her father and send him crashing to great injury. It didn't work. The thread just broke, and he didn't even notice. Her father worked in a foundry that supplied home appliance parts to companies like Whirlpool, heat-treating cast-iron rolls. Celine's mother, with habits of goodness and patterns of devotion, the enactment of which made her daughter seethe like a tempest, took care of the rest.

The factories were shuttering even then, hulking plants standing like an augur among ruined fields and echoing empty homesteads. Celine's father was pink-faced, with a booming voice, and would have looked at home onstage in Branson, Missouri, in a bedazzled Nudie suit. Instead, his world was gray, and he was somber. He trudged through the drudgery of mass production as a manufactory-floor overseer. He survived, later, on disability checks and painkillers, feeling sapped of use. How well she recalled it: the fading red star of his quick hand on her cheek.

Celine might have grown up with Chernobyl, Guerrilla Girls, AIDS, and Apple. Instead, she got Reagan, the Muffler King, parades, Eckel's Lake with its wobbly docks, cows with tails ticking, the Green

Gables. Festive libations out of tiki mugs at the Kahiki Supper Club was as exotic as it got.

Chagrin Falls, population 4,032, was a microtown made up of split-level houses, subdivided tract housing, and neighborhood retail properties, tucked between prairies, farms, and factories. Only a decade prior, industry *was* the town. At one point, the lithified bedrock had powered nine different mills. Origins of the town's name harkened from Moses Cleveland's frustrations over the river's shallow areas and sandbars, which were indeed of strikingly little depth. Day sailors scraped their hulls.

Celine's family lived in a modular home. She still remembered the day their house arrived on the back of a delivery truck. Celine's childhood was spent popping the batteries in and out of flashlights, disassembling radios, and digging for worms. And she had been attracted to grates. Any kind: manhole covers, curb gutters, storm-drain inlets. Been captivated by their portal-like quality. What if one fell in? They seemed to lead far and away, out of earth, to someplace inconceivable from which you could never again be found nor retrieved.

As if she didn't already know about men, she got married—and young at that, aged twenty-three. The dusky morning of her potluck wedding, Celine opened the minibar fridge and found her bouquet stock-erect in frozen water—the hotel guest before her, apparently, had cranked up the dial settings. Through the night, the flowers hung their heads. It should have been a sign, all those buttercups and hedgerow roses drooping like soft bells.

"I do," Celine said. Did she? It was an expedient promise to make. Looking back, she knew now that it was half-witted to choose a life to prove a point.

Celine and Adam had met through her mother. She had made a good enough social showing among her acquaintances that when one needed an eligible boy and one an eligible girl, notes were compared. Celine, with her tall bearing (which could be construed as elegant, if she would only remember to stand up straight), and Adam, with his expansive shoulders (which were out of proportion with his body, but were nonetheless handsome in and of themselves), were found to be narrowly satisfactory—even if both felt (he broadening his shoulders and she standing on tiptoes a little to gain those extra inches), behind closed doors, like they had inherited the bum end of the deal.

Adam had attended a Benedictine all-boys' high school in Worthington, where hormonal urges were eradicated through roughhousing and where glimpses of girls were apportioned in twice-monthly chaperoned functions, volleyball games and age-appropriate formal dances held from 7 to 10 p.m. Given all this withholding, Adam was understandably curious about girls.

Celine felt extraterrestrial. But she pretended to be like the girls he had hoped to know, smoothing mayonnaise onto her crazy hair in the hopes it would level out. "I love you," he had said, one day while they were playing a game of hearts. With a sweep of his hand, he collected the cards and shuffled, expertly wedding them into a single deck. "And I'm going to marry you." He carried through on the threat.

Celine conceived right away. She thought she would give her husband what he wanted, a child, and then be done. Mothering, she thought naïvely, was a task that could be completed, capped off, a checkmark on a to-do list.

Celine knew the very time Sadie had been conceived. In that empty hour of the afternoon between 3:30 and 4:30. Nothing happened in that hour, she had figured. Nothing of consequence. She had not really meant to have Sadie—yes, she *had*; it was not an accident—but she had not intended it to eclipse her life. Sadie was born in 1992, the Year of the Woman, with twenty-four women elected to the House of Representatives.

Celine's labor had been so strenuous that, now and then, she still started awake, blood rushing to her heart. "Imagine your cervix dilating like a flower," the midwife had counseled. Under influence of the hallucinatory pain, Celine had thumped with sweat, eyes pinched shut, braying, even her toes numb with exertion.

Adam had kidded that, approaching Celine's bedside, he had thought to himself: *Do not approach the animal.* Only Adam had seen her that way, but he was one person too many. And Celine always felt that Sadie had been witness, hawklike, to her own birth. Her intent eyes seemed to store away anything less than savory, to summon to memory later.

It was less difficult after that. Celine's mother would call to ask if the baby was colicky, whether she fussed. Fussed? Ha! Sadie was a tranquil observer, composed as a picture, unrelenting in the face of obstacles, be it when she tried to roll over or crawl backward. Strangers of a certain type would offer the highest commendation they could think of: she should be a model in a baby food ad.

To Celine, Sadie was a person, never a child.

And when she began to talk, Celine hung on every word. She knew, deep down, that Sadie was smarter than she was, born with essential seeds of intelligence one could neither earn nor buy. She would always remember when mop-headed Sadie broke away from her in a women's restroom, racing like lightning out into a public mall.

"I'm not a girl," she said, when Celine had chased her down. "And I'm not a boy. I'm a borl." Celine had laughed and said that was a made-up word. Sadie had looked up with her eager, young eyes. "Every word is made up at first."

Such brilliance! Celine would not be talked out of it, glowing with her daughter's wisdom and virtuosity. Uninspired, Sadie remembered it differently. "That was just something I said."

"It was brilliant."

"I probably heard it somewhere."

"No," Celine quarreled. "You had an original mind. Once you asked: 'If the universe invented everything, who invented the universe?' " Celine shook her head at the profundity.

Despite *parenting* with a capital P never being Celine's passion—her passion was for Sadie herself—Celine had been a good mother. Anyone who said otherwise wasn't looking closely enough. What about when she had rounded up all the kids in the neighborhood and carted them to the salvage yard, letting them peek in and out of decommissioned Jeeps and thread nylon cord through scabby slots and gaps caused by rust? Celine had shown them a great time. They said so themselves. No one had thanked her for that. Instead, another mother had repaid her with a droning lecture about tetanus.

For years now, Celine had endeavored to revise the chapter in her book called "Mother-Love." But the topic was too big. She'd never gotten a handle on it. Her feelings were bigger than words. One day . . .

Celine's devotion to Sadie never extended as far as her husband. She was a lesbian, of course, but had not known it yet. It wouldn't have occurred to her. For one, sex with a woman was not physically feasible. Surely, a man was required to complete sex. Otherwise, what was everyone doing, just slipping and sliding?

After Celine announced she was leaving, she and Adam slept together one last time, shyly uncurling like roots feeling their way beneath soil cover with such tender vulnerability that she had even thought she might stay. Adam, the first man.

Not enough to stay. They filed on no-fault grounds and completed the process without attorneys. What Celine had mistakenly perceived as his desire for a child was in fact desire for a life of plenty: he was happy to trade joint custody for a surrender of spousal support. He had pinned his hopes on the wrong female. He wanted family, intact, and said he would try again elsewhere.

When Sadie was five years old, Celine announced they were leaving Ohio. She had quietly applied to Cal Berkeley. To her amazement, on a Tuesday the acceptance letter arrived. She filched a sum of money from her father to finance their move to California. He kept a thousand dollars in his small steel Honeywell safe and she knew the combination: 122817. It was his mother's birthday. The embezzled bills, tucked into an open envelope in the glove compartment, looked faded, somehow, more gray than green.

Growing up, Celine had disdained her name. It seemed only to highlight the essential variance she already felt from her classmates. Couldn't she have been a Kimberly or a Jennifer, she'd wondered as a girl? Couldn't her mother have made life easy?

Mamie had baptized Celine with a rare pretension. The name must have sounded ritzy, like a swanky cultural benchmark. She would never have heard of the author. The Cuyahoga County Public Library holding the 1949 edition of *Journey to the End of the Night* under Dewey class number PZ3.D475 was not a ten-minute walk, but also an entire world, away. She would have been appalled to ascertain that the most famous namesake's most celebrated story was a lost soul's journey through violence, disgust, and cruelty, unto death.

Celine hunted out and procured that very Dewey class number PZ3.D475; the book served, against anything Mamie might have imagined, as a lightning bolt. It ignited in Celine a sense that she was someone different from what she had been told.

"I'd seen too many troubling things to be easy in my mind. I knew too much and not enough. I'd better go out, I said to myself, I'd better go out again."

The novel spoke to Celine, who felt *she* had better go out. The idea crystallized. It was the making of Celine who, by the same name, was suddenly entirely new.

"An unfamiliar city is a fine thing. That's the time and place when you can suppose that all the people you meet are nice. It's dream time."

Celine longed to dream. In unfamiliar cities, ripe with educated young people.

It was winter in Chagrin Falls and Celine, a young mother, was cold. Feeling awakened by her self-observation, her throat stung. The thermostat clicked gently. The daily newspaper displayed a hotbed of revolutionary unrest along Telegraph Avenue, sit-ins in Sproul Plaza, campsites of organizers occupying the San Francisco Civic Center in protest of H.W.'s latest attack on civil liberties or deployment of U.S. troops to the Persian Gulf. New leaves. Misty-eyed, Celine saw herself develop antiestablishment, anti-family ideas over Ethiopian and Thai food.

She decided: California, then.

And hadn't it been an adventure, to rise in the cold dark of early morning, to leave everything they had always considered essential—all their toiletries, namely, which Celine assured an anxious Sadie were replaceable—and to set out west on I-80 in Celine's Datsun Cherry as each day lengthened, taking the last summer peaches with them? Sadie had knelt on the sweaty leather, blinded by her hair, whipped by gale-force wind.

Sadie watched her mother, uncorked. Gasoline still smelled to Sadie like freedom.

Freedom and infidelity.

"Where's Daddy?" Sadie asked.

Last gas for 75 miles.

"Daddy wants us to be happy."

Sadie agreed this was likely true. That her daddy had always hugged her, sometimes leaving little notes in her lunchbox. Sadie accepted that adults sorted out the plans of life between themselves. She waited to see what was in store.

They advanced through Iowa, where drifts scraped the plains; straight through Nebraska for eighty miles; holding their breath in Wyoming's Green River Tunnel; admiring the snowcapped Great Salt Lake mountains, teeth chattering like castanets; slow through the Sierra Nevada; slow to marvel at Reno's jittering lights. "We're here," Celine announced finally, shifting gear into Park where the road ended in Downtown Berkeley, her spirits lifted like a hot-air balloon. Living in the Bay Area Sadie had often heard people say that I-80 *began* in Berkeley and ended in New Jersey. This was wrong. Berkeley would always be the endpoint.

"Is Daddy here?" she asked.

They sat together in the Cherry. "We don't live with Daddy anymore."

"Is Daddy bad?"

Celine looked seriously at Sadie. "Daddy reduces us. If one is not careful, one's whole life passes without incident."

So began the squalid days of waking early in the drab brown-shingle graduate family housing, where Celine and Sadie lived for a year, sharing a futon. Ancient, starved radiators seethed in the wine-dark corridors. Sadie remembered being unsure whether she and Celine had money or were poor; she learned later that if you were poor, you knew it. A discerning child, Sadie respected Celine's working hours. She would write notes, *i mayd diner*, and slide them under Celine's door.

Sadie even made a friend in this complex, who lived unintelligibly far away, across a series of courtyards and corridors, but who appeared daily in the complex playground, bobbing on the pale blue C-spring-mounted seal. They fell in with each other, though Sadie cared as little for her as for the outgrown toys conveyed from Ohio, untouched on the shelf in her room. In fact, she thought of this new friend as a doll. She dressed the friend, brushed her hair, imagined scenarios and assigned them each roles, even lines of dialogue. She sent the doll-girl to the kitchen as a mule for snacks.

Celine appreciated this new allegiance. Sadie could disappear for hours, Celine so tied up with discovery that she barely noticed Sadie had gone. Usually, children met their parents just as they were facing all they would *not* do with their lives. Sadie met Celine as she was beginning to understand how much she would. Sadie dimly recalled thinking that a mother was not supposed to be so jubilant.

Their only consistent male company was Jerry, Celine's writing lamp. Jerry was brass, with a round bonnet and a thick cord. He had accompanied them from Chagrin Falls to Berkeley. Every night of her life, Sadie had seen Jerry illuminated, positioned to stoop low, neck gently bent to peer conspiratorially over Celine's page as she scribbled with her left hand. Men, Celine tried to explain to Sadie, were ancillary. They would not be the major players in their lives.

It had taken Sadie years to surrender her childhood impression of the other sex. Dastardly grins, beneath razor-thin mustaches coiled like Dalí's, tiptoeing in every shadow, eyes like a ventriloquist's dummy's. She understood that the role of men was to serve as an obstacle for everyone else. For Father's Days, Sadie sat apart, allowed to spend the day coloring whatever she wanted. Her classmates, forced into fabricating stiff and gloppy handprint cards (just like last year; the teachers had not consulted one another), envied Sadie's half-orphan's privilege. She was dignified and solitary in her loss, policed by no one.

As a child, Sadie's prized possession was a ride-along Power Wheels Barbie Jeep, turquoise and hot pink with a working pedal, six preloaded "radio" stations—cranking out such plastic-pink hits as "Mermaid Party" and "Princesses Just Want to Have Fun"—and doors that opened and closed, hard-won despite it being used to begin with, passed along by the next-door neighbor—how could Celine refuse now that it was free? Equipped with wheels, Sadie had conceived of elaborate escape schemes. She would head for Ohio and track down her father. He would drive a Jeep, too, and they would park their vehicles side by side in his tidy, tool-filled garage.

Sadie remembered the day she had been seated on the floor of the dark graduate housing apartment, watching a 1970s Japanese-made cartoon version of *The Little Mermaid* that was marginally truer to its source, and which Sadie preferred to the Disney because the mermaid was less flashy, less bosomy red-green-amethyst, and because it had a tragic ending which it only hinted at, daggers and death denoted by seafoam. It was about the ocean and about sacrifice. There were no ditties, Sadie recalled, which she disapproved of in a story that was meant to be serious.

Celine had come in, interrupting the terrible moment of climactic self-sacrifice in which Marina stabs Fritz through the heart, allowing his blood to trickle onto her new feet. "Honey," she said, "your daddy died."

Pausing the film, Sadie thought there must be some mistake. She had never had a daddy. Why would Celine be telling her this? It was like learning your flight to the moon had been canceled. How could she grieve what she had never had? He was dead before she could get to him, stalled incorrectably by her mother's enigmatic and inscrutable motives. Motives that Sadie, all her life, had never decoded. Why keep Sadie from her father, except to rebuke one of them, or both, or perhaps the sum total of the entire male sex.

It was hard to know who Celine *did* abide. She and Sadie were members of the intelligentsia, but not of the community. Celine had little spare interest in "the theory blowhards," which was how she dismissed the academic elite, of which she and Sadie were only scarcely a part. Celine began packing up Sadie, a cherished burden, and hauling her to meet-ups in basement caves held by acronymical organizations, letters accruing like rings on a tree. PFLAG. GLAAD. IGLYO. She always brought Sadie's sleeping bag, in case she needed to nod off. Sadie would tour herself around the queer bookshop, navigate the maze of shelves; the small, sweaty crowd; the makeshift bar. She knew all the slogans, and even what half of them meant. *Rainbows reign.* Two, four, six, eight, how do you know your kids are straight? *Gays bash back.* A woman's place is on top.

If Sadie complained of boredom, Celine would admonish her. "Stop playing the child."

The truth was it was stirring. Durable women mounted the stage to expound on agitprop and the body politic, in hypnotic voices intoxicatingly sure of their own convictions. On one occasion, thrillingly, Sadie heard a soft-spoken female poet with a tweedy, grandfatherish aesthetic say the word *tits*.

"Cover your ears," Celine said. Sadie looked at her. "Or don't. I'll trust your judgment." Whenever the talk turned pornographic, Sadie pretended to be asleep so that Celine would not know she had heard. It would have embarrassed her if Celine knew. Sadie worried it would make her, somehow, in Celine's eyes, soiled.

Seated in the back row beside Celine, listening with her solemn air, Sadie waited with grave eyes for law enforcement to arrive, to point out the ADULTS ONLY placard plainly visible in the mullioned window, and to drag her out by the ears. But no one gave the patient young observer second notice.

It was around this time that an understanding rattled through

Sadie: Celine was irregular. Walking home with her mother after a members' meeting for Sister Spit, a Radicalesbian separatist spoken-word collective, with a bag of bear claws and elephant ears from Bette's Bakery, Sadie inquired what *queer* meant.

Celine chewed her pastry. She answered, lamely but honestly, that the word resisted definition. Seeing that Sadie was unsatisfied, Celine sighed and amended that, in her case, it meant same-sex attraction and same-sex sex.

What's sex? Sadie asked. She had still, then, looked to Celine for answers.

I shouldn't tell you this, Celine would often say, and then invariably go on to say it. Further, she would refuse to elaborate. *Stop me,* she'd say. *I've already said too much.*

Sadie was not yet a teenager when she realized Celine often generated feelings of contempt in others, even as, oftentimes, they held her in high regard. It was as simple as Celine saying, "A lot of people hate me. That means I'm doing something right."

But if Sadie hated Celine, then she would be like everyone else.

Those years, Sadie kept watch for another woman, her mother's age or preferably more senior, a suitable replacement. Someone who could actually *prepare* Sadie for life. There was so much escaping Sadie's grasp. She grew older by the day and increasingly less prepared for the future.

What were the retirement benefits of residual income?

. . . *Celine said the Fed would be bankrupt anyway.*

How did you achieve a smoky cat eye with a palette of bronzed eye shadows?

. . . *Celine said makeup was for wannabes.*

How did you balance a checkbook?

. . . *Celine didn't.*

The flotilla of other girls' mothers were the likeliest candidates.

Shelly, who tied gifts with lemon-yellow ribbon and fed other women's daughters forkfuls of key-lime pie. Or Masha, who indulged in a forty-minute Pilates routine every morning, glowing with moderation. Nina, who was delicate, who wore head wraps, and whom Celine wrongly had always assumed was undergoing chemotherapy or was in remission.

Mothers who conducted themselves like society said they should. It was funny, though: anytime Sadie had hit upon a potential candidate, the woman would go and say something like "Help others without asking anything in return," or "Dance like no one's watching," or "Kindness is its own reward," or admit to liking *Marley & Me* or Suze Orman. Something utterly pedestrian that would strike Sadie suddenly as drab and mediocre. Flat and colorless, commonplace. Why were people so endlessly disappointing? If they weren't rabble-rousing provocateurs, they were deathly dreary.

Now, age twenty-three, dodging her friend's play in an anxious remedial attempt, Sadie knew every in and out of 401(k)s—she didn't just balance her checkbook; she kept a ledger of every last expense, no matter how insignificant, and had filed her own tax returns since age sixteen (when she'd filed her babysitting earned income, all of $340, and received a humorless but complete refund from the IRS)—but she had never had a sexual experience. She was reluctant to parse how all this was associated, but she knew it surely was.

All right, sure, not exactly never. She had engaged in heavy petting with Damon, a synth-head from her Chemistry class who had pursued her, and who had insisted they listen to Kraftwerk's "Autobahn" together on a split headphone jack anytime BART ran parallel alongside the freeway. He liked to smoke weed and pretend, to the pinging electronica, like he was piloting a spaceship.

Did that count?

* * *

Celine remembered it differently.

After five days of Denny's eggs and gas station peanuts, she and Sadie fled the remote down-home backwaters of Ohio and *arrived* in the Datsun Cherry. It felt a little, there, like an aftermath. The Bay Area sixties were no more in evidence. No more Rainbow Gatherers toting rain sticks and sloppy felt pouches. No jangling leather boys. No hot Summer of Love. The Free Speech Movement was middle-aged and what was left was hippie tourism, outdated.

Initially, Celine felt misled, feeling she had gotten there too late. But soon she discovered that incense and flower power had given way to a strident, more radical feminist counterculture. Taking full advantage of the neighborly co-op nursery, Celine would walk the streets alone while Sadie mashed her fingers into floury berry-dyed dough. The first few weeks, Celine combed the teeming city, alert for the bogeymen sure to be lying in wait. To pounce on her and her girl, to send them scuttling, bridled, back home.

It was to this soundtrack that, at a worker-owned feminist co-op on Adeline Street, Celine met a songbird named Todd. Though her body was wiry and unendowed, Celine was still pretty enough back then—when being pretty actually mattered, when it might change the course of your life.

Todd wore patched elbows and a Women's Health Collective pin. He wrote soft ballads about murdering women and chucking the bodies into the bay. Sadie was snake-eyed, unyielding as pavement, butting in anytime he touched Celine, or else wedging herself between them. Once, age five and far too old for such behavior, she squatted over his guitar case, peed, and closed the lid so it baked. But he stuck around. Together, on weekends, after he returned from work, they haunted the Berkeley Flea Market, Olivia Records, and

Ollie's Bar. The Bacchanal and the Jubilee. Celine coordinated campaigns for the Lyon-Martin Clinic.

Celine dressed up to teach, button-downs layered over wifebeater tanks. She discovered that she could donate her shirts to St. Luke's Thrift, let them clean and press the garment, and buy it back two weeks later for three dollars, saving eleven in the bargain. Eventually, she moved out of graduate housing.

She and Todd leased a large apartment in the Flats' studio row because it was right on the I-80 turnpike, which would have made getting out of town a breeze, had they ever had any place to go. It had a sunroom! They were able to negotiate the terms down from twelve months to six—they already knew what little of this would last. They papered the neighborhood and found a third person to defray rent. In preparation for her arrival, she asked them to level the sloping, uneven floors with soft pine plywood.

Cassie, the third roommate, sculptress and a host of the local radio hour, materialized with an almost primitive body, tiny breasts, and fertility goddess hips. She had black hair and wore lime-green pants. She was a tough dame, a separatist feminist with a silver tongue, and had come from an educated home. Men were oppressors, she declared—which, unfortunately, she admitted could be kind of hot. Celine began sleeping with both roommates. Women, she discovered, were like guava to her parched tongue.

Together, living in a rigid sociopolitical harmony, the threesome of adults negotiated the tensions that arose when Sadie ran through the house bare-assed during the bedbug scare; when she left the front door wide open so that Cassie's free-roaming house parakeet made for the hills; when she licked the lid of the cream cheese; when she cartelized the television with *Barney and Friends*, wailing when she was required to turn it off.

Annually, Celine considered sending Adam Sadie's school

photos, a reminder of his almost-life, his near-miss. She thought of letting Sadie phone him on Christmas. She thought it was probably the Right Thing to Do. She even looked up his phone number, even *dialed* once, hanging up before the first ring finished.

Who was he, anyway? Just a guy who had disappointed her, whom she had disappointed, who had wanted to entrap her in the wrong life. Sadie did not know men, did not know the webs they spun. Give an inch, he'd take a mile. Celine was afraid he would try to keep Sadie.

The activist movement kept Celine busy. Political action meant signing petitions, renouncing mothers, demonstrating, applying mud-colored lipstick, singing, marching, dragging your feet, believing, not believing anymore.

"This may be a dumbass request," Celine said to Cassie, over the loud jazz Cassie always seemed to have on. Cassie smoked cigarettes after sex and during. "Feel free to tell me to fuck off. But I want to read something about what we're doing."

To her credit, Cassie did not laugh. She supplied Celine with names of the musclewomen, who, admittedly, Celine was supposed to have read for class. Over time, she supplied Celine with the books. Audre, Donna, Gloria, Angela, bell. Celine's skull was cracked, her mind opened, then opened wider. It was how Celine learned to study, by fucking and then reading about it.

"Are you a lesbian?" Sadie asked one day.

Celine pulled Sadie close and said that she loved women, but Sadie most of all. This answer had bothered Sadie. Celine could not understand why.

Celine's sexual awakening coincided with the onset of her intellectual life. Her days of blazing talent, when everything she touched turned to gold, when sitting down at her desk felt like diving into a glittering pool.

It had been life-changing, looking around with the newfound epiphany: everything is for me. Her mother had taught her that the world was for other people. That she was lucky to fit into an existing system. That she should be thankful. And on this point, she was not wrong! It was the nature of the gift itself that her mother had failed to grasp.

At Berkeley, Celine discovered that thinking could be said to be doing. She began to understand things. Experience was bracketed. History was falsified. Speech was gendered. Categories were a means to enforce compulsory action. Spinning-top inertia made sense to her. Trillions. The more she understood, the more she understood.

But no matter how much you understood, there was still always the messy matter of family. That was the thing Celine couldn't get right. Sadie's ride-along Jeep spent a few years gathering fallen leaves in the backyard, her plan to escape forgotten, or put on hold, or whatever happened to plans that never materialized, until, one day, while Celine was absorbed in one of her cartoons, bent down beside her. "Sweetie? Your daddy died."

Celine bore him little ill will by then, just a smidge. Enough not to attend the consummate celebration of his life with good conscience. Adam's funeral—after his idiotic death—started the tradition of Celine packing Sadie up and shipping her off alone to see her grandmother.

Celine had not had much feeling, as a girl, for her own grandmother, a Dickensian type, difficult to digest herself, who ate raw onion sandwiches. But Sadie was different. She offered to go visit Celine's mother alone. Celine always met her at the airport, Southwest brave solo traveler wings clipped to her sweatshirt.

Truth was, Celine could not bear to face her mother, shaking in her disapproval.

Less to fear now. Celine's mother had relocated from her imitation pine log cabin, so orange-stained that it looked like it had a spray tan, into assisted living. Medicare Advantage had covered her first hundred days in the community's memory-care wing, which had been motivation enough.

A few months ago, Celine had arranged a video call with Seven Oaks Elderly Care Center, downloading the center's video conferencing software, and the prim nurse, entering the screen with a sober face, had advised her in a tiny voice that the ruinous effects of her mother's dementia were so advanced that, putting on her shirt, the old woman did not know in which hole to put her head. It irritated Celine that Sadie had not given fairer warning of how severely the disease had progressed.

"If you came to visit, you'd see what I mean," the nurse said, with antiseptic implication. In lieu of that, the nurse set up another Skype call shortly thereafter, with Celine's mother this time. Mamie's shrunken image had resolved into slushy focus and landed in the pit of Celine's stomach. Her mother's new bedroom, fortified with locks and alarms, was spotless and as impeccably tidy as all her prior quarters, which comforted Celine. Mamie was in bed, wrapped in her sheets stitched with squares. She'd always been thrifty in her repairs. Mamie's weight gain had inflated her in a way that was pleasant. Her skin did not sag; in fact, she looked fresh out of the oven. Celine could do this. For a moment, Celine missed her.

Mamie's plump hands clutched a muff in the shape of a puppy. "Is that a toy?" Celine blustered, angry suddenly. Mamie's face was blank, uninsulted. Celine felt her blood darken. Yes, she missed her mother. The old one. "Who authorized that? This is an insult to her adult intelligence."

The uniformed nurse, seated just slightly in the background, had sighed. Prickly as splinters, Celine thought. Bedside manner must have been a nicety of the past. Celine could see the mind-numbing QVC home shopping network running behind her. So *that's* what they parked her in front of.

Looking fearful, sensing tension across the high-speed broadband, Mamie had stroked her pet absently until Celine relented and released her from the call. If only Celine had a sibling to help her with this. Her parents had tried, she knew, but it never took.

And now here Mamie was, on her way out, her escort at her side.

How had it become a war between Sadie and Celine? When *was* it that they stopped being a pair? When had the cord of life that coupled them become lace-pocked and degenerated?

It had to have begun around the time Sadie realized that, to Celine, she was an appendage. An extension of the mother body. All Sadie's childhood, everything was filtered through her mother, Celine always trying to tell Sadie who and what she was. Celine, a spokesperson for antiestablishment freedoms and self-realization, was in fact downright psychically oppressive.

"We don't like men," Celine said, when Sadie was eleven or twelve. They were in Ashby Plaza, trying out all the stock in the Mattress Barn.

For the first time, sloshing up on a waterbed, Sadie had spoken up. "No, *you* don't."

Another time, Sadie had thrown a fit because Celine refused to record her piano recital, wanting to intimately inhabit the moment, not spend the moment documenting it for some unspecified future enjoyment. For the rest of the evening, Celine had refused to let

Sadie out of her bedroom until she apologized. She finally had, so that she could use the bathroom.

"That's called child abuse," Sadie had declared, in recent years.

Celine shrugged. "No one's perfect."

All this begged the question, in Sadie's young mind: How *was* a mother supposed to behave? As a girl, Sadie had pored over the picture book *Are You My Mother?* The baby bird conducted a thorough inquiry. Over twenty-two pages, the bird needled hens, kittens, cows, and dogs with the same unanswerable question.

Are you my mother?

If not, then who is?

The page with the backhoe was sinister. How could a backhoe be a mother? If a mother could be mistaken for a backhoe, what then was anything?

Chapter Six

SADIE

To this day, Alice, with her easy faith, was innocent to the fact that her friendship with Sadie, down to their first meeting on the bus, had been carefully engineered. Even if they both nearly missed catching it, Alice by accident and Sadie by design.

Sadie had never left anything to chance, especially something so significant as a best friend. She kept to herself generally, preferring her own company to a friendship that would not be worth her time. Friends generally ran in packs. Sadie disliked groups, everyone talking over one another. How could anyone hear themselves think?

But friends appeared to be valuable assets in a life. Someone to count on, someone to call. They were an acquisition Sadie had fallen short of. And also, if she was being honest with herself, like something she would really like to have. Someone to see her, in all the ways her mother hadn't. See and appreciate her for the person she was, together with all her faults, not some idealized version.

The pursuit was daunting, though one friend seemed sufficient.

So Sadie gathered her gumption, went out, and with extraordinary effort, *got* herself a friend.

She had scoped Alice out for weeks beforehand. She liked her freckles. Accustomed to being looked at, of course Alice hadn't noticed. Alice drew attention, in her wrinkled men's button-downs, always slipped off one or the other shoulder. It wasn't difficult to strike up the friendship. Alice was quick with her confidences, with appreciation to the listener.

Sadie had the feeling that someone so beautiful should not be so happy.

In the establishing days of their friendship, Alice had still retained an after-school retail job in a small clothing boutique on Piedmont. It had overwhelmed her, she had confided in Sadie. The pathos of people eager and anxious to choose what might best suit them, to see themselves in the best possible light, had so overcome Alice that her heart would overtake her and she would cry bighearted tears in the stockroom elevator. Sadie did not understand such behavior but liked, with a hungry inquisitiveness, to hear about it.

In those first months, Alice still retained a debris of friendships from her former life. Teague, Mikey, and West. They wore all black, dyed their hair untame colors, and stalked the high school halls in tapered jeans and high-top Converse. They traced Anti-Flag and Penis Envy lyrics onto their shoddily hand-painted shock-pink bedroom walls with Sharpies and Wite-Out wands. The most persistent of these girls, Teague, stuck herself to Alice like a burr.

Alice had a good-faith belief in the innate value of any individual. And she was just easy. She wasn't choosy. She got along with everyone.

For a time, Alice hoped they could all be friends. Wishful thinking. "Why not?" Alice asked, and Sadie could see she really did not know. "They're interesting people," Alice said. She had read Thich Nhat Hanh and had a say-nothing-bad-about-anyone rule that year.

In their newly minted friendship, Sadie counted on being able to conduct Alice. Alice was an instrument, happiest when played. But strangely, given the facility of Sadie's playing fingers and the pliability of Alice's willing strings, sometimes, the instrument opted to play itself.

Honestly? Sadie was terrified of losing Alice. She saw her error in having chosen as a best friend someone beloved by all. She had to fend off a lot of pretenders to the throne. Sadie *thought* she and Alice were very close, but then again, Alice seemed to be close to all kinds of people. How did Sadie know she wasn't just another chummy companion, one of the pack?

Sadie became possessive. She began to want to know where Alice was going and why. She disliked hours unaccounted for.

But seeing that she had not yet secured exclusive rights to Alice, Sadie had agreed to attend one of Alice's interminable hangout sessions with her old, substandard friends, in an unsavory part of town. "I think I saw this street on the news," Sadie said, eyes small in scrutiny as the 57 bus let them off on the littered Talbot Avenue, tar and chip, rutted with potholes.

"We're here," Alice said, pushing open a dingy side-entrance screen door. Unmoored in the smoke-choked room, Teague sat propped disaffectedly against the blank wall on a naked mattress. Teague was pregnant, Alice had told Sadie in confidence, but had not made a decision yet. Her time for deciding was closing in.

Even when they entered the room, Teague did not lift her eyes from *The Animaniacs*. The small television's volume was muted, and Hole's *Celebrity Skin* was playing on a stereo. A few others were scattered on leaky bean bag chairs, beer cans parked on upturned cable reels-turned-coffee tables.

"Teenage wasteland," Sadie whispered. Feeling tart and tense, she secured an uninhabited corner of floor. Teague's cousin West was eerily energetic, bare-chested, wearing his orange T-shirt on his head so that it resembled a religious habit. He had a motorcycle shop and his specialty was powder-coating Suzukis. He tossed Sadie a pillow, which she turned over to the cleaner side before sitting on. She didn't want to be one in the sea of Alice's friends. She wanted to be *the* friend.

It struck Sadie as the sort of place a house fire was liable to break out—nothing as notable as an explosion from a failed experiment in methamphetamine or gang-fire ballistics. Simply someone nodded off with a lit cigarette dangling from their hand. The danger was ambient. This humid rat hole, Sadie thought, would be a stupid place to die.

"Something smells," Mikey said into the stale air.

You think? Sadie thought. Might it possibly be the brimming, sticky heap of hash, or maybe the morning's lingering hangover-induced upchuck, drifting in from the bathroom?

"Sadie farted!"

Sadie's heart pounded. "I did not."

Everyone laughed, except Alice, and Sadie burned.

"What the fuck are Animaniacs anyway?" Teague mumbled.

"This is totally weird," Alice whispered to Sadie, knowing it was what she'd want to hear. "We should go."

But they stayed. Teague dozed off, her tank top wadded up around her subtly pregnant belly. She had nice breasts, Sadie noticed, high on her chest. Sadie would have liked to have them.

"My dog is shoe-colored," West thought to observe aloud, over the music, puffing at one thing or another. He was twenty and supremely stoned. "And my shoe is dog-colored."

This made everyone laugh, even Sadie. Especially Teague, eyes fluttering open. Sadie watched as Teague's bowl of Fruity Pebbles turned soggy and infused the milk with a pink tinge.

"You get the BFFF Award for coming with me," Alice said afterward, sounding very Alice. They were seated on the bus, one of three they would take to recover the harmony of Alice's neighborhood, where the lawns were green, the houses historic, the views panoramic. Sadie loved the area. Soon, she assured herself, she would live in it.

Alice, on the other hand, hoped to leave all that privilege behind. She planned to move down to Los Angeles, to pursue her nascent acting career. All it had taken was one friendly compliment from her high school drama teacher and suddenly Alice thought she was Sarah Bernhardt. Sure, as an eager student, she had participated in chorus, dance, and the debate team. Her mother had enrolled her in summer drama camps. And yet, despite this sumptuous foundation, Alice was low on dedication. Sadie feared, privately, that Alice had outsized daydreams for a girl of her ambitions—especially when, for a girl like Alice, ambitions meant assumptions.

Alice was so impressionable. An agent had come to a film screening put on by the Berkeley drama department. After the Q&A, she had mentioned to Alice that she had a face for the screen. And that cemented it, being all the encouragement Alice needed. She was like a faultily magnetized compass, taking just a nudge to be set wildly off course.

Still, despite how unsuitable a career acting would be for Alice in certain respects—she lacked any dose of narcissism, grandiosity, vanity—it was perfectly right in others: she had a remarkable aptitude for identifying with people, she was charismatic, and most of all she was endowed with the innate charity that acting's self-effacement required. Sadie had noticed that, when they watched a movie, Alice could freely identify with *all* the characters. Sadie was not like that: she was a Charlotte, not a Carrie.

As a girl, Sadie knew, Alice had played the piano, then the saxophone. Then she figure skated, then she drew. She was gifted, things had come easy to her, and she liked having things to occupy her time. But she never bothered to *excel.*

"Sometimes, I feel like I'm faking it," Alice had said the prior semester, when she was still in the Bay Area, back when Sadie had thought Alice was bound to her forever. They were at Chito's, *their* Mexican restaurant replete with mariachi, red booths, a jukebox, and a palapa overhang. It was homey, under three generations of proprietorship.

"Why does public approval matter, anyway?" Alice asked, exasperated. She nudged the bowl of quartered limes toward Sadie.

"It's not for the public." Sadie squeezed a wedge of lime into her Modelo. "It's for yourself."

Alice clinked Sadie's glass. "I like myself as I am."

Sadie had complex feelings about Alice's immense privilege. She was all for license of opportunity. Why, then, resent the good fortune and warm lap her best friend had been born into—and was all too eager to share? It was something more complex, less explicable, than plain, ordinary envy.

It had to do with new ballet slippers, tights, tutus, wraparound Capezio cardigans, tennis rackets freshly strung; instruments nested into velvet cases, novel and gleaming, begging to be played. In Sadie's darkest moments, recalling her own budget magic kits and too-small secondhand Rollerblades, this litany of diversions struck her as plain, dumb luck: Alice all accolade and no accomplishment.

Celine had let her daughter develop without interference. Sadie would have welcomed a little intrusion. Preferred a mother like Alice's, who enrolled her daughter in an extracurricular each day of the week, just for her to quit them in succession. If Celine had enrolled Sadie in ballet lessons at age four? Today she'd be Baryshnikov.

"I'm an air sign," Alice said, "so I have a hard time committing to things."

"The problem is you're too happy," Sadie said. She felt that anxiety was a useful emotion. It forced a person into things. She dipped a chip into the mortar bowl of soupy salsa, more of a marinara.

Alice's contentment was preordained. "You have money, beauty, a perfect snow globe of emotional well-being." A snow globe Sadie sometimes wished she could crawl into and shelter inside. "What *else* do you have to offer?"

She prayed Alice would not say acting. Even as a child, Sadie had disliked playing dress-up, replacing your character with another's, putting on a hat or a feather boa just to take it off again and be who you'd been before. Where was the forward momentum? "Don't you have anything you like to do?"

"I like everything," Alice admitted, looking as directionless as a shattered compass. The enchiladas arrived, smothered in mole, and Sadie tucked in. "I just don't seem to like some things in particular more than others."

Sadie was different. She had always steered toward what she wanted, direct as an ocean liner aimed at a distant shore. Celine wanted to have it all. Sadie, having sensed the danger in that, wanted only a few things.

In sixth grade, turning a deaf ear to her teacher's guide to the mathematical expression of PEMDAS, Sadie had carefully demarcated in her Five Star spiral notebook a timeline of goals spanning a lifetime. She had slated her first kiss for age fifteen and, years later on the eve of her sixteenth birthday, had skillfully executed it with a seventeen-year-old exchange student, behind a gas station. "I just want to say," Per had said, "that I can't be your boyfriend. I'm a free agent. I'm still playing the field."

"I don't care if I never see you again!" He had driven her home in silence.

Folded inside Sadie, beneath the tenacity, was the anxiety that she was *not* good enough. Not spoken for. Her mother was someone, maybe. An arriviste, she had hoisted them skyward. But they had no *inherent* value. Despite all Sadie's outward surety, she wasn't wholeheartedly sure how she fit on the earth. Added to this preoccupation with origins that Sadie had not been permitted to know her father, an unqualified half of herself.

She remembered so little about him. Remembered him spooning onto her emptied plate the last of a spaghetti bolognese. Remembered sitting side by side at a tall counter, drawing goofy faces onto paper plates, him using a red-handled pair of child's scissors to furnish each expression with a different fringed haircut. Remembered he had corrected one of Sadie's portraits: boys, he said, did not have the eyelashes she had drawn. Remembered Celine having schooled him in turn, a premonition of the deluge to come.

Somewhere in the Claremont house, Celine still had those flimsy, creased plates. The crumbling mementos only served as an emblem of how many moments were forgotten.

Sadie tried not to think about that. She looked forward, never back. The timeline stipulated that Sadie would become pregnant by age twenty-three, catching the peak reproductive years when the body was at its most conducive to childbearing. Before everything shut down, grinding to a halt, the female procreative system's STORE CLOSED window shuddering to a locked conclusion. This would get Celine's goat: she spoke endlessly, with no regard for Sadie's feelings, about the pressure she'd felt, back in Ohio, to have a child; how she'd not been ready; how she'd still had her own youth to live when she fell pregnant with Sadie. Sadie could hardly wait for the day she'd make her own fresh-faced pregnancy announcement to Celine. Half of her wanted to seek out available semen right this minute. She could have a baby in college! Celine would be livid.

It seemed preposterous now. Unlike Alice, she had reached age twenty-three without even having had real sex. She did not have a career. She had not begun to pay off her Federal Student Aid loans. Her partner, Cormac, did not know how to operate a dishwasher.

Be all that as it may, Sadie liked plans, and she liked sticking to them.

Chapter Seven

ALICE

The only time Alice had spent alone with Celine—before going to bed with her—was idling in a taxicab outside a tattoo parlor, which was in a former auto-body shop, the street-facing walls soaked through with a thick layer of graffiti. A closer look revealed the spray-painted images to be sterile, almost antiseptic. They were advertisements, hand-painted billboards paid for by Coors Light and Foursquare.

Celine had inserted herself between the two girls, her long legs crowding every side. She sighed her disapproval when the three women pulled up. "It's just not the way these sorts of places were—"

"We know." Sadie cast Alice a look. *"In the nineties."*

"It was a great time." Celine was wearing a sleeveless T-shirt she might have had since then, Alice thought, with a grid of twelve grimacing luchador wrestling masks. She had minute but definite Popeye muscles in her upper arms, round as eggs. She said they were from writing. Who knew, maybe they were. "It was electric. I can't believe more of that feeling didn't filter down to you."

"I was five." Sadie had griped to Alice about that era with Celine. What kind of mother drags her child around like a piece of luggage? And yet, she said it with some pride. How many kids could say they had fallen asleep on her mother's lap while a Carolee Schneemann imitator unspooled a feminist manifesto from her vagina? Sadie could say whatever she wanted, but Alice always knew it was a matter of time before she and Celine made their way back into each other's graces.

"The sense of possibility was in the air," Celine insisted.

On the ride over, when Sadie had finally shared with Celine what Alice already knew, that her tattoo would read *No dads, no boyfriends*, Celine's brow had furrowed. "But you *have* a boyfriend."

"No consistency," Sadie said, with a tight-muscled little smile. And none of it looked to make any sense to Alice. Sadie with a tattoo? Her usual high-waisted trousers looked unsuited to the scene.

The tattooist had ensured Sadie it would be a short sitting. Though Celine had positively insisted on accompanying Sadie in case of calamity, Sadie had instructed her and Alice to wait outside. "What if you're bleeding out on the table?" Celine asked now. "And we're sitting out here like good dogs. What if your body rejects the needle and you go into anaphylactic shock?"

Sadie was unmoved. She turned to Alice: "This is so infantilizing. Crazy overmothering. The voice of feminist liberation, a helicopter mom." She turned back to Celine: "Presumably, they'll come get you."

Sadie couldn't appreciate her mother. Then again, who could appreciate their own mother? Alice had always felt that Celine was the ultimate key to her friend, that if she could penetrate Celine, she could understand some essential part of Sadie. From the street, she could hear the *Pulp Fiction* theme song. The parlor shared a garden-level floor with a B-rated falafel joint. Alice smelled the sweet ferment of rising dough.

Celine wasn't done. "And if you get contaminated with a blood-borne disease?"

"We won't know until next week. And then it will be too late, anyway."

Sadie opened the taxi door and slid out of the cab, leaving Alice and Celine clumped together in the backseat. "Okay?" Sadie said. "The meter is running."

A low rider sped by, thudding an abrasive rap anthem. Alice felt the bass in all her body's lowest places. Lately, Alice had stopped minding whether she looked pretty. Seemingly in the same moment, she also gave up the pursuit of *cool*.

"Make sure they haven't used the needles to shoot up meth," Celine had called after her daughter, at the closing door, "or take anyone's blood or give vaccinations! Ask them!"

Celine must have known Sadie would ignore this and she did. Without a last glance at Alice, Sadie vanished into the red-lit storefront, leaving Alice and Celine cooped in the idling cab. "I don't think those are the same kinds of needles," Alice said delicately. Celine grunted in response. Celine was not beautiful, per se, but her uncooperative outward appearance touched Alice. The tenacious, stubborn way she seemed to wear her tall frame, as if she wouldn't deduct an inch out of principle; the way her hair stuck out, growing outward rather than down; the way nothing about her was soft or powdery.

Celine read rare books, foreign books. She had quality conversations with high-caliber people. What small talk could Alice make that would begin to span the scale? Sadie referred to her mother as selfish beyond hope, a lost cause, not worth engaging with. "Don't feed the beast," Sadie had said, the few times Alice tried to engage Celine.

But these were words. Sadie and Celine orbited each other like stars; they always had. And Celine was Sadie's favorite topic of conversation. Many the night Sadie had unloaded onto Alice, regaling her best friend with a list of resentments she bore against her mother. At the bottom of which, least expectedly, lay a cockeyed loyalty.

"Watch him misspell something." Celine exhaled smoke through her nostrils. "Amazing what people misspell these days."

From Embarcadero, Alice and Celine could see the Bay Bridge and the swelling shore. At the razor's-edge of the continent, the waves fell in neat, ordered rows, like a tilled field. Sails leaned against the briny wind. Alice thought of her debate, once, with Sadie, looking down at the same view. She had thought a boat in the harbor was a toy. Sadie had been astonished that Alice could not figure it out visually. "If it was a toy boat, you wouldn't even see it!" Alice had taken Sadie's word for it, trusting her vision over her own.

"The bridge is beautiful today," Alice remarked.

"Of course, that's a misnomer." Squinting, Celine ashed onto the ground out the window. "It's really a *collection* of bridges. Not that I'm one for labels."

"I love labels." Alice laughed. "I like to get out my label maker and be like, 'What are we labeling this?' "

This made Celine laugh a little, until she slid out of the ticking cab to share a fresh cigarette with the driver. He quit the meter.

Celine leaned against a street-art-emblazoned wall and crushed the packet. "I only smoke when I'm really bored." Alice was not sure to whom the remark was addressed.

Celine released smoke in one heavy exhalation. It surprised Alice when, through the open door, she held out her cigarette in offering. Alice edged out, but admitted, "I'm trying not to." Actually, Alice had never had a cigarette. Raised in the sunshine, smoking had always seemed at direct odds with living.

"No boyfriends," Celine muttered, exhaling smoke. She squinted, as if the smoke pained her.

"Poor Cormac," Alice said.

"I should say so." Celine cracked a devilish smile Alice's way, cigarette dangling from her lips. Alice dropped her eyes. It was like looking at the sun.

Cormac had pink cheeks and a broad, harmless face. Alice had sometimes seen him at the rear of Celine's Cal Berkeley classroom, sniffing his fingers, when they'd all taken Celine's class. He had started to purposefully sit near them. Alice had spotted Cormac's interest even before Sadie had, though she hadn't said anything.

If Sadie stayed with him, she would be . . . fine. Celine took the last drag of their cigarette, crushed it out, and flicked it into the gutter. She slid back into the cab, disappearing. Alice stood, feeling deserted. She rounded the rear of the car and slid in, unsure if she was welcome. In the dark cab, Celine held her with her oddly bright eyes.

"His paper for my class was a flaming gob of hot garbage," Celine said, "but okay, so he's not a gender theoretician. Sadie probably has enough of those in her life. Probably one too many."

"He loves Sadie," Alice said. He had been an endlessly patient suitor. It had been touching to witness his serene, easygoing perseverance. A steadfastness that Colonel Brandon would envy.

Celine grunted. A bulb seemed to illuminate above her. "Do you think there's a chance she's queer?"

Alice glanced at the back of the driver's head.

"No," she admitted plainly. She suddenly felt guilty. The answer was the truth, but it was a cardinal rule that Alice not share any details of Sadie's private life with her mother.

"No, I don't think so, either." Celine fixed her eyes on Alice. "And what about you, Alice? Are you besotted with some blessed cornfed boy?"

"It never works out." Alice felt herself turning red. She stared at the partition, suddenly intensely aware of the driver seated in front of them, perhaps listening.

Celine interrupted, *"Uh-huh."* She helped people get to the point. You were afraid to bother her. Alice had noticed that this made a person an improved interlocutor.

"With guys," Alice added. "I never fall in love."

Celine turned. "Never. You already know that, at your age?" She contemplated Alice steadily, suggestively, for a long time. "Maybe you like girls."

Celine's eyes bored into her. Their gray burned almost yellow. How strange to suggest that, to speak such words, in the middle of the day, right there in the sunshine. Alice looked out at the bay, where the horizon seemed to broaden. She glanced into the mirror to see if the driver's eyes were watching. Sure enough. Unexpectedly, this gave her a frisson of nervous audacity.

Alice was straight. Still, she thrilled at the fact that Celine thought she could join her select club. "I love girls." Alice glanced at the red-lit door, in the direction of Sadie, her *favorite* girl. "But not in that way. I'm not a lesbian."

Alice had only ever known one other lesbian: her mother's dentist, a damaged old hippie who had once remarked, terrifyingly—with a tie-dye spiral blooming on her chest—that improving Alice's smile would require shaving down her teeth. "I wish I was," Alice added quickly, then feeling this was undue, amended: "What I mean is, I have nothing against people who are."

"Thank you, Alice," Celine said with a small, deriding smile, and Alice knew she had said the wrong thing, and felt any developing confidence between them ebb away like the bay tide. "That's *kind* of you to say."

Chapter Eight

SADIE

Sadie, loath as she was to admit it, had Alice to thank. First semester of their junior year, Alice had absurdly come up with the idea that she and Sadie audit Celine's class. It was a cracked idea from the start. They needed supplemental class time like they needed an extra hole in the head. However, in an uncharacteristic display of selfhood and nonalignment, Alice had coolly replied that, in that case, she would take the class without Sadie, without her company and even without her benediction. When Sadie pressed her for an explanation, Alice had enlightened her. "I think I have a lot to learn about being in the world as a female body."

Sadie couldn't argue with that. Like a gun, Alice's body was a loaded object that it would serve her to know how to handle. She was abundant, luxuriant, silk-stockinged in midnight-dark tights, with a profusion of freckles and bountiful thick hair. Always being chatted up by hopeful males. Mooning about with languid eyes, they would approach with the flimsiest excuse. *I see you're wearing blue jeans . . . I've never seen a girl who looks like you drink PBR! . . . How do you like the OpenSky Visa card? I've been thinking of applying.*

Alice sometimes did sleep with these clowns, but if she did, they were goners by daybreak. Sadie never had to worry about any of them putting her in second place.

Finally, in the face of her friend's determination, Sadie relented. If Alice was hell-bent on taking Celine's class, she would have to take it with Sadie.

Honestly, Sadie was curious. She had watched her mother progress from instructor to assistant professor to associate professor to the full-blown thing. And yet in all those years, she had never witnessed her perform in a classroom. She had resisted seeing Celine in her element, fearing she might actually be impressed. And then where would she be?

But Alice was so committed that she was left with no choice.

And so, on the appointed day, Sadie had slid into her designated seat beside Alice in Pimentel Hall, a battered sandstone building with a weathered façade and an interior that smelled like vinegar. GWS103: Introduction to Gender Studies had been relocated to a larger room, because so many students signed up for the class. "You know we're deep inside an echo chamber, right?" she leaned over to whisper to Alice.

On Sadie's orders, Alice had procured them a pair of seats so near the exit that they were under the radius of the red glow. "I reserve the right to leave at any time," Sadie marshaled. In fact, she kept her jacket on, eyes darting now and then to the sign marked STAIRCASE B.

Celine spent the start of class fielding admiration from a constellation of students. She requested help with the display-port adapter and volunteers crowded the front, crouching under the lectern, devoutly tracing extension cords, peering into output ports.

Celine was an ill fit with academia, nearly incompatible, having obtained her ride ticket by dismantling an ideology. By *dis*organizing thought, rather than organizing it. This imparted her a certain impunity, begrudged by her colleagues, who toiled under no such banner of liberation.

She was not a beloved professor, but she was a famous one. For some students, she was a momentous liberator, hailing emancipation. For others, she was a swindler, making off with sense. She was not on social media, which lent her a certain mystique. A few years ago, *Berkeley Magazine* had run a profile: "The Chaos Agent at Forty." If they only knew.

Sadie had still lived at home, then. Celine spent the preceding night preparing, well into the blue-gray morning hours. This wasn't just any class. *Sadie* was coming. Celine emerged from her bedroom in the morning, with hair specially washed and combed, wearing her favorite blinking orange trainers with lime-green laces. "See you there," she told Sadie, as if knowing her daughter was facing down second thoughts. "It will be nice to look out and see your friendly face."

Sadie wondered if, behind this bromide observation, there lay a latent trauma. She suspected that having accepted a professorship directly after completing her Masters meant that Celine lugged around a residual yoke of inferiority.

Now, in Barrows Hall, to light claps, a Pippi Longstocking type reported that the AV cords had been sorted: a four-way component splitter had been switched to a device that corresponded to another classroom. Celine beamed at her genius. She clicked on the slide presentation Sadie had assembled for her half a decade ago, and which she still used, with flow charts for gender identity, gender expression, biological sex, and sexual orientation.

Celine leaned on the desk at a casual angle, with no more pomp than if she were alone in her own living room. "Who here has been told you can be anything?" she inquired of all assembled, pattering her microphone. "Hold your hands high."

Sadie, feeling her mother's expectation of her, sat squarely, arms tight across her chest. Beside her, Alice raised her hand, eyes trained at the front of the room, chin in hand, admiring Celine in her eminence. What was she doing? Participating in the charade? Et tu. Glancing around the room, lingering just a moment over Sadie and Alice, Celine pushed up the sleeves of her jacket and began in earnest.

It was like seeing a snake oil salesman at work. For an hour and a half, graying hair silver under the fluorescent lights, Celine ignored the lectern and presided over the room, a swaggering cavalier, a pirate capsizing critical thought, dialectics and feminist sociobiology, a bandit upending binaries. The dowdy slide presentation was all but forgotten as the ample lecture hall electrified, full of her. Celine was robust; Sadie happened to know that she had not seen a doctor in two decades.

Firmly in her comfort zone, Celine crossed the room with decisive, shoulder-length steps in those tangerine-lime sneakers.

"Reality is socially situated," she was saying. She measured the room for her effect. And was rewarded: her influence rippled through it palpably.

Sadie hoped her gaze would not land on Alice.

It did not. It landed on Sadie. Their eyes locked, dueling, their usual battle.

"I trust you all did the assigned reading, chapter four of my book, 'Nurturance and Autocracy.' My daughter," Celine said, "is here today, up there, see, in the back row. In her frilly dress? She never opted to shed those femme signifiers. And that's *fine*."

A stir spread through the room, like a virus. A vague murmur, at least one titter, as the inquiring eyeballs of all assembled slid toward

Sadie, in her amoral outfit, hating her mother flagrantly, with a fresh zest. Sadie felt her lips quiver. She stared straight ahead with eyes hard as slate and did nothing to identify herself. Using her as an *illustration* in the lecture? How despicable.

"To her, I'm a mom," Celine continued as before, off to the races now, no longer gauging her delivery. "Am I, though? Is that *me*, in my totality?"

Alice, spellbound, finally glanced at Sadie. Whatever she saw intimidated her enough that she looked back at Celine without a word.

"Look how tall I am," Celine said. Somehow, in the tremendous space, she appeared doubly so. "Look at my dopey haircut." With her big red mouth, her tall, thin face, her crew cut, Sadie thought Celine resembled a gangly sock monkey. Other people, apparently, far-fetched though it was, found her sexy.

"How do you think my daughter feels?" When Celine said this, Alice snuck an abashed look at Sadie. "I'm the Phallic Mother." The room laughed, smitten, obeying Celine's compelling, authoritative thrall.

"What an unbelievably crazy person," Sadie muttered to Alice.

Scattered claps and that day's class was dismissed. The room filled with clatters of conversation.

"That was incredible," Alice said. "I learned so much."

Sadie groaned. "Please don't make me come back."

"I understand if you don't want to," Alice said delicately, the unspoken implication being that she *would* be returning in any case.

But Sadie couldn't leave Alice alone with her mother. God knew what might happen, in what ways Celine would manage to offend

Alice. Sadie would have liked Alice to share her dismal appraisal of her mother, but it would be inconvenient if Alice detested Celine beyond where they could share a room. Sadie waited, exasperated, to slip past the software engineering geek who sat in front of her and Alice, and who was now barrier to their exit path. Staring at anything but Celine, she had made mental note of the back of his head, his mop of mouse-brown hair, as, glued to his laptop, he noodled around on Bitbucket as he listened.

To Sadie's dismay, the nonconsensual outing had not slipped past him. He paused his configurating and turned around. "You're her *daughter*?"

Alice, even standing in the aisleway, was still taking furious dictation in her mini notebook, trying to recall Celine's lightning-fast wording. She glanced to see how Sadie would handle this.

Sadie stood and sidestepped to angle herself into the nook by the double exit doors. Celine was looking around wildly for her. Sadie confessed the association. Later, she would regret that the first words she and Cormac ever spoke were, "She's my mother."

Sadie saw that someone in the front row was wearing an iPhone charger as a kind of tech-grunge necklace. Celine was asking to borrow it.

Cormac was starry-eyed, still hanging over the aisle. He leaned sideways over his desk. "I can imagine it would be tough to be her daughter. Pretty crazy, right?" He looked at her. "Let's say half crazy."

Sadie was about to eviscerate him for his prying and presumption. But he had made an impression. No one had ever asked her this before. At the front of the room, Celine was tending her flock, seeming to have forgotten Sadie.

"Well," Sadie said, "actually, it is."

Cormac nodded. He revealed that he was a graduate student, halfway through his MSCS, taking Celine's class out of pure interest. He looked less than cool, but Sadie knew people could appear unassuming. If you had met a weedy Steve Jobs in 1982 on a bus, sporting dusty New Balances, elucidating on his North Indian spiritual pilgrimages, you could be forgiven for thinking he would try to sell you a multicolored friendship bracelet rather than a revolutionary iOS device.

Speaking of, Sadie watched Celine dial from her plugged-in phone, and then felt her own phone buzz in her pocket. "See you later," Sadie told Cormac.

"Really?" He wanted to know. "Do you mean that? When?"

Back at home after class, Sadie cornered Celine in the kitchen to let her have it for exposing her without consent. "You had no right." Alice listened unobtrusively. Celine barely listened at all, punching numbers into her Hello Kitty microwave.

"That was outrageously inappropriate," Sadie said. "You belittled me publicly."

"Sure you're not being a little dramatic?" Celine was wearing her Last Supper T-shirt, the host surrounded by his twelve disciples, throwing up a peace sign.

"That was a complete violation," Sadie said.

"I thought you'd be happy." Celine stood with a pose of defiance. "You were a VIP. I was sharing my spotlight."

"That, what you just said? Is so indicative of everything wrong with you."

Celine withdrew a foam cup of Top Ramen from her stash in the cabinet. "Want one? Either of you?" Sadie glared and Alice declined. She filled it with tap water, rapped shut the microwave door, and hit nuke. She would not allow Sadie to extract an apology. The most she'd say was "I'll try not to do it again."

"*Try* not to?" Sadie hated, in front of her friend, to lose.

Celine reached into the refrigerator, popped open a Dr Pepper, and took a long swig, her requisite late afternoon sugar rush. "Alice," she said, turning, taking a rare interest, "I'd love to know, what were your thoughts on the lecture?" Around the house, Sadie's friend was usually just that, merely decorative, discreet and deferential to her mother. Generally, Celine paid her little mind.

"Leave her alone."

"I, um."

Celine belched loudly. "You look like you might have some questions," she said. Her ramen was ready. She dumped it into a Darth Vader mug and went at it with chopsticks. "If you don't have any, you're not listening closely enough. This stuff should be blowing your minds." She crossed the kitchen counter into the dining room and reached to the shelf behind her, past the row of thumbed Vintage Contemporary paperbacks, pulling out a colorful volume called *Angry Women* with a writhing Medusa-head cover. "Required reading."

"Maybe twenty-five years ago," Sadie said, rolling her eyes.

Celine ignored Sadie, returned to her ramen. "This book set the precedent. If *The Second Sex* is the Old Testament, this is the New." She shook the book in her outstretched hand until Alice took it, then went back to slurping a bundle of noodles. "Meaning that it is still old, but eternally relevant."

It was an anthology of interviews outspoken against male domination. Alice accepted the book with holy reverence. The trouble, Sadie told Celine smugly, was that she and Alice weren't angry.

"That's alarming. Look around. You should be infuriated."

"Edifying as all this is, our generation is actually remarkably well-adjusted," Sadie said. "Thanks in no part to yours."

Celine shook her head, as if this attitude would condemn them to unspeakable misery. "You just *think* you aren't angry, because you've been sold a bill of goods."

After Celine released them, Alice squirreled away with the book in Sadie's room, where, with loving attention and careful scrutiny, she devoted herself to it. She read with two pillows tucked under her knees, saying it helped her focus, to assume the position. Occasionally, she solicited Sadie's tutelage. "What's *cis*?" Alice scowled, like she was solving a hard mystery.

The lexicon was not inconsequential, Sadie knew. But it could be dreary. Still, she grudgingly illuminated Alice. "A term for people who identify with their birth sex," she said through a yawn.

Through her bedroom window, Sadie watched Celine, in the overgrown backyard, now, on her knees, caked with mud, in a sweaty battle with burdock, her horticultural nemesis. She nosily weeded, yanking, uprooting intruders and the tenacious dead. She sat back, heavy-breathing, at the moldering picnic table, contemplating the uneven ground, pockmarked with dips and declinations. Sadie recognized her mother's brand of caretaking. Neglect, then attack, in a violent spasm of errant, conscience-stricken custodianship.

At the penultimate class meeting, out the window there was a rare, and light, slurry dusting of snow. It was mid-December. As students filed out around them, Cormac left Sadie his number. He rubbed his hands together, breathed to warm them, and told her to call if she would like to go out with him sometime, "on a date. I'm not gay, even though I'm in this class and wear pink socks. I'm a self-identifying male. I'm 99.99 percent sure I like to date self-identifying females. Sorry if that sounds stodgy and closed-minded."

Convention had the ring of the exotic for Sadie. And she was even thinking, lately, that a boyfriend might not be the worst idea. Lately—and infuriatingly it may have had to do with social media—an experience felt curtailed and incomplete if Sadie was its sole witness. Nice wines, good cheeses, an exquisite sunset, a great line of prose. If a tree falls, Sadie began to wonder.

And then, the following week, at the final class session, Cormac stood, tall, looming over them, and disarmingly crystalline in his intentions. "I hope you don't think I'm only interested because you're this famous teacher's daughter."

Sadie swallowed hard, wishing he hadn't said this.

"I wanted to say something before I knew that. I wish I had, so you'd believe me."

It was day twenty-two of Sadie's cycle and she had acne with a vengeance. She could scarcely believe a word this nosy, irritating guy said. "I'm not sure my mother is very likable," she said, "so, actually, I credit you on that front."

Alice stood with arms crossed. Cormac glanced at her a little awkwardly. "You seem cool, too."

Sadie's heart ducked beneath her ribs. Of course, he would prefer Alice. Who wouldn't?

"And beautiful, too," Cormac modified, with hands that said, *let me put it another way*.

Alice nodded, accustomed to this sort of male fumbling. How unoriginal, Sadie thought, to be sidelined by her best friend.

"But just somehow I looked at *her,*" he said, meaning Sadie, "and thought, just, if I could go on a date or speak to that girl for even like ten minutes, I would be the happiest guy in the world."

Alice laughed. "You would be." She seemed to like the guy. And she clearly loved the idea of Sadie embarking on an actual, real date with a live member of the male species.

He turned to Sadie, blundering on. "You're like a reverse Medusa. When I see you, I melt."

Sadie let out a burst of laughter. Was it mockery or embarrassment? Sadie herself wasn't sure. Still glowering, she was sure she burned bright as a tomato. "So you're saying you're not some psycho who wants to decapitate me?" Cormac just looked at Sadie, without trying to understand her. Simply taking her in like a view.

"By which she means: this is her phone number." Alice bent down to scribble it on a scrap of notepad paper. Beaming healthily, Cormac murmured that he would text her later. Sadie took this information to mean she should get her hair done and look up every last comedy show happening in town that night, and the restaurants nearby, and then sit up all night in her pajamas with her makeup on, waiting.

And then, of all things? At ten o'clock, he texted, saying he was just leaving the library after a marathon continuous integration session, "modifying commands to build his repository," and asking if she was up to join him for a late-night milkshake at Smoke's Poutinerie.

Sadie phoned Alice. "I shouldn't go."

"With Perseus?"

"He's too goofy," Sadie said. "Right? Not handsome enough. Too forward. Desperate for my attention. Trying to rush things. Certainly not suave. Shouldn't waste my time."

With the palm of her hand to Sadie's back, Alice gave Sadie an actual push. "*Go.* I'm driving past your house in twenty minutes with a carton of eggs. If your car is still there, I'm egging the windows."

Sadie scowled. "Because I'm desperate, I should go out with any inadequate guy who comes my way?"

"It's guys. You've got to give them a chance. He might surprise you."

"I hate surprises." Sadie glowered. This was seeming less and less like a good idea.

Alice assumed a person would prefer her company to being left alone. One afternoon the year before, at Montclair Egg Shop's Saturday bagel brunch, they had seen Robert De Niro seated at the corner table. To Sadie's mortification, Alice jumped up and introduced herself, presuming he'd be thrilled to make her acquaintance. The stupid-crazy part? He *was*. Sadie watched with her own arrested eyes as De Niro reached for her phone and requested a selfie with *her*. How could Sadie but feel fortified, having a friend like that? She made life on earth seem like a breeze.

"It's amazing," Sadie told Alice. "You could just do anything; I wish I could do that."

"You could!" Finally, Sadie didn't go. Though the thought of runny egg mucusing up the window glass made her gag, she knew Alice was all talk. She texted Cormac that she had a stomachache and that she would not be free for a few months, owing not to her stomachache but to her studies, and that he should not attempt to reach her after that, because by then she would be tied up with finals. When Alice rolled up that evening as promised, she tossed a disappointed egg into Sadie's hands. Sadie caught it, intact. "You suck," Alice said.

But Cormac was persistent, and patient. He was a suitor, tactful and old-fashioned, staying in touch with Sadie. He had nothing to prove, and he proved willing to wait. Sadie saw him sometimes, around campus, occasionally perching on the lip of White Memorial Fountain for brief catch-ups, once permitting him to bring her a panini from the Green Library café. She began mentioning him more often to Alice, puzzling over him. She had thought she knew his kind. Men who dressed carelessly, acting studiedly nonchalant, but who turned out to be neurotic and self-important. He turned out to be neither.

Finally, at the end of the second semester of their senior year, something gave. Realizing she was falling hopelessly behind on her schedule, or supplying Alice this excuse anyway, Sadie consented to go out with him. Alice was thrilled.

Sadie texted: "Remember those milkshakes?"

Cormac texted back: "See you in 15?"

And that was how it began. By some estimation, Cormac was a perfect man. By Sadie's estimation, appraised over hazelnut shakes, cherries on top, he could be a perfect man with a few alterations. She would ask a tailor to shorten the sincerity and let out the sex appeal.

It was not a fairy tale, but then what was?

Chapter Nine

ALICE

MONDAY

Alice had slept with Celine because she was famous, because she was sexy, because she wasn't that famous, because she wasn't conventionally sexy. Because she was twenty years older. Because she could see the girl in her. She slept with Celine because it was absolutely forbidden. She slept with Celine because it was suddenly possible. Because Celine was there, because she had come, because Sadie had sent her. Because Alice did not know why.

Alone in the Airbnb, after Celine left, Alice felt the thrum in her pussy, a consequence of being licked all morning by her best friend's mother. How could it be that downstairs, on Grove Street, under golden high-pressure sodium lights, pedestrians cast in a creamsicle orange were crossing the thoroughfare, hand in hand with their children, ferrying shopping bags, not even glancing up in the direction of the crime?

Alice saw that, already, in the heat, the anthuriums from Celine had bloomed past their healthy limit. The heads had fallen open like a hooker's legs, bloated and bloomed, showing their innards.

People made terrible mistakes. One erroneous turn in a car, and you are the arbiter of a stranger's life. One imprudent snip in the surgery room and you've severed the artery. For scale: the *Titanic* hit an iceberg. Nuclear equipment melted down at Chernobyl. Upturned seagulls lay obsidian with petroleum in the Gulf. The world kept spinning.

The Airbnb had not supplied a second set of sheets, still Alice began to make the bed carefully, like she rarely did. She tucked in each corner of the slept-in sheets, twice. She slipped a flat sheet between the mattress and box spring, and even a bed skirt. She had been too occupied, the past week, with rehearsals to throw in a load of laundry and now had no clean underwear. She rinsed her panties clean with dish soap. The natural thing would be to tell someone. To bring someone with her into the fold of misery and delight. But that, the person she would tell, was her best friend.

For the first time in a day and a half, Alice plugged in her phone. It lit up and she reloaded the missed calls, tugging the red list downward with her thumb.

Alice's manager at Shutters, assuming freely and frankly that the show had not been extended, requesting that she take on an extra shift the following week.

Her mother, saying she had a table by the window, their lunch date from another era.

Two guys, who seemed to hail from her deep past, hoping to meet up over the weekend.

Sadie's name did not appear. She and Alice spoke perhaps once a week by phone, and they had spoken only three days before. But suddenly Sadie's silence felt meaningful.

There was no sun today, wobbling everything, making it go bleached and zany. Celine and Alice had not discussed not telling. Although, of course, the embargo had been there all along, unspoken beneath every breath, start to finish. Celine would not be such a loose cannon—would she? Or would Celine do whatever Celine wanted?

Gingerly, as if Sadie were inside it, Alice took up the phone. It was ten in the morning. Sadie, an early riser, would have been awake for hours. The first blurry ring and Alice's body felt light and fluid as water. The second ring: sometimes, Sadie didn't answer. Alice was just drawing the phone from her ear when there came a soft click.

There was white noise on the line, as if Sadie were on an alternate terrestrial planet with a razor-thin atmosphere. Then came her usual placid voice, no more imperial than was habitual. "Yup."

Alice's puffed-up heart deflated, released. "Sup," she managed to say, blinking back emotion.

"What's crack-a-lacking?"

Alice let out the breath she had been holding, tight as a screwed-closed jar. Sadie sounded like herself. The banter picked up right where they left off. Verdict was out: she would not yet face her fate.

"What's cooking?"

"What's the dilly?"

"What's shakin,' bacon?"

When Sadie deigned to joke around, how dreadful to realize: she sounded a little like Celine. Which was funny, because Celine often said Sadie sounded like *her* mother. Alice plowed on, extending the banter. Finally, she closed out with "It's good to hear your voice." She asked how the weekend away with Cormac had gone.

Sadie took over the call as usual. Relaying a knotty saga of a dishonored brunch reservation that weekend at an eatery that she described as crab-shack chic. She described it as a place Alice's mother would approve of: "Underdone schmancy." A roadside lean-to that was nevertheless so pompous as to have refused to accommodate the couple. When Sadie could see the chairs stacked right there on the deck and they could easily have balanced plates on their laps.

If a restaurant failed to seat Sadie, even without a reservation, she took it as a personal slight. Why wouldn't they roll out the red carpet? Didn't they know who she was? (Well, and who was she?) Alice's perception was more straightforward. After all, a hostess could not produce a seat where there was none. Sadie said that, as Alice *must* know from Shutters, a restaurant could always shuffle things around, and that if she were Rihanna, they would have found a place. Alice refrained from stating the obvious. But you're not...

It occurred to Alice, while Sadie chattered, how impersonal the Airbnb was, each homey touch artificially engineered. The wallpaper was removable, peel-and-stick, with a second patterned roll on the top shelf in the laundry closet. A set of IKEA frames, meant for snapshots, instead displayed vintage postcards of Portland, Maine, and Florence, Oregon.

In the midst of Sadie's monologue, Alice's phone *beep-beep*-ed. She held the screen away from her ear, missing some of Sadie's words—all she heard was "blue crab beignet"—the phone's screen said *Celine*.

Alice fumbled, swallowing the grit of the name, managing to send the call to voice mail. How strange to think that the number Celine had stored in her phone, back in the days when she would pick Alice and Sadie up from the mall, was now being used for a postcoital postmortem.

"... an enormous slab of burl wood," Sadie's voice was saying, "that I hauled back from Marin—it tore Cormac's backseat, but he was nice about it—are you listening?"

Alice tried to tune in. She struggled to make sense of why she would be hearing these incoherent details. She sensed she was due to say something, to contribute to the conversation. "Burl," Alice repeated to show she was listening.

"The wood I'm repurposing as a bench seat. I stripped the bark," Sadie went on blithely, "and I'm going to sand it and use dowel pegs to . . ." Until, abruptly as if she had just thought of it, Sadie took it upon herself to shift subjects. "I can tell I'm losing you. Never mind all that. The real question is did she show? Did she behave?"

"Yes, totally. Except this one prop failure—you wouldn't believe it but a dog toy squeaked onstage. It was supposed to be the chicken dinner!"

"She didn't disrupt the play?" Sadie asked, sounding amazed. "She didn't boo or anything?"

Alice felt a slight irritation, in defense of Celine. "Nothing."

"Wow, I'm shocked."

"Very unlike her!" Alice knew that failing to say anything disparaging would stick out as uncharacteristic. "She was a model citizen."

"I had nightmares of her throwing tomatoes. Literally. I dreamt that."

"And how was *your* night?" Alice asked.

"It was fine."

"No news? No great tidings?"

Sadie's disappointment was palpable. So was her commitment to closing the subject. "None. I botched the whole thing. But that's all I want to say about it."

Despite her outward pragmatism, Alice knew, Sadie was an idealist and a dreamer. She lived a life of plans, but because life tended to interrupt those, in fact she lived a life of fictive imaginings. And Alice, who seemed so dreamy, was in fact a pragmatist in her way. It required little effort to be easygoing and let things roll off your back. Alice had strength, the strength of ease.

Beep-beep. Alice glanced down and reeled. Again. Fuck.

Alice cleared her throat. "Sadie?" The other line was insistent. *Beep-beep*. "The bench you're talking about sounds really cool. I'm going through one of these uneven Verizon patches. Losing you, breaking up, no bars, think the cell towers are far away. Ring you later?" She hung up, before Sadie could manage even a syllable of reply.

Alice did not immediately dial Celine. She left her phone charging and floated to the kitchen and back. She did not want a banana. She did not want a bagel. She mauled the shipshape bed, freshly made. She stripped the sheets, flags of ignominy. She set the wash cycle to heavy-duty, with multiple sluice rinses, and fired the water up to 150 degrees. Feeling only marginally sanitized, she returned to her phone. She sat a final, fleeting moment on the bed before she succumbed, touching her finger to the name.

Celine's throaty contralto was at her ear after the first ring. "I tried to call you."

Alice's panties chafed. Her voice cracked. "I was on the phone."

Celine made an offended grunt.

"With Sadie." There it was, the trump card.

A pregnant pause, fraught with Celine's wondering. Then, in a voice chastened and vulnerable, "And how is the dear girl?"

"She seems okay."

Celine cleared her throat and said, voice straining, "My good little daughter. I suppose she asked how the show went?"

"Just barely," Alice said carefully. "She's back from Marin. They had a good time. I let her do most of the talking, as I'm feeling a little drained."

Celine waited, breathless. And then?

"Not that she asked about me. She's making a bench, out of burl wood she found at Pescadero. She's using dowel pegs."

Celine exhaled an audible sigh, one of tremendous relief, even gratitude, and, like that, she and Alice had colluded without words.

Chapter Ten
SADIE

Probably, Sadie should have gone to Alice's play.

She and Cormac had pulled up in Marin, for their weekend away, only to find that a major lane fire had erupted on Highway 36, lighting up the shoulder brush all along Paynes Creek. They were redirected through Bowman Road. Outside, a fierce wind blew. Over the cliffs, the sunset was spectacular with Pacific violence, breathtakingly tangerine in a haze of smoke and fog. The County Fair was closed, due to hazard conditions. The vacant Ferris wheel rose high and purposeless, lit up orange.

Had it all been for naught?

After the detours, they arrived at the cabin past dark. Swatting at mosquitoes and flecks of ash, they found that the cabin was unerotically ornamented with wooden storks and browning prints of ocean liners. Wasting no time, Sadie set to work assembling the coq au vin she had planned to prepare.

"This is what I don't understand about cooking," Celine had mused recently, while Sadie was cooking for her, mandolining. "Why not eat the leek whole? It's the same leek."

Why not leave the paint in the tube? Sadie had asked. If it weren't for the hospital bracelets Celine had as proof, and their shared dislike of the Elena Ferrante novels, which everyone else seemed to love, she'd request a maternity test.

For the coq au vin, Sadie had fused two recipes, offsetting tart juniper berries with an oaky chardonnay. She would make it perfect. She would make everything about the evening nothing short of it. The pullet was just ready for retrieval—45 minutes at 350 degrees. But when she opened the door, a singed mouse fell out of the oven, scampering off, slightly crisped but nonetheless miraculously still alive. The kitchen filled with the smell of the charbroiled pelt of fur, the braised chicken was inedible, and they had no choice but to resort to Seamless and to order in local, three-star Chinese.

The most Sadie hoped was that they would not come across the damaged mouse, cross-eyed and belly up. It was a delicate balance. It was their one-year anniversary, and they were running out of time to have sex.

"It's a cool thing for two people who are in love to do together." Cormac was propped up on a musty floral-print pillow. "It can be very bonding. We could stop anytime you wanted, like even before we got anywhere. I could just put it up close and we could decide then?"

Cormac was like Alice in some ways, unoppressive and deferential. He really was just offering. But the more this incubated in Sadie's mind, the further convinced she became that the invitation was a kind of coercion.

Sadie sniffed. "If you pressure me, you see, I get weird. It won't help to rush me," she said.

"You're right," Cormac agreed.

"I feel sick," Sadie admitted, feeling she might dry-heave. Cormac went and retrieved Tums from the bathroom cabinet First-Aid kit. He fished past the lime and orange tablets, on Sadie's direction, and handed her two pink assorted berries.

"Better?" he asked after she had chewed and swallowed.

"Much," Sadie said, and soon after even reached for him. Tentatively, he moved toward her, beginning to kiss her slowly. But something else occurred to her. They might have left the car windows down. She pulled back and asked if Cormac would check. He searched her eyes: she was serious. He rolled out of bed, dressed enough to be decent, pants but no shirt, and ventured outside.

When he reappeared—the windows had been closed—Sadie was still sitting upright. She looked around her, mystified. "The lighting's not right. Don't you think?"

Cormac had no objections but, patiently, smiling slightly, he turned off the standing wicker lamp. Under Sadie's bidding, they experimented with the desk light, finally deciding that angling the swinging arm toward the floor was best. But when Cormac reached softly to finish undressing her, Sadie squirmed out from under. "Cormac, listen, the very landscape is on fire. All these things are not conducive. Doesn't it seem like a warning?"

"A warning?" Cormac looked unconvinced. "Of what?"

Sadie knew she was just looking for excuses, but could not stop her diligent mind from working overtime.

"Is it helpful to take a look at it?" Cormac held his penis with his hand.

Sadie regarded it skeptically. It wasn't so bad-looking. Still, she negotiated. "How do you make sure it pushes in properly?"

Cormac showed her his penis, as if it could explain anything. He wagged it from side to side. "You just kind of do it."

"I don't like it."

Cormac smiled. "Sorry. It's not my design."

"I didn't mean that. What I mean is I don't understand it. When you were with Laura," Sadie began, then stopped herself. "No, don't tell me. That image won't help." Cormac smiled gallantly. Sadie was glum. "I don't know what's the matter with me."

"It's all right." Cormac pulled the floral sheet over himself and leaned back against the headboard. "There's no rush."

"No, I *do* know. It's my stupid mother. Did you know I secretly read her book? I didn't even tell Alice. I knew I shouldn't. Obviously, it was psychologically damaging. Oh, god. Her passages on the centimetric complexities of her labia are coming back to me." Sadie buried her face in a pillow. "I really wanted to this time!" She began to cry. "I really wanted to make it work out."

"We'll try again." Cormac reached for Sadie's hand. "Tissue?"

Sadie sniffed. "You don't have to be so boundlessly considerate, you know. You can melt down, too."

Cormac turned out the remaining lights, snuggling close to Sadie after she had wussed out at the last minute, after any reasonable person ever would. Sadie turned off the bedside lamp with a disquieted click. "Don't worry," Cormac assured her again, tousling her hair gently as they fell asleep. "There's always tomorrow."

Chapter Eleven

ALICE

My god, Alice thought, feeling pulverized. What have I done?

She groaned aloud, agonizing over the coming days, the requisite lies. Just when she was starting to panic, thinking about how she'd have to return to the scene of the crime for the week's rehearsals, she received a phone call. "I've got the most unbelievable news." It was Darius. Alice's heart pounded. Though it made no sense, she assumed the only thing he could be calling to say was that Sadie knew. Had caught wind somehow and the jig was up.

"No one was hurt," Darius assured her. "But the theater burned down." He explained that the stage drapes had encountered a stage light someone had inadvertently left illuminated, setting Brackendale's wooden stage on fire.

A member of the janitorial staff had smothered the flame and the wooden stage was damaged only minorly, just enough for the theater's insurance company to prohibit the show's going on. "I'm so sorry, Alice."

That's great! Alice almost shouted.

"How awful," she said, grinning as she processed this miracle. "How disappointing."

"A theater fire, can you believe it? How very 1800s of us."

With gratitude for fate's hand, Alice escaped down to L.A. But escape didn't bring with it consolation. It was demoralizing to return to her anonymous, windblown Marina housing complex, to her dim and vague-feeling garden-level apartment with blurry, hazy light—while conjuring images of hollyhocks and gentle breezes off the nearby jetty, a garden apartment only meant you were a subtenant, enclosed with mothballs and drainage. Alice had made attempts to infuse it with personality. But it never seemed to adhere. What type of person was she, she wondered now, and when would she know?

Alice spent three jittery days straight trying to bleach her body clean and bake it dry. She bought Groupons. She waxed and lasered. She went to Meisner-technique class. She considered phoning handsome, eyes-untenanted Tinder Thomas for distraction. She attended barre class. "Tuck, tuck, tuck, tuck," the instructor said in time to aggressive pop melodies. She attended spin class, staring herself down in the glittering mirror while an instructor shouted at her about her best self.

It was one evening, as she was leaving SLT, a hard-line fitness studio that offered boxing and smelled like asphalt, that Celine phoned, checking to see how she was doing "after the play and all." It would be rude to decline the call. Alice had never learned how to be rude and live with it.

"How-dee-do?" Celine asked.

"I'm fine."

Celine discounted this. "You're not beating yourself up? I would hate that. Thinking you're deceitful or anything? A bad friend?"

"No."

"I'm sure glad to hear that. You bring out the protective instinct in me, that's all."

Still breathless after muscling through a series of full-body intervals, lunge slides, and what her instructor called "playful plank," Alice deposited her TheraBand into the bin.

She should not have answered the phone in the studio, where anyone could hear her. She began chattering manically to Celine, about nothing consequential, as she rolled up her springy foam mat and tucked it into its cubby. She whispered into the receiver that SLT charged an annual mat storage fee, but staff did not know who had paid and who hadn't. Alice had been careful not to make herself memorable at the sign-in desk, so that the next year she could purchase another introductory special using her middle name as her last.

"I take it back." Celine chortled. "You *are* a naughty girl."

Alice, feeling defiant, blinked into Pico Boulevard's stony light. The sky was streaked with colors like a child's waxy drawing and threaded with opalescent gold; only the smog wreaked such beautiful havoc.

Alice had parked outside a cash-only watch repair that also offered nail and eyelash services, and clicked her car unlocked. Only then, out of doors, with no one around, did she admit to Celine, "I'm practicing selective amnesia."

"There's always electroconvulsive therapy," Celine suggested.

"Is there a Groupon for that?"

Celine grunted. "What does SLT even stand for?"

"'Strengthen Lengthen Tone.'"

"Those are verbs, by the way. You can't verb a verb."

Celine called the subsequent day to ask by what degree Alice had lengthened since they had last spoken. "Centimeters? Inches? Just checking your progress. Did you figure out how to verb a verb? Or is that still verboten?"

Alice made the mistake of laughing, and Celine loved to make people laugh. Before long, they were speaking regularly. Alice pressed softly in a way that would not commit her. Like pedaling in the proper shoes in spin class, without clipping in. "Hi?" Alice would answer. "Hello?" She was useless on the phone.

"Hello there!" Celine would bellow into the receiver. She was even worse.

On the third call, Alice pulled herself together. She was occupying herself with a heavy round of sit-ups on a foam pad. "We shouldn't," she gathered the courage to say. She sat up and patted clean the foam pad with a towel and spray bottle.

"Shouldn't what?" Celine tested.

Alice wasn't sure what. "Talk like this," she decided.

"We've always talked, in our way."

This was a bald-faced lie, entirely fraudulent. But Alice felt safe, in an obscure corner of Los Angeles, giving Celine a wide berth. No FaceTime. No physical proximity, nor even a glimpse. What had happened—*if* it had even happened; the night was so dreamlike, so starkly outside of time that Alice could imagine she had only dreamed it—was an isolated incident.

Sadie had become unspeakable, profoundly avoided as a topic of conversation.

They talked instead, circuitously—about how *Meisner in Practice* spoke of finding character as if it was a matter of scrounging around with a magnifying glass, and university politics. "I have to change my life," Celine groused. "The whole thing. I'm lonely. Even Siri 'isn't available.' "

"You can adjust that in Settings," Alice said. "I can walk you through."

"Don't bother. I think I'll relocate to the Desolation Islands or Tristan da Cunha, go off-grid, forfeit my phone."

"What are you going to do with it?"

"Drop it into the ocean. Put it in a drawer and never see it again.

But then how would I phone you?" Celine was silent. "So I'll have to rethink that."

Once, Alice conceded to a FaceTime. Only because she was dressed for an audition in a bright blouse with billowy sleeves and Celine demanded to see, to assess whether it suited the character Alice had described. "I suppose it's all right for the role," Celine said after the chime that meant they were connected. "But pepperoni red is not your color."

Alice studied herself. "I like it."

"Good, then. Forget I said anything."

"Except now you've ruined it."

Celine cautioned Alice against letting things be bankrupted so easily. On these calls, Alice said little.

They were worst at goodbye. Alice got quiet and Celine got boisterous.

"Okay," Alice stammered. "Okay."

"Bye-bye!" Celine nearly shouted.

It had been a week. To take her mind off things and to keep herself from calling Sadie, Alice accepted an invitation to an industry party from a Shutters regular who put his clients up at the hotel when they were in town. "A-listers," the agent promised, as the lobby bar's piano player looked on. The party, at a sleek and unfeeling mansion up Beachwood Canyon, was allegedly hosted by a prominent producer who was nonetheless nowhere in sight and appeared not to have bothered to attend.

Still, Alice could not wait to tell Sadie she had been to Stan Donner's villa, overlooking the Hollywood sign. He had produced the latest six Marvels, for god's sake. Alice had liked the films, but after Sadie called them waste for the masses, she hadn't said so.

The agent had invited a gaggle of actors, "new associates" he had met at Sundance. Festival hoppers, hanging on one another's arms, the actors had just returned from Coachella and still sported VIP badges from a corporate-sponsored party. Someone wielded photos, circulated about the party on a passed-around phone, sharp, sunny shots with heavy filters.

Alice confessed that she had never been to Coachella.

"That's okay," the actor with the photos said, struggling, smiling dimly. "Some people enjoy festivals, and some don't."

The actors were like puppies, eager to arrive, then seeming to sigh and keel over with the exertion. Realizing the party could offer them nothing concrete, they deflated. They sat on couches and rested. Zoned out, tried and failed to scroll their phones. There was no cell reception in the house; that was the quality of the concrete.

Alice found the actors to be tranquil company. They, like her, didn't ask prying questions. No one had to explain they were not presently employed, currently out of work. People, Alice knew, could wrap their minds around what a person had accomplished, not what they were capable of.

A Benz-worth of executives arrived, unfolding out of a gleaming E-class with enormous purses and bamboo latte cups in hand. Alice tried to text Sadie but could not find the bars. She fell in with a child, Akiko, a bouldering phenomenon. "I am the youngest rock climber to climb a 9A-plus." Akiko was fourteen. Her father was diligently working the party, occupied with trying to secure a bit part for her in the new *Green Lantern.* Outside, on the viridescent lawn, two standard poodles belonging to the house were leaping and rearing like a pair of enchanted unicorns.

Alone at the bar, Alice drank until her cheeks felt like two puffed pink hot-air balloons. She began hitting on the bartender, thinking she looked too cute to lose the night. He decorated drinks with parasols and fruit kebabs. His shirt, loose, much washed, fell off his shoulders. He plucked a lemon off a two-tier stand.

Alice was testing, debating with herself. Did she not sleep with guys anymore? Unless this guy could be deployed as a palate cleanser, a neutral flavor used to mitigate any stronger flavor that might be lingering. Could you mop up one human soul with another?

Until she noticed his wedding ring.

Just as the party should have wrapped up, a young movie star materialized, straight from the San Vicente Bungalows, injecting the place with life. The assembled actors stood up straighter and the bartender restocked the dwindling reserves. Drinks were poured, glasses clinked once more. Voices raised, as if everyone wanted to prove they had been having a fine time without her.

The movie star strolled on her toes like a dancer, though it was well-known she had given up dancing when she was cast in a commercial for M&Ms at age twelve and caught the attention of Martin Scorsese. She stuck to the outside, where she flung sticks for her dog, both bounding across the ample, well-kept lawn. She kissed it zealously on the mouth. Even the poodles stepped aside. A caterer, looking like the king's page, brought out a bowl of water for the dog. "Thank you so much, I so appreciate it." Behind her, Alice could see the sun's big, bulky light, descending.

After the movie star slipped off, closing the security gate behind her dog, the staff cut the music, and there was a flurry of leaving. No guest wanted to be the last. A rush of apologies for forgotten names, of promises of touch-keeping, coats retrieved, contacts bartered. Even the host, producer Stan Donner, emerged in the final hour.

"I'll send you an invite to the show."

"Love it. So excited. Will be there."

"So so nice to see you!"

No hugs—vocal enthusiasm took its place. Outside, long fronds were sage pale. Shadows shimmered gently beneath them.

Utterly placeless, knowing she should leave but feeling she was leaving something unfinished, Alice fled into one of a maze of guest bedrooms, where she found an assembly of fellow idlers. She was plied with a joint, introduced to her as quad-grade California kush. Feeling heady, Alice thought about Celine, how she had said she was lonely. She wondered with a start whether, having had sex with a woman, she was now a marginalized person. Whether she occupied a different place in the social order. Did she, daughter of privilege, now number among the vulnerable in society? Or was it the opposite, that her privilege was what allowed her to experiment without danger of repercussion? It occurred to Alice that, as perplexing as all this was, none of it compared with the prior week's disorienting unreality.

There was a kind of order to the evening now, Alice felt, if she could only grasp it. She did not feel that way about what had happened with Celine. That was inexplicable.

The agent, Alice's tether, must have taken his leave at some point. Alice understood she was one of the last remaining guests. She had stayed until such twilight that the hosts were visibly locking up. She followed the weary producer and his wife down their own stairs, into the laundry room.

The weed spoke for Alice. "I know you're casting for the new *Redividers*. Can I send you my demo reel?" the pot said. Alice felt suddenly like she was drowning and needed to seek out anyone who could help. She propped herself up against a shelf of organic laundry products. "I really think I'm right for the part. I wouldn't chase you down here to say that otherwise." Alice addressed her entreaty to the producer's wife; she seemed the best bet.

When Alice suggested she could text them her information, after a few whispered words of debate with her husband, the depleted wife supplied Alice with Stan's assistant's email. Alice clutched it like a prize.

"I've met your daughter," Alice called to the wife as she went up the stairs in a pair of hostile high heels. Alice had suddenly remembered this fact and lurched after the woman. "I went to drama camp with your daughter." The daughter was anorexic, smart, and, according to Instagram, was now completing a social work degree. Alice had sat out the drama camp play—sat it out!—and instead spent five days in the arts and crafts tent, fashioning bumpy Plasticine ladybugs.

They did not seem to hear Alice. Alice watched opportunity ascend, just out of reach.

Soaked in guilt for two weeks, Alice tried to outrun it. She spoke intermittently with Sadie, feeling duplicitous. She bagged her shifts at Shutters. She scurried from Burbank to Culver City. She aimed doggedly for three auditions daily. Alice knew that many actors struggled and toiled for longer than a year and a half before making it; nonetheless, she was restless. And if she was honest with herself, she cared only marginally about her career.

"You haven't phoned back," Alice's mother scolded.

"You only called once," Alice said, out of sorts.

Hadley, wrapped in alpaca, had always maintained an eminently *appropriate* distance from her daughter. Was she disapproving or simply reserved? How, after so many years together, could Alice still be powerless to recognize the difference?

Hadley had supplied Alice with all the trappings: sparing no expense on daily comforts, lessons, and tutors. And yet Alice could not recall ever having spoken to her mother about any topic more personal than her daily homework. Alice was an uneasy only child, unlike Sadie, who took pleasure in her solitude. Hadley's voice reminded Alice of those tedious afternoons she had spent as a young girl, floating all day in the pool as the sun crossed the sky, trying to think up a game that would require no playmate. Where was her mother? Golf club, lunch club, garden club. She was gone by 9 a.m. Winter mornings, it was 6 a.m.; she did a polar bear swim, alone.

Nothing like Celine and Sadie, always together, on an adventure—even if they fought like wildcats, it was still better than the void Alice faced with her mother.

"I figured you saw the one call," Hadley said, "so there was no need for others. Am I wrong?"

"No," Alice admitted. "You're right." She asked where her mother was.

"The brown-and-blue room."

The brown-and-blue room was a room in her mother's house. Speckled with shade from the leaves outside, the walls were like the surface of a quail's egg. They were hung with oil glaze studies of birds and monkeys. The room had an open fireplace so grand that, unlit, it kept the room chilled as champagne. All the heat escaped out the fireplace, so there were always two space heaters running and the room hummed.

The room, like all the rooms, were Hadley's. She distinctly drew the edges of her life. Even things that could not be owned were referred to proprietarily: it was "her" kitchen counters and "her" gardeners. When Alice mentioned to her father that this made her feel as if she and her father had encroached upon her in occupying their own home, he had remarked, "It is hers. Her family bought it. We're just temporary tenants."

Hadley was the one person Alice's magic didn't work on. She had seen Alice sow too many unsprouted seeds. She felt acting, especially, of all Alice's pet projects, lacked taste and sophistication. She found it common, just as she found heels a centimeter over two inches, boisterousness, flaunting, any clothing article with a discernible label, poinsettias, carnations, talking on the phone at the club, purple, orange, farting, bronzer, potlucks, anything diamond-encrusted, anything silver-plated, the entire metropolis of Los Angeles west of old Pasadena, any piece of furniture conceived after 1982, any president after George H.W.

Still, Alice wondered what she would have to say about a lesbian fling. Funny thing was, she might even get a little thrill out of it.

Now, Alice could hear her mother's footsteps. While on a call, she routinely mounted the stairs and paced the third floor of her house, a wing she never otherwise had a chance to survey, checking grout and caulking, once-overing the guest rooms.

"How's the acting thing going, dear?"

Hadley was mortified that Alice had taken a job at Shutters and would not ask about it. What if she served one of Hadley's friends? It was a fine job for a teenager, but Alice was a college graduate.

"Fine," Alice said.

"When I was at UVA," Hadley said, tightening her voice like the strings of a corset, "I had no idea what was ahead. You'll come around to your calling, dear. When you're ready." For Hadley, life was a regatta. It had been all tomato salad at the table, cliffside Cape

Codders in a Collins glass, cycling to the local museum with fresh pink peonies in the basket of her single-speed Bianchi Pista. "We hope, of course, for *your* sake, that day comes soon."

Hadley took care of people by serving the useful purpose of teaching them to take care of themselves. It struck Alice that Hadley looked twenty-five years older than Celine; she looked like she was from another century.

Teeth locked in exertion, Alice pried the recalcitrant bag out of the under-sink pullout trash bin and hoisted the heavy, damp package. Generating garbage satisfied her. She liked reaching the ends of things and throwing them out. Kleenex boxes, vitamin jars. Using the last of a product felt gratifying. Soothing. Alice did not know why she was so irritable. She was on the phone with Celine.

She knotted together the trash bag's twin plastic ties. "Do you ever think about what we did?"

Celine answered softly. "Of course." She was mute for a good while. "Do you have any plans this weekend? Because I don't." She was circling her subject, warming to it. "What if you came up for the weekend and we tried to figure it out?"

Rancid juices were pooling at the bottom of the bag of trash, hanging in Alice's hand. It was pooling, beginning to seep, would drip imminently, should she fail to act soon.

"Never mind." Celine was brisk, impatient to forget the discussion. "Bad suggestion. Weird. Don't know why I said it. Just thinking out loud. Forget it."

"No." Waking into motion, Alice padded to the room at the end of the hall. She tossed in the malodorous bag of rubbish and felt immediately lighter. "Tell me."

"What if you came back?"

Alice made her way down the open hall.

"So we can actually talk about it," Celine said. "This dodging isn't like me. It's great to spend time together on the phone, but it feels a bit like treading water."

Alice opened the door to her apartment and blinked in the aggressive sun. "What about her?"

"Nothing about her. She's at Cormac's. She hasn't been here in a month."

LAX's long landing strips began a few miles from Alice's apartment block. From the service roadway above hers, you could see the runway illumination lights. Just then, a westbound airplane rumbled past overhead, on its way to an unknowable destination. Its jet engine shivered Alice's coffee table. She reached to steady a glass vase.

"Fly here," Celine said simply. "Tomorrow. This weekend. I'll pay the ticket. I'll buy it right now. It wouldn't cost you anything."

Alice wasn't so sure. "For one day?"

"We'll resolve this mess, and all get on with our lives."

For the second time that month, Alice flew north from Los Angeles, her life gathering speed. Alice was portable. Having come from a family of standing and status, an *established* family, she enjoyed feeling rootless as a cloud.

A soft marine layer blanketed the bay. In this mist, the trees were wisps. Alice's taxi driver eased up on the gas pedal as they passed over the elevated Central Freeway to the sunny side of the bay, where she and Sadie had vowed one day to live together. They passed the cheerful Star Grocery, which sold asparagus strapped into blue elastic; bright pink irises, still closed; California artichoke; stacks of sun-ripened satsumas.

The taxi stopped at the train crossing and Alice thought of her mother's friend who had driven across the tracks, trusting the green light and the upraised entry arm. The system had been nonoperational, and she had been slaughtered by the approaching train.

They crossed the tracks. As the taxi drew closer to Celine's home, the medians grew broader. Walnuts and sycamores gave way to redwood trees, towering over the Mediterranean Revival homes that Sadie faulted for blending too many styles. Alice knew every navigational turn to the trim, compact shingled, topsy-turvy cottage. Fitted with cedar siding, it had an unusually broad face. She knew where the road dipped upward, the houses looming, trees rising into view.

She knew the extra set of keys lived under the sparrow pedestal, in the dry, sloped-front garden, tucked into Celine's patchwork of Mexican grasses, her eccentric landscaping. Celine was always trying to force things to grow and her plants had a high mortality rate. But those that did survive thrived, budding frenziedly and developing to immense proportions. Sadie said that, like Proust's housemaid strangling a chicken, she tried to wrestle rewards out of nature. She played god, pretreating bulbs, inverting tubs over rhubarb crowns, cheating with artificial light, blitzing the plant beds with phosphorus and potassium.

Alice bet she'd been the last person to use those keys, visiting with Sadie a few months back while Celine was away at a dreary conference. But today, Alice was not letting herself in.

* * *

Celine's house was deep and narrow, tunnel-like. Sounds echoed. Of course, everything was awry.

"Is the house tipping?" Alice asked, when Celine approached with two steaming, fragrant mugs of tea. One shaped mug said "Pug of Tea" and the other showed Smurf cowboys lassoing a bull. Celine had peered out behind closed blinds at first, then answered the door with a one-armed hug and an air of bravado. She had dressed for the occasion, it seemed, in a Western shirt with a bolero tie.

"That's just the floor," Celine said.

She had a doughnut chandelier hanging from the ceiling. It seemed to beg for a comment. "I'm a hundred percent about this sculpture thing," Alice remarked. Maybe, Alice reconsidered, what she'd thought was a sculpture was only a lamp.

Celine laughed sharply and shifted from foot to foot. "You're just noticing it after a decade?"

"I'm just . . ." Alice was at a loss for words. What she was doing defied identification.

Hadley maintained neat cabinets, a tidy row of five collectible Herend china plates on display. Celine had no such thing, no cabinets to contain the debris of kitsch spilling over every surface. Her trio of purple suitcases were assembled in the corner of the front hall, as if the place were provisional and she might bolt at any moment. Alice set her own duffel bag beside them. Alice felt sure now that she had made a mistake in coming.

"Making conversation?" Celine supervised Alice. "I know. Things will be funny for a minute. We're both nervous. We'll sort ourselves out."

Alice was in a familiar place. She knew the house, size medium, a three-bedroom (third turned office), inside and out. She knew which floorboards squeaked. She knew which cabinet door harbored the Tom and Jerry jam jar glasses and which the confetti tumblers. She knew which plate set—an annual Christmas gift from Sadie, trying inoperably to impose order—was a set of six and which a set of eight, and which seven because one had cracked in the dishwasher.

Alice's eyes drifted around the room, finding her bearings. It could have been occupied by a teenage boy, so dwarfed was it by PEZ dispensers, Chairman Mao statues in various imposing poses, and busts of lesser-known presidents wearing Christmas tinsel.

Like a beacon, Pearl, Celine's cat, moseyed in. Alice had been the one to find her. One bronze-lit evening headed up Camino Real, noticing two eyes, sleek glints, in the headlights that cut across the snaking curve in the darkening night. Sadie had coaxed the downy silver kitten out from under the arid-reserve bushes. Where she had taken pity on the creature, Celine had gone a step further and had become completely enamored with it.

Alice waited now, hand outstretched, for the cat to come by for a scratch. "Shh," Celine said sharply, prying open a half-eaten can of Purina. Pearl rubbed against a coffee table. "You eat that."

The cat looked on and, with a start, recognized Alice. It dodged her hand, staying just out of reach. Alice coughed on her sip of tea. It was strong as petrol.

"I added a splash," Celine admitted, "to take the edge off. Hope that's all right."

"Some people ask first."

"I'm asking now."

Alice downed her cup in three scalding gulps.

"Okay, then." Celine seemed to admire this.

Pearl finally made amends and rolled onto her back on the floor, showing her white belly and bubble-gum-pink paws. The cat liked to have her ears smoothed, gave Alice whale eyes.

Celine shooed the cat. "You get comfortable," she proposed to Alice. The cat stretched and yowled once. "Take off your jacket. If you want."

Alice, under the best of circumstances, did not like to be hosted and to choose among a host's limited offerings. She did not like being subject to the host's timing of *her* wants and desires. *Would you like a drink? Yes, and I have for forty-five minutes.*

"Feel free to freshen up, use the restroom."

Just when Alice dutifully struck off down the hall, Celine called after her, "Use mine!"

This stopped Alice in her tracks. Celine's en suite bathroom was unspeakably foreign. Oddly, to enter into it struck her as the most glaring breach thus far. To reach the bathroom, she'd have no choice but to negotiate Celine's bedroom, a place she was not sure she had ever set foot in. Alice had always found parents' bedrooms creepily off-limits. She avoided looking at the bed, noticing instead that, on the deep yellow walls, twin mirrors hung at the bed's head and foot. Alice kept having to satisfy herself that she was not in Sadie's house. She was in Celine's.

Alice did not need to use the restroom. Closing the bathroom door behind her, she splashed cold water onto her face. She uncapped and applied a deodorant she found behind the mirror, gone clayey. She scrunched her toes in the woolly bathmat. She had stopped in at a bathroom less than an hour before, catching her breath at the airport. Two slim, tailor-made accent chairs flanked the sink. How many people needed to sit in Celine's bathroom at one time?

Yes, she *had* been here, in this bathroom, once. Sadie had dyed Alice's hair cinnamon red. She had still worn retainers, then, and had asked, "Doesh it look fantashtic?" Sadie had cocked her head, fluffed Alice's hair, and declared the change unsuccessful, then dyed it back again. It was the path of least resistance to submit to Sadie's supervision. Alice had even convinced herself she liked it.

Alice turned off the faucet. She rubbed her brow, the skin sore from yesterday's wax. Sore and naked, a little gummy. They had ripped off too much. If Celine noticed, she didn't say so. Alice had not waxed any other area. Why would she have? She had no plans for anyone to see it.

When she opened the door again, her heart danced like a jumping bean. Celine had taken off her shoes, was in her socks, reclined upon the bed, directly across from the door, a smile playing at the corners of her lips. A feeling of warning crept over Alice. She wanted this. And she was going to do it.

"Splash?" Without waiting for reply, Celine poured Alice a glass of scotch from a decanter, casting reflections onto the white bedsheets.

Alice accepted the glass. Celine took stock of Alice. Those burning eyes, charring, watching Alice's throat when she swallowed, as if she could see the liquid go down. See the tendrils of nervous energy. It seemed to fuel her. Alice grimaced, uneven, feeling the kick. "Should I sit next to you?"

"I won't bite."

But minutes later, Celine was pinching Alice's nipple, still tingling, rising again to her unexhausted arousal. Her body was dazzled, going wild anytime Celine came near. "Is this," Alice murmured, her body swelling. "Okay?" She moaned, up against the outsized bureau.

"What do you mean. This?" Celine licked, innocent as a kitten. "This?" With industrious hands, she brought her own nipple to Alice's mouth. Alice noticed that the flesh of Celine's nipples tasted the same as her lips. "This?"

Sex meant disappearing into another person. You were most alive at your most negligible, when you felt your entire self nearest to death. You were least yourself. It was such a relief not to be herself. Celine's fingers staggered into Alice. Alice felt a grip in the place where she had let her feelings collect. It was softer, coming by Celine's mouth, like shivering water.

In the two dizzying mirrors, Alice stared back at her many selves, fallen back in Celine's bedroom. "I was worried I smelled, from the flight."

"You did," Celine said, inching closer to her by degrees. Everything she was, all the legend and actuality of her, was there, in her body. She carried herself, it seemed, deep in every atom of her being. Alice wondered what it must be like to feel so embodied. "Hey, do something for me. Stay for the weekend."

Across the room, Pearl was ticking her tail, eyes yellow as two moons. The dual mirrors reflected dozens of themselves. Such was Celine's bottomless ego. It was in that instant, seeing herself folded in with Celine, shone back, redirected, reproduced in infinite multiples, that Alice understood she would stay. That Celine would have whatever she wanted.

Wishing she had any idea what she wanted—she must have wanted this, if she was here; if she *hadn't* wanted it and had done it anyway, what hideous light did that reflect on her?—Alice left Celine contemplating her tufty hair in bed. She slid open the door to the deck, eyes trained on the wooded area at the far end of the property. A string of hanging chili pepper lights glowed. The raucous garden, which Celine tended meticulously, if peculiarly, bobbed in the evening breeze. Seed-eating sparrows hopped in and out of foliage. The amaranth, which Celine loved for being unruly. Celine could cultivate all that, by sheer force of will. Couldn't she unscramble this?

"What are we doing?" Alice turned to ask, catching sight of herself, disheveled in the mirrors. Suddenly feeling she had no right to be there, let alone for tens of her to. She slouched to make herself small. "Are we insane?"

Celine groaned, almost happily. "That's a nighttime conversation."

In the sky, darkness was gathering. "Almost night," Alice said. "Glass-of-wine conversation."

"You said we were going to sort this out," Alice said gently.

"Let's not push it," Celine said, putting it off. "Can't you stay for the weekend, so it'll come naturally?"

"We weren't supposed to be doing this again."

Celine reached for the box of Chex Mix on her bedside table. She turned to Alice. "We were lying to ourselves. If all we needed was to talk, we could have done that on the phone."

"I have a theory," Alice admitted, deciding not to point out that she had come on Celine's insistence. "You're trying to solve *her* by spending time with me."

"Are you kidding?" Celine pressed a cluster of nut mix into her mouth. They were flirting. "You are the great complicator. You're taking me back to square one." She turned to face Alice. "Do you think you're looking for a mother figure?"

"Me?" Alice choked. She thought for the first time of her mother, in their stately home on four acres in Lamorinda. In her mind, she traveled the Highway 24 corridor, eastbound through the Caldecott Tunnel, until the streets were lit by ivy-choked streetlamps and turned into the tony cul-de-sac at the crest of the hill. She thought of what in the name of Nelson Rockefeller her mother would think, if she knew. It was even kind of funny, how defective this situation was. Did she have to spell it out for Celine? "*You* came to see me, remember? You came three times. You hunted me like a poacher."

This was funny to Celine. She nodded in lawless approval. "Fucking fuck." Alice jumped at a sound coming from the street, a car driving past the house. Celine noticed. "You can relax," she said after a moment. "She has never once just showed up. She *always* calls."

The light was blue-gold as the sun melted over the crest of Panoramic Hill. From the steeply ascented angle, the shoreline was obscured. The city below seemed to bathe, comfortably, in water. From a corner of the lawn, from one minute to the next, crickets started up all at once. The chorus sounded bracing and manly.

Celine reclined, hands splayed on her belly, an amphibian in repose. "Okey-doke. If you don't mind, it's that time I usually shut myself into my office. You okay to hang solo, maybe watch some TV or something?"

Sure. It was where Alice and Sadie had watched *Killing Eve* and *Euphoria*, and where they had sighted their first lesbian porn, having accidentally logged into Celine's user account. Sadie had closed out of the window fast, not daring to look at Alice. Alice couldn't help asking fifteen minutes later, "Wait, was that a carrot or a parsnip?" To which Sadie replied, "Shut up."

"Pour yourself something to drink," Celine said. Alice rose obediently. "If that sounds nice. Only if you want to."

"I do." Alice thought she did. An appliance churned, somewhere deep in the house. Pearl raced around the hallway corner and eyed the intruder.

"If it creeps you out to be alone in here, I can knock off for the night." It was a symbolic gesture with no intention of fulfillment, like when someone said *please, don't get up*. "Of course, I'd have to do double shifts tomorrow. This book is killing me. I'm desperate to get this motherfucker done."

Alice insisted and Celine let herself be talked into working. She quit the room, trailed by Pearl. This left Alice seated on the bed, springs still bouncing. Her half-packed duffel bag lay open in the corner, spilling its hopeful contents.

The cottage was small enough that Alice occasionally heard Celine in her office, drumming on the typewriter keys, punctuated by "Pearl, what are you doing?" And "You're just a little grain of sand that got trapped inside a mollusk and irritated into luster, aren't you, girl? That's all you are."

Celine had weaseled cheerfully out of the conversation, but they were *going* to have it. A drink, that was what Alice needed.

She rose and found that the only mixer in the fridge was cranberry juice, which she had not been able to drink since it was all that had sustained her grandmother in her final days, starched with Thick-It for smooth consumption. No mixer, then.

Pearl appeared, seemingly from nowhere, and made herself snug. Alice rubbed her soft jelly paws. Generally, the cat could not be induced to lie on Alice's lap. Today she did, contributing to the sense that today was a different kind of day, one in which everything was changed.

Alice knew what she would do. She would call Sadie the next day. Let her know she was in town. Seeing her best friend would drive all thoughts of her mother's sex organs from her mind.

Deciding this, she felt much better. She was going to close the conversation with Celine, do recon with her friend, and put everything back in order. Easy as pie. She poured a pair of gleaming brandies, as celebration. One for Celine, before thinking she was not in on the scheme, nor would she want to be disturbed. Alice held the twin set of Tom and Jerry glasses, one in each hand. In her reeking shirt, without anything else to cover her, in someone else's underpants, skirting her potential, skirting her friend, Alice downed both pours.

Chapter Twelve
SADIE

WEEK TWO

Sadie was miserable. Only when it transpired that Alice had come back into town—there, she said, to petition her mother for money; two walk-on parts in one year did not pay the rent and she said Sadie was right; why be so proud?—did Sadie manage to drag herself up and out of the house. She knew Alice would have just the right thing to say. She would assuage Sadie's concerns. She would treat sex like she always did. Like something easy. Nothing to worry about.

The best friends met up at Judy's, a campus coffee shop located down a narrow alleyway, only four feet wide. It had an unofficial *Twin Peaks* theme, outfitted with hanging traffic lights and cherry pie memorabilia, even a trickling waterfall in a dark corner booth. The police procedural's instrumental soundtrack, saccharine and soapy, was on loop, rendering any conversation dreamy and atmospheric. Judy's had a daily special on two coffees and the slice of pie du jour.

For once, Alice was on time. This was unlike her. Usually she was, if Sadie had to hazard a guess, twelve minutes late on average. Sadie hated down time. Today's punctuality gave Sadie a private gratification. Alice missed her.

Not only was Alice on time, but she had traded in her usual

slouchy, drooping garb and was dressed for business, in a checkered blazer and a crewneck sweater over a pressed collared shirt.

"Someone take the wrong turn from Vineyard Vines?"

Alice just smiled slightly. Ordering at the counter, she declined the pie, which bothered Sadie marginally. Alice never dieted, blessedly faultless without effort. But she signaled a no-thanks when Sadie handed her a fork, mumbling something barely intelligible about her stomach being a little jumpy today.

The pie had a lattice crust, which Alice pointed out was a discrepancy. "Dale Cooper's was a sealed crust," Sadie said.

"Should we leave?" Alice asked.

Sadie wished she could. At the booth, Alice sipped her drip coffee.

Sadie started right in, pulling off the Band-Aid. "It was horrible. It was so awful. Tums!" Sadie groaned at the recollection. "Can you imagine? Munching on Tums in the middle of my bodice-ripping romance?"

Tums! It did not seem inconceivable that Sadie could die an Emily Dickinsonian self-elected virgin, unimpeachable, isolated and brooding, sequestered in a lighthouse tower, a castle built into a cliff where no one could contact her—not her manipulative mother; not her vacant, needy grandmother; not even her flighty, promiscuous friend—and devote herself to the pursuit of knowledge and knitting. She could already hear the waves crashing against craggy bluffs, sending up sea spray.

"That's okay," Alice said, as Sadie knew she would. And she dipped her fork into the pie, just as Sadie *also* knew she would. Sadie pushed the plate toward her. "It sounds like you weren't quite ready."

The feather-haired waitress promenaded over to refresh their coffees. Sadie waited to speak until she retreated, tapping her knife lightly against the table. "I disembody," she said. "My brain gets in the way." She tried to put it into terms Alice would understand. "I feel like I'm acting, trying on a role."

Alice validated this, with an ardent nod of agreement. Finally, something she seemed to agree with. "Sex can be complicated." She fidgeted, turning over the tines of her fork in the pie filling. "In the best of cases."

This surprised Sadie to hear. Alice owned her sexuality. She didn't judge herself for relishing it. Sadie would pay to adopt this position. She wished she could. It was something her timeline simply had not accounted for: sex phobia.

"Listen, sex is probably the last thing you want to be hearing about," Alice said, seeming hopeful to be let off the hook.

Sadie could not bear to admit that was precisely why she was here.

"Sex," Alice said reluctantly, taking a sip of her coffee, swallowing, "can be destructive. It can bring out people's worst impulses." Alice seemed to be talking to herself. "Very often, it can feel guilty, or wrong." She fidgeted, like a child, Sadie noticed, crimping the edge of a sugar packet.

Sadie stared into her coffee grounds. At the counter, a customer was asking who killed Laura Palmer and the barista directed them to the fan theories on the *Twin Peaks* Reddit. In the booth, Alice was rocking back and forth, side to side. She cleared her throat. "There's something, uh . . ."

"My timeline is all fucked up," Sadie interrupted. "I need to up my sex-o-meter. How? *Cosmo* would call it *boosting my libidinal instincts*."

"Um." Alice stared into her coffee. "I've heard people talk about oysters."

Sadie nodded, taking note. "I did mix maca root into my smoothie."

Alice smiled slightly. "That sounds like a good start. Maybe lingerie?"

Sadie frowned. Easy for Alice to say. Late at night the year before, tipsy after riding the steam train at Tilden Park, under a toothpick-sharp crescent of moon, the two best friends had skinny-dipped in the Lake Anza dam—well, Alice had. Alice never looked indecent when nude. It was her natural, proper default state. Sadie had taken off her top and retained her undies. That was the most naked she'd ever been in front of Alice. "I've just never understood what you're supposed to take off for sex. Or when. Do you wear lingerie for thirty seconds? Or slide the crotch to the side? There are all those snaps and hooks."

Alice tossed her hair over her shoulder. "Just don't think about it so much. Let it be easy."

"This was not an answer. Do *you* wear lingerie?" But Sadie knew Alice always slept in plain old boy briefs. "You don't, because you don't need it. You're a natural sex bunny. It's innate."

"I wouldn't say that."

"We all know you'll fuck anything!" Sadie laughed at the thought, like they always had. But this time, Alice didn't join her. Something about Alice was definitely off. Ordinarily, she would have offered the line herself. "I mean that as a compliment. I wish I could be a sex gymnast like you. You know so much about men. You're a man whisperer." Sadie secretly felt that Alice embarked on so many affairs out of a lack of conviction.

Cormac and Alice had always gotten along; they shared a certain tranquility that bordered on irresolution. Sadie had always felt the two would have made a better match. Though Cormac had never given her reason for concern, she never felt entirely comfortable when he spoke of Alice. What a relaxed life the two of them could have, easy-breezy, affable, laid-back, the twin *bon humeurs* smiling upon the world, seeing the best in everyone, uncritical of motivations, trusting their first impressions, never second-guessing, let alone third, fourth, or fifth.

Oh, to be oblivious to one's own shortcomings—and those of others!

"Men." Alice sighed heavily. "I don't know. Men are simple."

Men were simple. Sadie's story was so pathetic. It was so humiliating, it looked to have embarrassed Alice, just to hear it.

"Are you okay?" Sadie asked Alice. "You're chewing your lip like it's bubble gum."

"Fine."

"Good." Sadie knocked Alice's forgotten mug with her own. "Coffee's cold. Are we done here? Are you going straight home? Should I come with you and say hi to Hadley?"

But Alice said Hadley was at her figure-drawing class, would stop afterward for a glass of wine with her fellow trainees, and would not be home all evening.

"Am I going to see you again before you go back to L.A.?"

"I may have to stay a few days," Alice said, fiddling with the saltshaker. She was talking very fast now. "Hadley and I are opening a joint bank account, and they require two forms of identification, which means I need to renew my passport."

Sadie looked skeptical. "I thought you renewed for Barcelona."

"It's invalid for some reason." Alice perked up, swallowing the last few forkfuls of pie in rapid succession, as if someone had a gun to her head. "Anyway, red tape. I'll let you know."

Together, they walked to the marina, where Alice pointed out a cormorant just as it was swallowing, in one gulp, a striped bass the length of its body. Sadie thought about it all the rest of the day, pondering the improbability. Sorry, a little, for the fish, but more for the bird's indigestion.

JULY

Chapter Thirteen

CELINE

On Alice's fourth night in the house in Claremont, Celine was not, as Alice believed, working in her office. She had gone to her office to calm down. She had gone to congratulate herself with a fist pump. She felt exultant and limber, her dwindling body rejuvenated with the infusion of new blood.

It was like a man looking at the moon and thinking, I could go there. She was so enamored that she had to keep from yelling it out on the street. What if she *could* have it all, the little life *and* the big; the stricture *and* the emancipation; the fish and the chips?

Celine thought this might even get the creative juices flowing. Allow her to finally write this flipping thing.

"A guest is like fish," Alice had cautioned. "I'll start to stink after three days."

"Honey," Celine said, "you're roses."

There was the word *desire*—it had always knocked about—but had it ever meant anything before? That beauty, Celine had to possess it. She felt it would lift her up, give her access to a pillowy feminine splendor she had never permitted herself to yearn for. Seeing it in her mind's eye, there in her office, suddenly was not enough. Feeling like a stallion, Celine galloped back to the bedroom.

Abruptly self-conscious, Alice covered her bare breasts, feeling Celine's sweeping eyes. Alice's hair was piled into a mountain on her head. She was a dewy slab of ruby-red tuna, iridescent, stripped clean. Celine felt herself grow larger, harder. She understood in these moments what it must feel like to be a man.

"Am I fat?" Alice asked, sensing the appraisal. She reached to cover her pouchy nipples, a shocked raspberry red.

Celine's gaze softened. "You're perfect." A stir went through her. Alice's bottom was soft as Japanese mochi cake. It was hard not to objectify her. Anyone who alleged not to notice the change in a young girl as she metamorphosed into a sexual being was a downright liar. Nature was not subtle. Even after no less than a week in Alice's company, Celine still felt she should look away. As if to have no witness, she always shut Pearl out in the living room, dozing in a patch of sun.

But Alice just kept watching steadily, holding Celine's prying gaze with round eyes, almost obscenely large. Alice was guileless, so well-adjusted. Celine felt there had to be a dark underbelly. There *had* to.

"Aren't we going to use a strap-on?" Alice asked, with jarring directness. Discreetly as she could, trying not to laugh, Celine explained that she generally reserved prosthetics for special occasions, because it was kind of a hassle. "But if it's important to you that I have a cock, I certainly can."

"Well, do you have one?"

"It's possible. Unless it's disappeared."

"Where would it have gone?"

"Let's check."

And so she pulled out her Magic Box. Together, she and Alice contemplated the crammed-full box. Alice recognized the basic internal vibrator, the standard clit stimulator, the clamps. But Celine's zebra-striped bullet surprised her.

“That was a gift,” Celine explained. She caught herself in the mirror opposite the bed. She frowned at her reflection and fluffed her hair.

Alice scanned the drawer with apprehension. “What’s that bug with arms?”

“Hands-free vibrator. You put the wings . . .”

“I get it.”

Celine held out the box, but Alice wouldn’t touch it.

“And the one shaped like a J?”

“Shared vibe. Dual motor.”

“And the L?”

“Finger extender. You—”

“I can Google it.”

It felt peculiar to introduce Alice to all this, delivering technical tutorials, dispensing knowledge. The girl was almost like a virgin. Celine felt tender, to be a part of this journey. Not so long ago, she was learning herself.

The following evening, confidence swelling, Alice set off to the Wednesday farmers market. She returned home with a paper bag of plums in one hand and in the other a set of shining handcuffs, made of cheap die-cast metal.

At the moment, Celine was in the grip of an attempt to brush the cat’s teeth, having been accused by the vet of tartar accumulation. “Wow,” she said. She relinquished Pearl, whose head she had been endeavoring to grip at forty-five degrees. “Are these for me?”

Pearl tore out of the room, like this intimacy was beyond witnessing.

“Actually, I thought you could put them on *me*.” Alice placed Celine’s hand on her breast. She liked to have her nipples suckled. Celine did not especially like to grant this pleasure. It made her feel like a nursing baby. The anatomical metaphor that Freud had overlooked.

"What I mean is, is this a gift?" Celine pulled back. "Are you going to take them with you when you go back to Los Angeles?"

"They're for us and I don't know when I'm going back but I suppose I'll decide then."

With a start, Celine realized Alice was committing.

Alice was congenitally cheerful, even when her pride was hurt. "Just call it a trophy," she said drily. "When I leave, you can pack them away into your box next to the zebra-striped bullet."

Celine turned over the clinking cuffs. "I'm afraid these won't work." She had a hard line on safety. "We don't want radial nerve damage. These are designed *not* to feel good, you understand? They tighten if you tug."

Alice couldn't resist the urge to ask, "So you've used them before?"

"Possibly."

"I like when you discipline me," Alice said. Coyly, she pulled Celine's faux-suede whip from the box and tantalized it over Celine's thigh. Celine had taught Alice about dom, sub, and switch positions—and invited her to assign the roles. Alice clapped her mouth shut with the palm of her hand, a bit of a slap. "Maybe I was bad to get those bad handcuffs. Maybe I deserve a spanking."

This was not how Celine wanted it. "I would never spank you," she said desperately. "You're my daughter's best friend."

Alice stiffened. She pouted. "That's not very sexy."

"Isn't it?"

Celine sat back on her heels, twirling the faux-suede whip. "We still haven't had that talk, by the way."

"We will," Alice said crossly. "Now, please stay in character."

So Celine tabled the discussion, yielding with a flush of confused affection. Disoriented and heady, she spanked her daughter's best friend—Alice liked that—then petted her with a soft article that resembled a cat toy. Their safe word was *safe word*. Their four hands raked the sheets.

Mornings, with the sun, the bedroom's deep yellow walls lightened to chamomile. Alice and Celine both often woke with iMessage flags raised. Sadie had insomnia and would text Celine gripes about her scattered medical records or the whereabouts of her birth certificate, and Alice about the latest celebrity-marriage gossip. This didn't disturb them; both Alice and Celine slept like logs.

Afternoons, the walls turned buttery. In the evenings, under stark light, the walls were the color of egg yolk.

Soon, Alice was ushering Celine out of the house for brunch and gelato. At home, because neither cooked, they ordered takeout. Celine discovered the delivery apps and, because it was so easy to pile on order items, with no extra delivery fees, they began ordering tacos *and* hamburgers *and* ramen. They had the best time.

Time strode on. Celine could not be blamed for that. After all, she had no hand in time. Celine liked feeling the house activated, hearing Alice's footsteps in the next room. She saw Alice's body the next day and the next, every time they slid into bed. Each time, the misconduct dismantled Celine less and the infatuation gripped her further.

"I never noticed your ears before," she said, petting.

"Your shoulders are so beautiful," Alice said, stroking.

Celine squinted. "I love that little thing at the edge of your mouth."

After sex, Alice quivered. Her wide eyes looked at Celine too directly. "Your love and kindness and heart are beautiful."

Celine kissed Alice's forehead. And yet, to Celine's surprise, the words nauseated her abruptly, mostly, she thought, because she felt their untruth.

Celine, dizzied, tried to take a broad view. Only a priggish moralist would deny that mothering was tantalizing, even erotic. Years prior, those far-off hours, back in Ohio in the laminate kitchen, in another lifetime, Celine had kissed Sadie's succulent, luscious skin and felt it all through her body, like a power surge. Warm as good bread. Fat thighs like a steaming bath, toes cool and juicy. Freud's baby at the breast, clamping to latch. A closed circle of want: Sadie suckling contentedly, knowing exactly what she wanted from Celine and getting it. What could be sexier?

"Hate in the Counter-Transference," a hot polemic in 1949, and required reading for Celine by 1991, was not wrong in recording that an infant excites a mother and also "frustrates—she mustn't eat him or trade in sex with him." Celine had not eaten her daughter, though tempting. Estrogen, progesterone, adrenaline were pumping, increased lubrication, increased sensitivity. Birth's sweet release. Don't blame Celine, blame physiology. Nothing was more primal.

In Celine's eyes, then, it was in fact one turn *less* on the dial to be attracted to the friend of the offspring. One notch closer to natural.

Alice was alight, eyes like butterflies. She looked up from the tangle of sheets. "Am I gay? I don't look gay."

"Is that significant?"

"Not really."

As it grew dark, under creamsicle skies, whole evenings were spent parting the seams of lips, both sets. Celine chided herself. She woke up swooning, unaccustomed to sex blurring at such velocity into love. The bed was like a ship, Celine thought, lingering inside the metaphor, sheets billowing like sails. She could feel the ocean rocking.

It was like a honeymoon. It was them against the world. The cat blessed Celine's lap, landing squarely, warm as pie.

"Pearl is eating well," Celine remarked. "She thrives when you're here."

"And when I go away?"

"She suffers."

At night, Celine was at war with pillows, always feeling Alice had too many. Celine said they were for propping up, not sleeping on. "It's too many. Awkward for me on my side. It puts us on uneven levels. I don't like that."

"Sadie taught me that it's better for your back to sleep propped up," Alice said, bewilderedly blinking awake. Pearl was parked at her side. "It reduces the collapse of the airway."

Celine scowled like her daughter's name was a bad word. "Is it really time to bring her up now?" She didn't mean now, she meant ever. Sadie was a bridge Alice and Celine crossed on their way to each other. The bridge was unstable. Sadie was the hump that had to be gotten past; she was the high road. So long as they did not talk about Sadie, they stayed well.

"Well, okay, but are we ever going to have that talk?"

Celine rummaged in her side table and lit a rare cigarette. "Are you really that eager to have that talk?"

"No. But I guess we should at some point."

Celine had never cared to interrogate what she was doing as she was doing it. Where was the fun in that? Besides, Celine thought to herself, she hurts me all the time. Every day. Every other line she said to Celine was hostile, critical, and unkind—and Celine didn't even call her on it!

"Have you ever noticed that her farts smell like celery?" Alice asked.

Exhaling sweet smoke, Celine allowed herself to laugh. Maybe even Sadie could find the humor and pathos in the circumstance. So long as they hadn't told her, Celine could imagine the telling a success. What if Sadie could let this be unifying?

Alice retrieved the pillow from the floor, fluffed it, and propped herself up suitably. "Inevitably, she will have thoughts on the matter."

Celine knew this was true. But Sadie did not have a private monopoly over Celine. And what Sadie didn't know couldn't hurt her. This thing would probably wear itself out, go away without her ever needing to know about it. Just a little wonderful thing that had happened, just a twinkle, and that would be it. She would run into Alice at Sadie's wedding someday, far into the future. Maybe they would catch eyes across the ceremony, maybe even wink. Alice would be on the arm of some fine-looking guy her age with whom she'd lock eyes when she caught the bouquet.

Celine fell asleep, still sitting up, drooping against the sconce lamp, her tufty hair dangerously close to the hot bulb. When she woke, she found that Alice had lovingly covered her with a blanket, turned off the light above, slipped off and folded Celine's reading glasses and placed them neatly on the bedside table. Celine stared up at the ceiling. Sadie was not like other people's daughters—whom Celine had never thought much of. She'd always had a sensible head, a remote fairness. All their life together, Celine had sought a meteoric rise out of her. Sadie was immune to Celine, sensible and dispassionately nonpartisan even to her mother, and this pissed Celine off.

Alice scratched Celine's back lightly. When it began to grate on her, Celine shrugged free.

Was Sadie's self-mastery such a virtue?

Once, for fun, Celine had dressed her lover-du-jour in Lucite platforms and a fishnet top and installed her outside the window of Sadie's third-grade class. Like a sea of pansies, phototropic, perceiving the sun, the children all faced the front of the room together. Sensing activity behind her, Sadie was the only one of the flock to turn around. The tall woman positioned her fluffy permed head in the classroom window and waggled her fingers. Sadie buried her head in her workbook, refusing to engage, to look up again, implacable as ice. The girl had willpower.

Celine knew Sadie wouldn't say a word to her teacher. She had a healthy disrespect for authority; Celine had taught her that. And Celine was careful to never take things too far. *She* never wore the fishnet top, for instance.

That day, after school, flapping out the corridor into the learning commons courtyard, in the woven leather sandals Celine had lovingly selected for her at a stall on Sixteenth and South Van Ness, Sadie had gone home with another girl and her mother, supposedly to work on a project for the science fair. Back when Sadie idealized those other women, just to try to break Celine's heart.

Maybe if she had had a father. It had been with a heavy heart, sodden with guilt, that Celine had learned, four years after leaving him, when Sadie was a nine-year-old girl, that Adam had died, not yet having found the family he sought. It was the early days of the camera phone and he had taken a grainy selfie on his Kyocera flip phone while driving. Cost him his life: self-absorbed, he had lost track of his surroundings and careened off the road. He had snapped a succession of shots, including mugging next to his shopping bags in the passenger seat from the local golf club's shop—here, Celine winced—which he was proud to have joined.

Maybe it wasn't true, what Celine had always told Sadie, that the only place a man led was straight off the path. Nevertheless, his means of death was silly, comedically stupid, and not the example she wanted set for her daughter.

Chapter Fourteen

ALICE

The days continued to accumulate until they were two weeks, and Alice had quit her job at Shutters remotely, and sublet her lease to a fellow hybrid actor-waiter, and suddenly she and Celine were spooning, and it was the end of July. Alice should leave, she knew that. She did not fool herself into believing this could have a happy ending. But, like a fly stuck to paper, she could not seem to lift a leg.

It was a baptism by fire. The sex was electrifying, seeming to expand Alice. She had begun saying words like *pussy* because Celine liked it. She was working up to *cunt*. Saying the word aloud seemed to require a latent muscle.

Alice had so often taken up things she was not committed to. She wondered vaguely if this was just one more half-done thing. Had she been locked inside her heterosexual orientation like in an iron closet, her precise orientation embedded inside, pinned fixed and dormant all these years like a butterfly mounted to board? Celine took exception to the inquiry and questioned why Alice cared to think in those terms.

Sex had never been a source of heartache. Alice had always had a simple good time. It was not fraught, the way it was for Sadie. Alice thought of her former, retired lovers. Like sleeping marionettes lining the wall of a dark room, hung by their handles. Jason, Brian, Kevin. "It's so easy for you," a stranger had commented once, a guy she had met at the gym—whose handsome, vacant eyes she could see straight through—and nonetheless spent the rest of the day with between the sheets. Or the capoeira instructor who Alice noticed never used a fork, preferring to eat everything, including Alice, with the assistance of his strong hands: "It's like an ignition. I press a button and watch you turn on."

Still, this was beyond easy. Alice felt that, as long as she kept this up, she would not be fit to live among children and reputable society. It was almost like a sex crime.

When you read about someone doing something like this, you'd think, *What an idiot, to risk everything that way.* When it's you, it was, *This is so beautiful. This is something different. This is special.*

"How does he always smell so good?" Alice asked, wadding up Meacham's beagle ears and inhaling the scent like a drug. It made her want to cry. Good, simple-hearted Meacham, unlike the cruel Pearl.

She was home, across town from Celine's, visiting her parents, trying to regain a little taste of her old self. She claimed to have just driven up from Los Angeles for the visit. This pleased Hadley. She'd been there since mid-morning. Hadley, peering stolidly out from behind her tortoiseshell glasses, dressed in oatmeal alpaca, had welcomed her guest into the fusty home with cheek firmly bared and open arms.

It was a cold morning and all three were bundled into sweaters. Alice clipped hydrangeas by the small, reed-fringed pond, and they ate on the screened-in porch. Alice looked out at the blurred view.

Alice's mother was perched on the rattan outdoor sofa, staring at a photo her sister, Alice's Aunt Bunny, had attached to an email. "Are they cute?" She held the phone out at an angle. "I'm not so sure."

"Mother!"

As it turned to afternoon, the trio moved to Hadley's game room, which had jigsaw puzzles and playing cards displayed under a glass table, a lamp stand fashioned out of dice, chessboards hung like paintings, Scrabble on the lazy Susan.

"Tell us, Alice. How is Los Angeles?" Beside her father, Meacham, the beagle named for Thomas Jefferson's biographer, was at work bothering a button on the back of the Chesterfield sofa, nibbling its edges and trying to get a solid enough grip to pry it free.

Alice frowned. They had no idea that for nearly a month, she had been not fifteen minutes away. "I don't like how palm trees are always leaning sideways."

Her mother sipped out of her blue-and-white Royal Copenhagen mug—she'd switch to scotch on the hour (the house dictum was "we pour at four")—and considered this. "I like that about them."

"I just don't know if the acting thing is really it." Alice suggested that she might like to be a marine biologist, work with whales, study mating and sleep habits. But reconsidered when she registered that would require years of school. Hadley patted Alice's lap with those shaky hands and reminded Alice that they came from strong stock and could not be so easily vanquished.

Alice's father glanced at Hadley from the overstuffed Cheltenham sofa. He was head of brand restructuring at a large multinational consumer goods corporation, which meant he kept his job and divested others. He was well-enough salaried to keep Hadley, despite a dwindling family reserve, ensconced in the life she was used to, albeit a decidedly less-storied West Coast version. He was a large, square man, built like a unit of geometry.

But where had she *been*, her parents finally wanted to know,

Hadley sipping her scotch and soda out of her signature tall Collins glass. Two weeks prior, Hadley had slipped on a ruffled silk pillowcase, bashing and skinning her shinbone, requiring six stitches. Why hadn't Alice called?

Alice did not know why not. She must have missed that message. Lacking the energy to conjure any other myth, she almost buckled. "You want to know what's going on with me? You really want to know?" Alice almost even told them. There was something so comforting about being here, visiting her childhood bedroom, the evidence of all the people she had been: the horse trophies, the faded yellow ribbons.

What would be the point? Alice leaned against the damask wallpaper. She watched the dust motes floating in a shaft of sunlight and, instead, conjured a white lie.

They'd begun to get sick of takeout. "Is there anything that looks remotely homemade?" Celine asked Alice, scrolling the delivery menus. When they tried their hand at cooking, it was inedible. Alice had not noted the difference between corn oil and olive, and Celine had not seasoned as she went. "Griff's for hamburgers?" Alice finally suggested.

Today, Celine had ordered Szechuan pepper noodles for breakfast. She was sitting with a gallon Ziploc plastered to her head. She had gotten into one of Sadie's home-beauty books and read that a yogurt-and-honey mask could be used to deep-condition hair.

"Let's have a marvelous time," she suggested. It was late afternoon. Feeling festive, she propelled open the sliding glass doors. She lugged the flat-folded deck chairs, feet scuffing as they skidded over the wooden deck, into the sun. She hauled out accent lamps and nestled them into overhanging foliage, plugged into extension cords, missing shades. Next, the padded chair cushions. Now she was bare-breasted under a drowsy string of dim-wattage bulbs, wires slung low. Her breasts shone in the sun's low light.

Alice hoped the scene could not be observed through the latticed fence by the neighbor to the left, a solitary misanthrope with a menagerie of ten-foot-tall ornamental rocket ships decorating the yard, or the couple to the right, who had a trampoline and three children.

"More?"

Alice ran a finger over the deck table's weathered wood. It came away with a film of gray dust. Alice felt Celine's sinkhole gaze, stockpiling details. She wondered which of her own idiosyncrasies might end up in Celine's book. She couldn't wait to read it. "Just a drop."

Celine raised her stemmed glass. "Down the chute." Her small breasts wagged to either side as she got comfortable. She made a little joke of it, swinging them around. Alice noticed that humor, with Celine, worked differently than it did with Sadie. With Sadie, sparkles of wit had been observational, darker, more adult. With Celine, anything funny was ribald, bodily, childish.

"Be a lamb," Celine said. "Hand me that hat, would you?" She had left her hat outside for the season. They joined hands.

"This is so nice."

"Don't say anything, don't ruin it."

The fresh air carried a peat smell. They watched the disappearing sun. A small plane drifted overhead, exhausting a billowing contrail. In the paper-white sky, the contrail was fuzzy, all but disappeared. "I want to hear the story of when you landed the plane in Buchanan Field," Alice said.

"Wild but true," Celine said. She lay back in the sun, eyes closed.

"Really?"

"Do you want it to be?"

Alice sat up. "So you *didn't* land the plane? Did you fly at all?"

Celine swished her glass of wine. "What do you think?"

Alice studied Celine, whom she knew so much about now. Celine was a thrashing sleeper, spinning like a dolphin. Nightly, she rolled herself up in the duvet so that every morning Alice woke cold to find the bedsheets a gray-tuft-stuffed burrito. It amazed Alice to think you could be this intimate with a person, but still not know who they really were. "I think it's completely fabricated," she said.

Celine was inscrutable. The plane was now almost invisible overhead.

"Is it?" Alice asked.

Celine sipped her wine like a cat. "I'm not saying I *didn't* get my pilot's license at the Alameda Aero Club." Her eyes were still closed. "But I'm also not *not* saying that."

Alice rubbed her temples with both hands. The wine had a steely finish and she felt an oncoming headache. She could not see the plane anymore.

"There may be a kernel that's true," Celine said. "Maybe I landed and it resulted in this scar." She held out her inner forearm, which had a protracted scar. She spoke authoritatively: "*'Contact. Three miles, nine hundred knots. Closure.'* Convinced?"

Alice searched her eyes. "You're infuriating. You know that?" she said, the matter no more clarified than when Celine had been a stranger. The relaxed feeling had faded, replaced with an eerie sense of how little she knew Celine. Everything looked different suddenly. She saw that Celine's nasturtiums had bloomed. She watched the plane disappear into the evening sky.

After a moment, Celine said, "You're all right, know that?" Her voice was soft and lazy. "I think I'd like to go on being with you in just this way."

She leaned in close and patted Alice's hand familially. "I know it's too soon to ask this. I shouldn't. But do you love me?"

Celine's hair was sticking out in all directions. Alice reached over and rumpled it, hoping that would be enough of an answer.

But Celine's eyes opened, her gaze surprisingly serious. "Do you?"

Alice waited, as if someone else might answer. But she looked at Celine and saw the girl in her. "Yes," Alice said, hearing the truth in her answer. She saw that, as the sky had darkened, a few fireflies had materialized, light fading in the evening glow.

"How much?"

Alice struggled with this. She cupped a passing firefly and guided it to the tip of her finger. It thrummed its wings, glowed green, and disappeared.

"More than . . ." Celine tried to think what. "Your own mother?"

Alice burst out laughing. Celine's expression was serious.

"Why are you laughing?"

"Because . . . I mean, do you love *me*?" Alice had had the right amount of wine to ask. "More than *your* mother?"

"Yes."

Alice let this sink in. A cute bug waddled across the deck. "Okay, do you love me more than your daughter?"

Celine coughed on her wine. The phone rang. Who else but Sadie? Alice silenced the call.

"Forget that." Alice kept her eyes on the cute bug, still watching as it marched straight into a barred drainage grate. "I didn't say that."

Celine's eyes flared. "Not a great place to go." She wiped her mouth with the back of her hand. "Little hostility there. I can't be everything to you. We've got to limit the scope here."

Then came a text chime. Sadie. *"Where are you?"* Then another: *"Call me, I have something to tell you."*

Celine slid into her flip-flops and gathered up her hat. "You won, fair and square."

Chapter Fifteen

SADIE

Tonight, after tidying up according to the new crackdown regime Sadie had imposed, an acrylic chore chart she had unpopularly, and to negligible success, posted to the refrigerator, she and Cormac settled in in the main room. They were in the grotty dorm-like apartment he shared with his roommate, Dennis, all of which Sadie did not know how much longer she could go on tolerating.

Sadie preferred her tiny, foreclosed bungalow with a front porch in Menlo Park, situated just behind the forty-acre campus of Saint Patrick's Seminary. It was the falling-apart variant of the house of her dreams. The neighborhood was active in the day, with tire fix-it shops and greasy-food bistros Sadie frequented only because she hoped they would stay open, hoping the neighborhood wouldn't begin to change. It was quiet at night, near enough to campus but blissfully withdrawn from Fraternity Row's theme parties and stereo-blaring kickbacks.

The extra half hour away from her mother, headed south, gave Sadie a sense of peace.

But Cormac had class in the morning. She and Cormac watched the big TV only when Dennis, tightening his drawstring shorts, had not monopolized the sofa, munching on Chicken McNuggets.

Watching true crime shows—the more heinously dreadful the misconduct, the better—left Sadie and Cormac feeling safe. They had watched five series in the week since the farcical failure in Marin. Tonight, *Making a Murderer* bonded them in a common cause. They joined in outrage.

"Avery is categorically, indisputably innocent," Sadie said, through a fistful of microwave popcorn. "Period. There's no doubt in my mind." Steven Avery had been accused of murdering a magazine photographer and incinerating her remains. It was all but certain, certain surely in Sadie's mind, that he had been framed. It was a show everyone had watched years ago, contributing to Sadie's sense that she was behind on everything.

"That may be," Cormac said equitably. "Sure looks that way."

"Looks?" Sadie wiped her slippery hands on the ragged dish towel in her lap. She'd toss it into the bin later. "Consider the prosecution's evidence, what they actually have." A filmy sliver of popcorn kernel had lodged in her tender gum. She fished at the back of her mouth with her finger. "Teresa's car, keys, and bones were planted. They have nothing!"

"We're not criminal investigators," Cormac said, vexingly evenhanded as always. Was he incapable of taking a stand? He punched the remote until they were returned to the home page. "We're two kids with a Netflix password."

It was spine-chilling. If Steven Avery didn't murder Teresa Halbach, then that meant someone else, still at large, *had*. Sadie buried her head in Cormac's shoulder, then pulled back, feeling something she had not felt before. She and her boyfriend eyed each other, bathed in the soft light of the red screen. She felt anticipation heighten like a thermometer. She felt the dial crank up. Was it time?

Cormac had begun tracking his sleep metrics. He was oblivious to Sadie's portentous, private conclusion, scrolling through the gradations on his watch. Giving herself a brave little nod, Sadie touched Cormac's belt; she freed the loose end. With dawning awareness, Cormac closed his metrics and his eyes. Sadie traced her hand along the belt's length, backward and forward, up and down. He breathed heavily, like a bear waking from long slumber. It was not the first time they'd come this far. Sadie tickled the buckle with her fingernails. His bear breath deepened.

Sadie thought about what not to think. Do *not* think about the past failures to finalize. Don't think about Steven Avery. *Do not* think about sex. Systematically, she recalled her favorite spreads in *World of Interiors*. Imagined she was there. The gleaming white hamlet in Greek Patmos. The sprawling pigeonnier-turned-wine-barn bordering the Dordogne.

All the while, Cormac and Sadie advanced. She felt him beneath her, very still, just barely breathing. He assisted in unhooking her skirt. Sadie envied his craving, his desire. Sadie told herself she was not in Cormac's main room, on the grotty sofa. She was in the Greek hamlet. She shivered in her tights. The thin material would partially reveal the raised blemishes on her bottom, mottles of pink rosacea on each cheek. She had kept them, so far, from Cormac, with strategic angling. She could actually feel the region of her brain—Biology 101 came back to her: her amygdala—pulsing with self-judgment. She hated to be imperfect. But then, she was not here. She was in the Dordogne.

Cormac gaped at her, probably clocking how she was cockeyed: one breast smaller, the other lower. Don't think about that. The very fact of Sadie's anxiety was making her anxious—but she would get through this. She was resolved. She reached for him, unzipped his penis, sheathed in silky skin. Sadie babied the member, touching gently as a deer.

"It's cool," Cormac murmured. He bent down and kissed her. "Really, you can kind of knock it around. It's sturdier than it looks."

Sadie could not believe she was doing it *here.* She screwed her eyes shut tight. When Cormac began to grow, and a feeling of inevitability took hold, she suggested that he carry her into the bedroom. The thought flashed in her mind: she could always tell him to stop. If she got cramps or if nothing fit together properly. If she had to pee. If she farted, a thought too awful to bear. They bumped down the hallway. He set her down, eyes open wide, almost disbelieving. After acres of false starts, he probably couldn't.

What if his erection melted into flaccidity?

It would be mortifying. There were so many ways sex could lead to humiliation. As a rule, Sadie never subjected herself to a scenario where so much was out of her control. Sadie backed onto the saggy bed. A wooden slat was missing from the base. Her ribs rested faintly lower than her other bones. She could feel the springs beneath her. And suddenly, to her astonishment, Sadie was doing it. And she wasn't dying. Relaxing into it, she was like Wonder Woman. Her instincts kicked in, washing away all her planning. She was feeling it, the thing she was supposed to. Pleasure, washing over her.

Pleasure? In all her preparation for this moment, it was the one thing that had never crossed her mind.

They had gone the whole way, Cormac checking in with Sadie all along. She had managed to do it. And then do it again. And then . . . again. Sadie relinquished all control. And she was overflowing. To be well and truly satiated, for the first time in her life, was the most wonderful thing. It was like discovering that she could fly. Sadie soared, nourished by a secret superpower. Some essential part of herself melted away.

They stayed up most of the night doing it. In the morning, they did it again. For the first time, she recognized she had a body. Each session was better than the last. Cormac broke away, reluctantly, bolting to prepare for class. He would be late even if he left that minute, but figured he'd better at least rinse off.

While he was in the shower, Sadie fished out the soggy, drooping condom he had chucked into the trash. It sent her stomach for loops. Cormac's secret dominance: he showed up and discharged, a discharge that could set all of life into motion.

As soon as he left, Sadie picked up her phone. She reached Alice's voice mail: "It's Alice. Am either not here, busy, or avoiding you. Leave a message!"

As if Sadie would dispense such tidings by voice mail. *Call me,* she texted, *have something to tell you.*

For the next three days, Sadie, a surprisingly sensitive instrument, entered the garden of paradise to which Alice had held the keys for years. In this new arena, Cormac, ungainly though he could be, showed astonishing dexterity. He was empathic, an extraordinary communicator, transparent and honest. And he proved to be a great lover.

He varied his approach, listening to her body. They were in incredible sync. He was sensitive enough to help Sadie navigate the new territory, sensing when she might prefer to move from slow and sensual to a little more rough, when nothing would make her feel more secure than being screwed blind, in the most respectful way.

Over the next week, Sadie strained to care about anything else.

But you couldn't have sex twenty-four hours a day. So, the following Monday, she showed up to work late, her hair a mess. She was so full of infectious jouissance that she was unimpeachable. And she tore through her morning's tasks. Her designs were usually assured and rigorous, pared down to what was constitutive and essential, almost structural. But where she'd always been careful, today she was loose and inspired, resulting in the most sumptuous pattern she had ever produced.

"Wow," a senior designer said, looking covetous. "What happened to *you*?"

Now, head resting on Cormac's belly in bed, Sadie wanted to tell *someone* how she was drenched in happiness. Celine would just ruin it. Alice, for some reason, wasn't returning her calls. Suspicious. She had probably begun sleeping with one of her co-actors, some loser understudy, and didn't want Sadie to know.

Sadie picked up her phone. She was tickled enough at the thought that Cormac was going to hear her say, "Hi, Grandma, guess what? *I've fallen in love.*" A little gift to him. He would think it was cute.

Mamie, old-fashioned and unfussy, tucked into her cabin, neatly constructed out of imitation logs stripped and smoothly rounded, had mostly embodied comfort. It wasn't a perfectly cozy and secure grandmother relationship—but at least it wasn't fraught. She and Sadie had never had a fight.

Sadie held the phone to her ear. It rang and then seemed to pick up. "Mamie, are you there?"

"Mm." A voice just like Celine's, and at the same time not at all.

"I think I hear you," Sadie said, hopeful.

"Err."

"It sounds like you're listening."

"Eh."

"Hello? Hello?"

The phone clicked off. Sadie sat with the phone in her lap. "Weird."

Cormac sat up a little, extricating from Sadie. "What was that?"

Sadie told Cormac about Mamie. How in a remarkable act of foresight, the year before, true to her ways, Sadie's assiduous grandmother had anticipated her deterioration—"when I reach this stage of dementia, I want you to do X, Y, and Z"—booking herself into Seven Oaks before it was strictly necessary.

"She wants to die in a dump," Celine had said. "To punish me. She wants to eat deviled eggs and rot away, drooling into mashed peas in a dormitory that smells like piss. To *punish* me. How petty is that?"

No one involved had listened to Celine, least of all Sadie.

Seeing what was coming, like Ulysses, Mamie arranged to have herself shackled to the mast. It amazed Sadie that someone so closely related to Celine was capable of behaving with such prudence and reason.

"I'm afraid her dementia has really set in," Sadie told Cormac.

She relayed to Cormac how she had visited once a year, in lieu of Celine. "I was sent there because my mother wouldn't go," she told him. "It was one of my childhood chores. Not that I didn't like it, kind of."

First to Mamie's home. The rooms were cheerful places of industry, unlike Celine's fraught dungeon office, infused with umbrage, where she struggled to create. Sadie and her grandmother would take the short walk to the streambed where the swift-flowing Aurora Branch dipped down away from the Chicago River. Sadie loved to run her fingers between the grooves of ripple-marked sandstone.

Then to that assisted-living center that smelled like Kleenex, glued to *Jeopardy!* on ABC, switching to CBS for the Saturday reruns. Mamie persevered, one eye squinting at the screen while she darned and mended, snug as a granny in a fairy tale.

Mamie's instincts were admirable, even if the methods were sometimes self-defeating. Once, while visiting, Sadie had run an errand for Mamie, dropping off a pair of boots at her grandmother's local shoe repair shop. "Your grandmother," the cobbler had said, "once brought me a rubber dog toy to repair. Repair cost thirty dollars, the toy still had the sticker: ten bucks from Petco."

Later, things had changed. As a teenager, down at the streamside, Sadie listened patiently as Mamie babbled a butchered Scripture: "If you have faith like a mustard seed, He will make your path straight."

She lamented her daughter: "Celine was always a selfish child," Mamie would say, the fairy-tale granny slipping away a bit more with each unkind word. "I always knew that she would never take proper care of anyone but herself."

Mamie seemed to think that Celine lived a considerably different life than the one Sadie knew. "I always felt she was surprised I had clothes," Sadie told Cormac. "She had gotten it into her head that I was an abuse case, barely fed."

It was as though Mamie couldn't see Celine. It dawned on Sadie: what if Celine's world-class narcissism was a natural result of growing up in a household where she went unseen? Her mother always patching up something tangible, in the household or at the church. As a girl, Celine must have wondered, what about me?

"Celine and I weren't *so* dysfunctional," Sadie said, while Cormac stroked her hair. "I always had what I needed. Now and then, we even had a good time."

As a girl, Sadie had relished the private assemblies with her grandmother, the corroboration of everything she had observed. But at a certain point, an unfamiliar feeling had crept up on Sadie. "It literally has never happened before or since," she told Cormac. "But I actually began feeling defensive of my mother." Still predominantly wishing Celine would disappear off the face of the planet—but also sensitive to unfair slights against her.

As a little girl, Sadie had bought the granny performance. She hadn't questioned anything. But later, perhaps around the time Mamie casually remarked that Celine was probably a lesbian because she had failed at sex with her husband, Sadie realized that *her* fairy-tale granny was *Celine's* dangerous, embittered mother.

Sadie had even stopped visiting for a while, out of unspoken protest. She could not let either Celine or Mamie know how much she cared—she'd risk losing her dignity. Lying in bed, she stopped short of revealing this facet of the story to Cormac, her blissful new love. She would save that, maybe tell him in a year or two if they were still together.

Soon enough, though, after Sadie's stark realization, Mamie deteriorated and when Sadie next went to visit, it was at Seven Oaks. And, in light of her infirmity, spurning her grandmother for her past errors of judgment didn't seem so pressing anymore. Together, they ate sour-tasting spinach in the dining room, and mashed potatoes and hamburgers. "What is this?" Mamie had asked Sadie, becoming agitated.

Sadie wasn't sure what Mamie was asking. "It's hamburger." Even if it was more like cardboard.

"No, what *is* this?"

Sadie realized what she meant to ask was, what was everything? What was anything? She was at a loss, seeing her grandmother so exceedingly battered by her disease. "It's us having dinner."

They returned to Mamie's room to play Rummikub, more difficult as her mind had begun slipping away, gentle as water down a drain. She began confusing 6s and 9s, placing the tiles upside down. "It's a subtle distinction," Sadie had said, correcting the tile on the board, "but it's different."

It was gloomy to see Mamie sapped of all her characteristic vitriol and vital energies. Was it enough of a life, placing game tiles end to end?

"Some days, she would seem to be doing well," Sadie told Cormac now, "and I would leave hopeful. Then, when I returned the next morning, I would hear her distraught voice, accusing the nursing staff of incompetence, because they couldn't move the ball of sun from one window to the next. But it's never been this bad."

Cormac offered to visit with Sadie, saying that Sadie's presence would be a balm for even the loneliest of cases. To be loved this way, Sadie felt, could make anything tolerable. Anything in the world.

AUGUST

Chapter Sixteen

CELINE

On campus after her lecturing, heading down the pathway between Alumni House and Zellerbach Hall, Celine admired her campus. She thought she might grab a quick bite at the Golden Bear before heading home. It was a windy day and the Memorial Pool looked beautiful, even the ripples rippling.

Celine dodged a faction of dissatisfied young citizens, staging a sit-in, hoisting signs. The usual local uproar over whatever was most current. BE A BODY! At one time, Celine had felt the weight of the organizing world on her shoulders. Now, permeating the hedgerow of protestors, she had accepted who she was. A certified stakeholder in the system.

And the term seemed to be going well. She found that, in recent years, she was unable to tell one term from the next, which meant no fiascos. If something had gone tenure-imperilingly wrong, you remembered every face and name, the group of students adding up to a sentence that spelled disaster in front of the committee and provost.

You'd think, teaching a class subtitled Patriarchy and Power, Celine might have been *spoken to* by her department head, for not notifying students that her course content might be disturbing to some students, but it hadn't happened.

Contrary to intuition, Celine had found herself becoming tamer, more gentle, as she became less liable to firing. The three-year review, the six-year review. A date had been set for the upcoming assessment. Celine had embedded herself in the department. She was confident that the review of her performance resulting in the prize of security was a certainty all but enacted.

This thought comforted her like a snug fire, when her phone suddenly buzzed.

Sadie writing, at exactly noon, to say: *Coming over to grab something.*

Celine stopped short, in the middle of the walkway.

"On your left," barked a passing bicyclist, pedaling with ferocity.

Celine blinked at the flip phone, then whipped it open. *Don't come now*, she texted, never more expedient. *I'm busy*. She tried to dredge up something she could be doing. *Prepping book.*

A batch of girls passed Celine, clad in plush bear ears and sets of face-paint whiskers. They looked too healthy, with cultishly bright eyes. Must be a game day. Once, a student had confided in Celine, "On game days I have to tiptoe around whispering *bear territory, bear territory*. They won't win without it."

Need something, Sadie texted, six minutes later. Time she had probably made maximal use of to proceed from her apartment. One thing Sadie did not do was procrastinate. *Will be quick. Won't distract you.*

Bear territory. Bear territory.

No time for the bus. Celine texted Alice a warning, full of typos, nonetheless conveying the message. The message was *Mayday*. Speed-walking, heart thudding but freshly energized, as ever, by trouble, Celine flagged a passing green cab.

Celine let herself into the cottage, only to collide with Alice, arms encumbered with a bundle of clothes. She was scrabbling around the room, blind with unthinking. She balanced a pair of canvas tote bags. She grabbed a fistful of patterned nylon tights. "We're toast. I'm going to cry, actually *cry*."

"Don't do *that*," Celine said, and kissed Alice's forehead. "Deep breaths."

Alice sipped steadying air. She had been there for what, three weeks, but Celine was surprised to see the extent to which her personal belongings had accumulated in that short time. Alice jumped when Celine slung a loose foot of tights over her opposite shoulder.

"Good enough," Celine said.

The clump of tights hung like a pageant sash. Alice wadded and holstered them into the crammed-full tote, slung over her shoulder. A person couldn't go anywhere without being gifted a tote bag, Celine thought. ALA, MLA, 2008, 2006. Before she'd started declining them. Some had zippers, some inside pockets. One contained a vestigial USB drive. God only knew its contents. Alice yanked in the dangling nylon foot, then wailed, switching to a major key, "What are we *doing*? Together, all this, what is this?"

Celine tried to stay focused. "Let's hide these remaining things."

Alice lashed out at Celine, her huge eyes round. "Do *you* know where she'll look? Are you a mind reader?"

While this was not as tactfully stated as it might have been, Celine understood. Pearl dozed in the window, looking like the eye of a hurricane.

Not being shouted at for a minute gave Celine a chance to think. "Here's a thought," she said. "Before you say no. Should we just tell her? Just have her find you here? Everything aboveboard. Couldn't that be fruitful?" Celine saw this as a teachable moment. She held out her hands, like a peace-bearing Buddha, around whom the storm raged but did not touch. "This is love. Why treat it like a virus?"

"Love?" Alice turned her back, trying to stuff her plain navy parka into a packable nylon pouch. "God*damn*it," she said, with her back still turned. She careened toward Celine. "Help me shove this in here."

"At least consolidate. And I think you could leave that puffer here. Something like that, she won't even—"

"You're not helping," Alice said. "At all." On the ground now, Pearl, sphinxlike, shifted her haunches so she was symmetrical. The parka defied its travel pouch. "This is supposed to fit! Uniqlo has all these ads: *pocketable parka*. My ass."

"Why don't we make something up?" Celine said. "So you can stay? We tell her you just stopped by. To give me something. A gift. A gift for Sadie!" She looked around. "Is there anything here we can give her?"

Alice closed her eyes. "Sometimes I can't with you."

No room in the travel pouch. Alice would have to wear the parka. Celine helped her into it, becoming practical. "Go down to Rockridge," she counseled. "Take a left and wait at the bus stop. I'll hurry her out, promise. You won't have to wait long."

Alice faltered, lacing her boots. "She'll see me."

Celine tutted. "She never takes Claremont. She'll take the highway."

"There's construction blocking the overpass!"

Alice was beside herself, but she was right. Celine had forgotten that Claremont was impassable, temporarily. Panicked, Alice tripped over a tumbled sweater. Celine stooped to retrieve it. It *would* be risky to leave that one behind. With unique appliques, crystal stars embellishing the neckline, Sadie would identify it immediately.

Celine tucked the incriminating sweater into Alice's bulging load and glanced at her watch. Alice was not wrong. She had better scram. "This is almost too ghastly," Celine said, "but you'll have to hide out at the playground."

Celine had photos somewhere: it was the park where Sadie had her legendary eighth birthday party, with aluminum pans of dill-flecked potato salad, with piglets and a clown—and her fifth and her sixth, though those had gone admittedly less well.

"It's pleasant, actually!" Celine was cheerful, maneuvering Alice toward the door. "Swings and stuff. But, then again, maybe you won't fit on those. Listen. Stay low, in case, because she could take Ashby. There are hedges—you might just stick close to those."

Alice slid her reluctant feet into a pair of sandals. "This is so tawdry."

"Come on, it's just life."

"Not mine."

"You'll find the park on the map on your phone," Celine said. "Green area. Follow the green. Bring a book."

Alice looked forlorn. "What book?"

"Never mind! Let's not worry about that, if you haven't got one in mind." Sadie had been on the San Mateo Bridge, "No Fishing," when she last texted. Her car still just a speck. She would be paying the toll on the turnpike by now. Then, any minute, she would be there. "Catch." Celine tossed Alice her phone.

With a rubber band, Alice cinched closed a tote with a torn strap. Celine led Alice to the porch and gave her butt, which Celine noticed for the first time was looking perky-cute in a pair of vintage Levi's, a friendly thwack. "Let's get cracking."

"I'm walking, then?" Alice asked in disbelief.

"Afraid I didn't book you a limousine."

"Don't kiss me." And Alice sailed off, out the back door, tipping sideways with her sad packages like a paper boat. Celine watched her go, then stepped off the porch to wait for Sadie.

* * *

It was serene to be in the garden, Celine's own, where nothing bore allegiance to either girl. She had started the project with a narrow bed of young plants, not seeds. She had whacked at existing roots, untangled bound radicles, erected bird barricades, dug in peat moss with a forged-steel flex-rake, mowed down ragweed and burdock. The plants had suffered Celine's interventions that first season. The weaklings died.

However, a few clumps of the hardiest plants did not acquiesce. These Celine tended with a renewed devotion. She accepted that she had an unconventional gardening style. She lacked the patience of Lady Londonderry. She ignored the advice of the sunflower-bedecked nursery owner in the Oakland Hills. She did things her way.

And now she toured her bravely glistening grape tomatoes, her valiantly resplendent dahlias. They had survived, despite her. In the scrubby weeds—that endless, thankless task—a dandelion had stretched to thrice the length of the others and was growing sideways along the ground, head pushing toward the sun. Her nasturtiums, grandmotherly, were finished for the season, parched on the stem. Celine shuddered. *Grandmother*: a designation that, knowing Sadie's penchant for maturity, Celine would probably be fastened soon. A galling thought.

Pearl observed coolly from the hyacinth bed, ticking her tail.

"What?" Celine asked. But even she knew it had been a sorrowful sight: encumbered Alice wobbling off with her bags, proof of their treachery. Celine congratulated herself on having handled the stressful occasion well.

When Celine kicked a fallen branch to the northernmost edge of the sloping lawn, nudging it over the fine blades of grass with her foot, Pearl leaped out of sight. Celine scooped a handful of soil. It soothed her. She slid the soil into her pocket. For later.

She had just hung up her trowel, her spade, which last time she had left out to rust, when, from behind the gardening shed, Sadie's sedan appeared—and then she did, pulling up to the curb in blazing white silk, untouched by the summer's last heat. Celine's daughter: hers. In all her goodness, meanness, and glory. Celine cried out a greeting.

"Grass looks good," Sadie said squarely. She unfolded herself from the car and pressed her cheek to her mother's. "You've been working. Don't touch me with those hands."

Something was wrong with Sadie. She was eerily perky. "What's the matter with you?" Celine hardly dared to ask. Her skin burned where Sadie pressed her other cheek. "Are you on drugs? If you are, share."

But Sadie just danced in the direction of the house and wiped her shoes on the front mat. Celine had a fresh memory of how, even as a mop-headed child, Sadie, never deviating, had always wiped her little buckle Mary Jane shoes before entering the house. "Can't stay long."

"I'm sorry to hear that," Celine said, escorting Sadie through the door. Sadie sidestepped fluffy tufts of sheep's wool that Pearl had clawed off Alice's slippers. Bad Pearl. "Wish you could stay a while." Clean and crisp, in her whites, Sadie felt to Celine like the calm after the hurricane.

"I thought you were engrossed in prepping your book." Sadie brushed past, disregarding her mother, headed down the hall before Celine could stop her. "There's a funny smell in here." She wrinkled her nose but swept past the radioactive bedroom without a glance. "Something feels different."

Celine lurched after her daughter into the kitchen. She took a quick survey of the yard, half-expecting to catch sight of a nosy Alice peering out from behind the hedges.

Crookedly, Pearl circled Sadie's legs as she expertly sliced a peach. "What's new with you?"

"Nothing!"

Sadie popped a slice into her mouth. "Ever going to hand in that book? Or going to beat it to death into eternity?"

Celine sighed. Those ostensibly disheartening paradigms of lifelong genius unsung, those authors upheld as the most pathetically ironic, appreciated only posthumously—Dickinson, Van Gogh, Poe—were Celine's beacons of hope. One's undifferentiated scribblings could, with the aid of an industrious descendant, be resurrected. One's yearnings, fantasies of success, belatedly fulfilled. Unlikely Sadie would ever bother. Fat chance.

Sadie blinked. Mascara. Celine had always liked watching Sadie make herself up. It was as foreign to Celine as eating a tapeworm for weight loss, or binding her feet. "How long overdue is it now?"

"What can I say?" Celine said, looking away from her daughter. Shuffling letters and keys, making tiny adjustments between the stacks and piles. She folded her lobster apron, tucking in the antennaes. "It takes time to make a good thing."

Sadie slid open a drawer and began sifting among the scrambled assortments, irrelevant small parts, uncritical bits and bobs. Celine inched closer, angling to peer inside the drawer, to see like Sadie saw. If Sadie wanted to ferret something out, she would. Eyes in the back of her head. Celine could make out box cutters, defunct remotes and tangled cords, batteries depleted of life. Any one of these could be the thing to expose her. Probably several.

"It's like you've never heard of a drawer divider."

"Careful with your fingers," Celine said. "Beware the stray X-ACTO or rusty Cuisinart blade." And *what if* Sadie bayonetted herself, and Celine had to ferry her to the hospital, and Alice was stranded in the playground. Just imagine. Who knew if, in the mayhem, she had thought to carry her key? If we have to go to the ER, Celine thought, I'll leave the door unlocked.

Feigning boredom, Celine leaned against the doorframe. She picked at a loose thread on her sweater. "Is the spare key still under the sparrow out front?" she asked Sadie, straining to sound casual. "Do you know?" She hoped Alice knew it existed.

But Sadie was foraging in the drawer, the forensic senses in her long fingers surely detecting traces of wrongdoing. "Mexican *pesos*? You haven't been to Mexico since the nineties." And how many times had Sadie told Celine that the long-handled scissors were for opening packages; the orange-handled were all-purpose, meaning never for herbs, hair, or fabric; the serrated were for the kitchen; and the squat shears with a safety clip were for clipping flowers? The shears with a bent angle of 150 degrees, Sadie said, were for emergencies: cutting through denim or a seat belt.

Sadie reached into the drawer and pulled out a stalled kitchen timer. "Don't try to tell me this works."

"I don't see why it wouldn't."

"You are not allowed to keep this." Sadie strolled to the garbage, and tossed the timer into the bin with a jingle. "You have a timer on your phone."

"Hanged if I know how to use it."

Something Celine had meant to do for weeks suddenly, in a flash, took on a fresh urgency. Trying to go unnoticed, she used her fingernail to scrape at the obdurate candle wax that had dripped and hardened on the linoleum counter. She never lit candles, having bad associations ever since Mamie had lit one, neglected it, and almost obliterated herself. Alice. It was Alice who lit candles.

Sadie turned to lean against the kitchen counter. "Ice removes wax."

So, then, Sadie hadn't noticed anything odd about the candles. She hadn't made the connection. Despite her relief, Celine was a little affronted. Did Sadie not know her at all? Sadie was inattentive today. Why?

Sadie stood before the open freezer door, the crisp light illuminating her hair, silky as butterscotch pudding. Her stern voice was diluted, unexpectedly, with humor. "You *freeze* your *mayonnaise*?"

Celine accepted the extended tray of ice. "Would that be so wrong?"

"That is psychotic. But not out of character," Sadie said fondly. "You've always had the most awkward refrigeration habits." She expertly, even jauntily, popped the frozen cubes from their silicon tray compartments.

"I have, haven't I?"

Sadie even laughed a little as she doled Celine an ice cube. On the rug, Pearl had quieted, curling around herself like a cozy doughnut.

"And you've always noticed minor oddities of character." Celine's fingertips froze as she pinched a cube, dabbing at each blot of wax.

"Especially defects," Sadie said, with a barely perceptible smile. "They're my favorite thing to notice."

At first, Celine thought she had misheard. But no, Sadie was poking fun at herself. Emboldened, Celine bumped her daughter with her hip.

"Yours in particular," Sadie said, bumping back a little, as she pretended to need to slip past Celine. "You were never sure if eggs should be refrigerated or kept at room temperature, so you were always shuttling them back and forth."

Celine could not believe it. She wedged a knife under Alice's coin of wax, and it lifted right off, as if it had never been there to start. "Look at that!" She laughed at the ease of it all.

". . . Incredible that we never got salmonella," Sadie was saying, then interrupted herself, brandishing the antique cast-iron corkscrew she'd been pursuing. "*Got it!* Still here after all these years."

Celine vaguely recognized the rusted handle, engraved like a fishtail. Celine never knew where her daughter picked up these trinkets. If it wasn't a corkscrew, it was a geometric Bauhaus nutcracker, a hammered-copper watering can, or a Viennese toast rack. Only Sadie.

Only Sadie. Only. Wasn't this all Celine wanted, right here in this room? Suddenly, she was flying high as Icarus.

And she realized that at that moment, the greatest thing that could happen would be if poor Alice—staggered off with her every earthly possession, a boat without a rudder—never rematerialized. Abruptly, Celine had not the least desire to do what she had promised. She did not want to hurry Sadie away. She wanted to divert and stall her, no matter the cost.

"Do you still have that extension ladder?" Sadie said, voice swelling unaccountably. Then her face lit up like a Christmas tree: "Don't make an occasion out of it, but Cormac and I decided to move in together."

Suddenly the corkscrew, Sadie's loot, seemed unimaginably precious. It pained Celine to imagine it gone. "That is *mine*, you know." She came beside Sadie to contemplate the handle. The trout's scales were meticulously hand-wrought.

"Mom?" Sadie tried to catch Celine's eyes. "Did you hear what I just told you? Any reaction?"

Celine pulled back to look at her daughter. Who was moving on. Leaving her for a new life, with a new person. "Isn't that a little premature?"

"We've been dating for a year." Sadie seemed to decide something. When she spoke again, her voice was softer and her words felt like a warm bath. "I think I'm going to be a much happier person. It just so happens that I've discovered love. And all its remedial properties. You and I, I know we have this habit of going straight into defense mode.

But what if we tried to resist that temptation? Do we really want to do battle the rest of our lives? What if we lay down our swords?"

Sadie was inviting Celine into her new life, to tag along beside her. Sadie struck Celine as being like one of those Renaissance mothers, cold and collected, with stern appearance, but who proved to be mild, capable of infinite mercy.

"I want you to be happy for me," Sadie said when Celine didn't say anything. "It would mean a lot to me."

Visions of a harmonious new era of love and peace danced in Celine's head. They would confide in each other, express their feelings. Order Chinese takeout, paint each other's toenails, and talk all night, feet in laps. Have picnics and watch rom-coms beneath a shared duvet and make fun of the cheesy final wedding scenes.

"I'm really happy for you, Sadie." Celine felt the truth of the words in her bones. Sadie smiled back. Together, they beamed. It struck Celine: she was loved, filially, despite all her warts, all her failings. And that it was time to come clean and start anew. The moment opened like an oasis, in which forgiveness might live and breathe.

"And I want you to be happy for me, too," Celine said. Like an ocean trawler heaving up a net filled with pearls and debris, Celine dredged up the words. *Have to tell you, that night, the play, came back up, been here since.*

Sadie's eyes flickered slightly, as if calculating an equation she was trying to solve on a chalkboard that lay just over Celine's shoulder. After a few frightened tacks, they came to rest. Very carefully, as if it required utmost thought, Sadie adjusted the shoulder strap of her bag, which had slipped down her arm. "You're having an affair with Alice."

Celine nodded. Only a small twitch in the crook of Sadie's smile as she glanced inquiringly around the room, which must have held a new significance. Then she asked, as if inquiring after something of no more consequence than a lost button, or a mislaid corkscrew, "Where is she now?"

"Errand, she had to run," Celine fibbed. Then, thinking of this clean start she was making, she contradicted herself: "No, that's a fib. We hid her. Sorry."

"Wow. Wow, Mom." And Sadie started to laugh.

Celine smiled, feeling desperate to catch up. "Yeah, it's kind of funny, isn't it?"

Sadie bent over, laughing, her hands on her knees, wiping her eyes.

Celine tried to join in.

"Now *you're* laughing?" This made Sadie laugh more. Celine did not know what she was witnessing, if not a complete and total breakdown.

Chapter Seventeen

SADIE

"You are not going to believe this," Sadie said, bursting into Cormac's apartment, divesting herself of her bags. She had rushed home. She wished she had come from her favorite overlook at the Shorebird nature preserve, not stopped in casually at her diabolical mother's house. Wished she had never recalled the corkscrew. Stopped instead at her seat on the pebble beach, where she watched the sandpipers teetering in their long black stockings, skipping over the wet sand. Instead, this.

Even after Sadie told Cormac in the plainest possible words, he could not absorb the information. She thought even this was cute, his not understanding. Everything he did was the best thing she had ever seen. His eyes became suspicious, like someone fed something they did not want. "Alice who?"

Sadie smiled archly. Life, for her, had always been a question of how she could hold on. To her identity. To sanity. To the threads of actuality. Now here was this. She felt a quick chill in her arteries. Celine's words came at her with a meaty fullness. What Celine said, all Sadie's life, had always felt hardly real. And yet no matter how outlandish, Celine's truth always permanently replaced whatever prior reality Sadie had lived and breathed in.

"*Alice* Alice? *Your* Alice?" Cormac was still waiting for Sadie's confirmation. "Holy shit."

They sat with this.

"Want to know the batshittest part?"

Cormac swooned, falling back against the sofa. "That's *not* the batshittest part?"

Sadie's eyes fluttered. "They think they're in love." The world around her seemed to tip forward, like a tablecloth off of which everything could slide and crash together in a symphony of destruction down to the floor.

"Fuck *them*!" Cormac sank against the couch, then leaned forward. "Jesus! What did you say when she told you?"

Sadie was almost embarrassed of her reaction. It had been so flagrantly inappropriate. "I started laughing and couldn't stop. Sure, she's the scourge of the earth. But do you know how much of my psychic energy I've given to my mother? This is my escape hatch."

It felt strange to Sadie to be so impermeable, protected by the cushion of first love. Everything slid off of her. The betrayal felt abstract: Celine and Alice had overridden their two loyalties to Sadie and come together, without her, despite all they knew. But then, unsolicited, for the first time, a hellacious thought occurred to her. One that was decidedly *not* abstract. "How bizarre to imagine them having actual *sex*..." Sadie shuddered. She felt the residue of her old self, who would allow this to corrode her like hydrofluoric acid. "Rubbing vaginas."

"Sweetie," Cormac said, knowing Sadie so well. "Are you sure you want to go there?"

Sadie's mind seethed with a lewd *Fantasia*-like vision of long-legged dancing blades, bows garishly colored, sharpened and sliding raspily against each other. The gears of her mind began to grind. "No," she said.

It helped to have Cormac there. Her best friend. Sadie backed away from the thought. She let it fade far, far away, becoming a vision that did not concern her. "Right now, honestly? I couldn't care less. I'll think about it later. They missed the deadline by a week. If this had happened a month ago," she said, "I would have been so fucking pissed off. I would have shattered their lives in retaliation."

"And now?"

Intellectually, Sadie recognized that Celine and Alice had committed an unpardonable act of barbaric treason. Of course, her mother was morally deficient. But in her heart, it was difficult for her to give the blow its due weight. Who *was* this new version of herself? Unconquerable. The kind of girl who could lose her mother and her best friend in one blow and laugh in the face of it, and say only, "Go to hell, motherfuckers."

She felt a little bit sorry for the entire human race. What else could they do but pitch themselves headlong into sordid interhuman dilemmas? Celine's flailing attempt, stooping to such a bitter low, struck Sadie as naïve, childish—and in this regard almost quaint. Even imagining them in bed only made her feel sorry for them. Not that it would last. Celine's infatuations were tacky and defective, like cheap craft store glue. Sticky until the adhesive wore off suddenly and absolutely.

Meanwhile, Sadie had everything she needed. She rolled back and let Cormac wash over her. If they were expecting a whopping response out of her, too bad, she was otherwise absorbed, sheltered far away from them where they could not reach her, lost inside a kaleidoscope of delight.

Chapter Eighteen

ALICE

Alice had been relieved to find the playground deserted, abandoned on a weekday. One little boy plucking his wedgie, then even he was gone. Lying prone in the sandbox where she would not be seen, her parka repurposed as a pillow, Alice racked her mind for anything she had left behind. She could not think of any. The frenzy of earlier had passed and she felt at peace. The sand beneath her body was comfortingly cool to the touch.

How little Alice could have imagined this, back when a stranger had his tongue in her mouth a few months before in Los Angeles, during Alice's throes of fevered Tindering.

"You're someone who has standards," Sadie had said, frowning at Alice's matches. "Don't forget that."

But, playing angel at the gate, Alice began saying yes with more frequent regularity, testing out her theory that almost anyone, randomly selected, could make tolerable enough company for a single night's date. She was not even wrong.

"Me, too," she said, failing to disclose that she had been on six dates in a short week and a half. Alice liked meeting people. On these dates, she tried to intuit whom he had hoped she would be and fulfill his expectations. It felt good to give people what they wanted. But there were so many things that could be infelicitous. She could either come across too outspoken or too reticent. Too ambitious or not enough. Anytime you opened your mouth, you were torching someone else's dream.

At the playground, Alice had picked up a pine cone and absentmindedly begun plucking off its scales one by one, when she was overwhelmed with a cast shadow, unsure what had overcome her with such sudden violence. It was an unleashed dog, of a mottled and indeterminate type, barreling over her. There was some grappling, and all was put to rights. Alice sifted sand through her fingers, jumping again only when another tall, unintelligible shadow passed over her.

It was only Celine, no one more hazardous, not Sadie, not the dog or wedgie boy, not a vagrant with criminal intent. "You scared me."

But Alice noticed that there was a cloud around Celine, her hands deep in her pockets. The cloud darkened when Celine said, "I told her." She was short-breathed, eyes trained in the flattened patch in the grass where Alice had lain earlier.

Alice scrambled to a stand, like the countless children who had done just the same when an imposing figure appeared above them.

"Don't look so tragic," Celine said. "No one died."

For a moment, Alice felt something like liberation. Sadie knew. Sadie would fix it. Sadie could fix anything. But then, like surfacing after a dive underwater, the sounds of earth flooded Alice's ears. She turned her head to look at Celine.

"She started talking about Cormac and how happy she is, and I wanted to share my happiness with her." Celine stared back, with gray eyes, blind to so much. "I did it. The words just came out."

It was evening and the sidewalk had seemed to sink, warm from the day. The light had turned a sun-washed lilac. Alice dropped into the sand beneath her feet. She was beneath ground. She was subterranean. *"And?"*

"Let's go home."

At home, Alice made Celine sit in the big chair and tell it all again.

"What do you mean she *laughed*? That can't be true." Alice had begun unloading the bags at random, flinging bras and cosmetics. "She laughed, okay. And then what? She had to have said something."

"She said, 'I have to go.' " Celine frowned. "Or maybe it was 'I've got to get going.' "

"Because she couldn't deal with it?"

"Impossible to know." Celine seemed stumped. "Maybe it was an act. I don't know what to make of it myself. I am cautiously optimistic."

Alice threw a fistful of underwear into the top dresser drawer. For an intellectual heavyweight, Celine was pathetically clueless. "And her body language?"

"Self-composed." Celine reached down to her toes, stretching her back. "Controlled. Usual Sadie."

Nothing about this was usual. When Alice yanked the top dresser drawer, it slipped its tracks. She jammed it back in. She realized they were operating individually now. Celine was withholding; she didn't want Alice in on this. Suddenly, Alice felt desperate. "You had no right to tell her without me. You probably threw me under the bus. Blamed it on me."

"What?"

"You probably both did." The truth of this hit Alice. She contemplated her beribboned intimates, tipped out of the bags and over the floor. She did not recognize herself in the mirror across from the bed, the chain of innumerable selves, like a strand of cut-out dolls, a crowd of people she had never known. What did they want? Maybe they each wanted different things. "Do you *care* that I'm here? Do you *notice* that I'm here?"

"You're getting hysterical." Outside, an ambulance siren blared. "I don't know what you're talking about anymore. I think we've lost the thread."

A tear pitched from Alice's cheek to the floor, and she stared at the spot where it had fallen with an absent look. "No." She sniffed, feeling chastened by her outburst. "I want you to tell me every last thing Sadie said."

These words quieted the ambulance siren. It seemed to turn a corner, recede into a middle distance. Alice sat, surrounded by her sorry garments. Celine made a clearing in the debris and scooted closer. "What if I make us some nettle tea and we sit down, and I'll try to remember?"

"I would have been able to," Alice leveled. She reached up. She had grass in her hair and sand in her shoes. She rubbed a blade of grass between her fingers. "Because I would have known that you would want to know."

"I think I can do it," Celine said resolutely.

Alice sat very still, and the tension diffused, deflated like a hot gas balloon. "Every word?"

"I think I've told you everything, but I'll try." Celine stroked Alice's hand. "I hope you won't be disappointed."

Alice regained some composure upon hearing an exact, meticulous account of Sadie's few words during the minutes in question. Celine was right. These words were not damning. The nettle tea tasted like honey and hay. In the wake of this, she and Celine lit candles and watched a funny movie. They even laughed.

At one point, Celine nudged Alice. "Hey, don't get your hopes up," she said. "I'm not sure we're out of the water yet."

But Alice's hopes were ballooning. Though she certainly did not hear from Sadie—and this set her wheels spinning: maybe this was even a good sign; meaning Sadie was processing the news calmly and would reach out when she was ready—the next day was surprisingly serene, the sun slanting peacefully in lace-carved sheets across the living room.

And Alice got an idea. She'd go see Sadie. They'd talk it out. Like adults. Like best friends.

Alice approached the porch steps of Sadie's tiny, charming bungalow to the heavy tolling of seminary bells. She felt a pang, having no idea what was inside the house, its contents unknown to her. This was how quickly things had gone wrong in their relationship. Normally, she'd have helped her move in.

For a moment, Alice let herself imagine that maybe she'd even be invited in. She was halfway up the steps when the front door opened and Sadie came out onto the porch. She was on her way somewhere, evidently, winging into her trench coat, car keys in hand. She stopped, seeing Alice, looking down. "If it isn't the ghost of friendships past."

When Alice began to advance toward her, Sadie stopped her. "Be right back. I have something for you." She disappeared into the agreeable-looking rental. To retrieve what? A buzz saw? A hand grenade? Alice braced for the crash of recriminations. For the bill of indictments that she deserved. For a chance to make her defense, even having no idea what that might be.

When Sadie returned, it was with a folded sweatshirt. "You left this here. Not *here*, in the dorms. I borrowed it the night we went to Tilden Park. Remember?"

Alice remembered. They had ridden the steam train, sipping from a spiked thermos, just the two of them on the covered caboose, feeling like kids. They rode the merry-go-round and took each other's photos. Sadie had sent hers to Cormac, smiling privately into her phone.

Sadie laughed. "I eviscerated that ride operator who asked you on a date? I thought he was going to melt into a puddle. You were going to say yes! That's very you. You always say yes."

"Not always," Alice said, smiling tentatively.

Sadie turned the sweatshirt over in her hands and cut to the chase. "Listen, I'm not going to turn this into a melodrama. Obviously, it's categorically creepy that I met you at Judy's, you sat there giving me sex advice, watched me eat pie, then scooted home to service my mother. That's objectively hair-raising."

So they were diving right in. "I'm sorry," Alice said. "I should have told you. I was scared." It occurred to Alice to crack a joke: "Didn't you always say you wanted me in your family?"

Sadie shrugged, looking down from on high with level eyes. "In the end, I should probably thank you. Because now you're going to deal with her. She's your responsibility—good luck." Sadie turned toward the house. She tossed the sweatshirt over the banister.

Sadie lobbed a last few terrible words, which Alice, like someone hit over the head, barely heard. Alice bent to collect the sweatshirt, the spurned goods. And when she stood up, the door closed. Sadie must have decided to can her errand, whatever it was.

* * *

Alice pulled into the drive. Celine was waiting at home, cloaked and furtive, coiled like a snake, like a granddaddy longlegs anticipating the seizure of its prey.

"Hit traffic?" Celine smiled crookedly. "You took a while."

"I stopped at Dumbarton Bridge," Alice said.

"But you decided not to jump?"

Alice gave her a look.

"How'd it go with my daughter?" Celine opened the screen door and swept Alice inside. "What did you two decide?"

Alice dropped her keys into the small bowl and plopped onto the divan. She was exhausted. "You were right," she said.

What Sadie had finally said, just as Alice was leaving, was that she wasn't in the least surprised. That Alice and Celine deserved each other. Alice almost related this now, to Celine, but she stopped short. It simply wouldn't be kind. Sadie had always been unfair to her mother; she didn't understand that Celine was actually, on the whole, a sensitive and loving person. And now she was lumping Alice in with her rote vilification? Honestly, screw her. "She basically seemed to take it in a weird kind of hostile stride."

"Can I interrupt?" Celine asked. "Why do people use the word *basically*? It's a filler word. Anyway, go on."

Alice sighed. "She wasn't hysterical." It was Alice's turn to stop short of relaying the complete transcript. Alice had just been told that she and Celine were the kind of scum who deserve each other. Alice wondered why this had made her so angry. She would not allow herself to imagine that it might have gotten under her skin because it was the truth.

Celine shook her head in disbelief. "So, we got away with it?"

"No, we didn't get away with it. It's more like she's written us off."

Alice had always been Sadie's antidote to Celine, the remedy to her mother's poisons. Instead, now, Sadie had called Alice and Celine a perfect fit. *She's your responsibility—good luck.*

If Sadie had been raging, it would have been understandable—Alice was expecting it—it was the coldness that was so hard to take. Alice had behaved badly and hadn't been rewarded with rugged behavior in return. Sadie was so far above her.

"I think she'll just get used to it," Celine said, smiling broadly, a smile of someone in complete, reckless denial, "and then everything will be just fine."

Chapter Nineteen

CELINE

It seemed they had gotten away with it. It should have been Dodged-a-Bullet Day. But over the next day it had begun to bother Celine.

It preyed on her: Sadie didn't care. Celine felt like a clown—worse—a clown with no audience. At age forty-seven, she felt about four centuries more ancient than that. She felt bereft, stripped of her powers. Unable even to scandalize her daughter.

From her desk on a Thursday evening, she watched the sky darken outside. Lately, she had been sneaking away to her office to plow through crinkled papers. Writing was like a puzzle she had to solve. She knew if she kept figuring, she'd eventually disentangle the equation.

Celine had never managed to re-create the conditions for her career's magnum opus, *The Body Borne*. The book, hardcover, was on her desk, facedown. On the back cover, a self-important version of herself, a young phenom, recently promoted to associate professor on account of her bestselling almanac, here in its fourth reprint. A barrette secured her permtastic curls to one side of her head. She had rushed out the gate a prodigy. She had run her mouth and broken the mold. She hadn't planned to teach. She had planned, simply, to be brilliant.

In her next author photo, a little older, heavier, and grayer, Celine vowed that she would not be so laissez-faire. Not behave as if influential books were birthed effortlessly every summer of her life, as if manuscripts grew on trees. She would smile in gratitude.

Since the book's publication, her once-disruptive contributions had become axiomatic, their lifeblood sapped by that most fatal of toxins: widespread acceptance. Her previous book had been about slipping out of the carapace of sexual identity. This new book would be about slipping out of *all* the roles and living free. About peeling back the layers of self, about the exfoliative process of new growth.

To refuse definition is to step into a new skin, she wrote, her writing hand moving swiftly over the page. She swelled with generosity as she synthesized what the past year had been about. Thinking of her readership, devoted after these years—not *so* many years after all—absorbing all she had discovered. *To cast off your outer layer, vulnerable as a skinned lamb, and prepare for new stages of growth; for a new skin to surface. One that can glitter or spear, poison or invite. To jettison the categories of Mother or Woman or Friend or Lover is to inhabit the skin of Life Itself.*

Emerging from her office in a rosy mood, Celine stopped in the kitchen to pound a Dr Pepper from one of the tall pink flamingo glasses. Helped her think. Thus fortified, she found Alice in the living room, wrapped in comforting quilts like the mummy Hatshepsut.

"I'm going to bed." Celine waited in the doorway for Alice to follow her. "What's your plan, to rage against the dying of the light?" Alice had spent the past several days loitering around the house and yard, pottering to the kitchen and back, dissolving abruptly into tears. Lighting heavily scented candles that perfumed the air and made it catch in Celine's throat.

"Something like that." Alice was round-shouldered, clicking her laptop keys with a slow gravity.

"What are you doing?"

"I'm looking at audition listings. I'm thinking of going down to L.A. for a few days."

No doubt Alice, prone to spasmodic exertions, was clutching at an escape. But if she wanted Celine to beg her not to go, then it wasn't happening. Alice was wrapped in the frayed fringe blanket, Pearl's really. Alice wore a tear-stained cashmere sweater, pajama pants, and a glut of accessories. She looked out from her cartouche. Celine did not own a scrap of cashmere. Think of Alice, all her life, enshrouded.

"Listen to this." She held open her quilt in invitation. Celine slid in, feeling slightly sour. " 'A call for women whose feet are super sexy and want all of YouTube to see.' "

"Ugh." Celine might have suggested that Alice author her own parts and stage them. But she knew it was as far-fetched as Alice winning the sexy-foot role.

" 'Seeking Beautiful Females. Seeking Hot Wife. Damsel in distress. *Nonspeaking role.*' "

Celine listened attentively, indulging Alice. "Exploitation of women is alive and well."

Even though Celine herself participated in that misuse, to a degree—that afternoon, rather than bedding Alice, Celine had snuck into the bathroom and clicked *hentai* from the dropdown menu, for the sake of variation. She felt a stirring when the flat-graphic male hero caressed Mariko-the-silent-schoolgirl's galactically upright breasts, sprung free from her crisp button-down. Mariko blushed, with brimming eyes.

I think you're cute, the scholar-hero whimpered in subtitles, tugging the end of Mariko's long pigtail as he annihilated her, sweat drops dripping down his chest. It turned out Mariko found her voice, had lots to say when it came to cocks and cunts.

"It all seems so meaningless," Alice said, staring at the castings page.

"Welcome to life," Celine said, feeling privately that Alice reduced herself. She thought of how Sadie had been in the school play once but been mortified by the whole thing, refused to allow her to invite anyone. This seemed, to Celine, evidence of sound judgment.

"You need support out there," Celine said, thinking that it wasn't brain surgery. "Why don't you hire an agent to look through this crap for you? Can you possibly land a good gig this way?"

This was a bit subtle for Alice. She pouted. She let her hands fall into her lap. "Easy to say. Plus, he'd take fifteen percent. And what if it didn't work out?"

Celine considered this. "You could always fire him."

"Why would I fire him?" Alice was testy. "I haven't even hired him yet."

Celine got a bright idea, thinking it would give Alice a vote of confidence. "Couldn't you deliver your headshots to a casting office in person? Put on something pretty and introduce yourself? If you're not standing out, then you need to go off-book. I tell you, if you walked in, I'd be happy to see you."

This didn't land. "I can't just show up like *ta-da!*"

"I don't see why not. It can't be unheard of. That's what I would have done at your age." Celine felt she might say something inspirational, to inspire Alice. "All that shit they say. It's worth repeating. About dedication and commitment. About hard, honest work."

But Alice was out of reach. Celine had poked innocently and awakened a misanthrope. A bad feeling twinkled inside Celine as she took inventory of Alice's stringy hair, her PJ pants, the blanket, and now her cashmere sweater matted with Pearl's silver fur.

Having initially believed this dalliance would take twenty years off her life, Celine saw with a sudden clarity: She had let her sex drive do the thinking for her. Had allowed her midlife crisis hormones to convince her that this inept and moody amateur was a brilliant performer. The revelation was sizzling to her mind's touch. Celine's whopping transgression, her big coup? To become madly infatuated with a nobody! A nobody with a lack of character. Not that it was such a feat, either, Alice being so readily available the night she had bewitched Celine.

"You know something?" Celine asked. "I only wonder if you might not be as cut out for this as you think."

"Say that again?"

"Maybe not. No, never mind."

Alice said nothing.

"I said—" There was no easy way to say it. "Don't take this the wrong way. But have you ever considered the possibility that acting is not for you?"

"You loved *The Winter's Tale*." Alice scrolled down the page, eyes fixed more intently. "You said that."

"You were good," Celine said, leaving intimations tacitly implied, "even if it wasn't the most significant company on earth."

"It's one of the best on the West Coast." Crimped by the words, Alice closed her laptop. Her eyes rested on the maidenhair fern, struggling in its clay pot. "It's rated four stars on Yelp," she insisted, still grandiose but with slightly less gusto. She stood, thumped over to the litter box corner, and began spritzing her room spray. How many times did Celine have to tell her? It smelled more ammoniac than ammonia.

Celine winced, her frustration building. She was feeling spicy.

"I saw you three times. The first time, I was captivated. I thought it was a great performance, very natural."

Alice huffed. "You certainly came back."

"The second time," Celine sallied on, carried as if by force, "I thought *hunh*."

"Stop it," Alice pleaded.

"And the third time, I thought, 'I can see the Scotch tape holding this thing together.' "

Celine watched Alice's face, enjoying the hurt she had caused. Alice was surprised by the cruelty, when it came to her. Apparently, she'd thought she was the exception. Alice was winding up to say something when the phone rang. Celine held up a hand. "Hold that thought. I'll be right back."

Chapter Twenty

ALICE

But Celine was not right back. She had been outside in the garden on the phone a long time now. Pouting, probably, sulking. How had Alice, generous and kind, agreeable, *pretty*, adored by all, allowed herself to develop a relationship with this person? Wasn't Alice a prize?

I hate this person, Alice thought, for the first time. Celine's flame warmed you at first, but, left unattended, it could devour the world.

The Shakespeare she had committed to memory in Mr. Cady's high school drama class, a few lines from King Lear that she had not needed the Folger edition to parse, came back to her in a fell swoop: *I will have such revenges on you that all the world shall—I will do such things—what they are yet I know not, but they shall be the terrors of the earth. You think I'll weep? No, I'll not weep.*

Alice would have her revenge. She paced the garage, stepping around the roll of AstroTurf Sadie had forbidden Celine to install in the living room. She would unleash on Celine terrors of the earth, and she would not weep. She would solve what, precisely, these were later. Bursting with malignance, Alice stalked out and back through the claustrophobic house, shoving open the screen door to the front porch.

She found Celine squatted low on the stoop, cradling her phone in her hand, like it was something delicate, hurt beyond revival. Celine's eyes rested in the middle distance. Her voice, very small, cracked the silence like a sheet of glass. "My mother is dead."

"What?" Alice asked, her gun of revenge still cocked.

Everything seemed gone out of Celine's eyes—they were two gray sheets. She held her phone in her clenched fist. She explained that the old woman had died of a small sack of a tumor, the size of a cut sushi roll. Large enough to do it. "So. I did not see that coming."

Alice sank onto the last stair, close beside Celine. Like a warrior in chain mail forced to sit down just as the battle heated up. And then she felt ridiculous. It was a mystery of life, Alice thought. Why did we squabble, pick at, and destroy each other when life was so cruel anyway? In the face of death, under its grim spotlight, her hurt feelings about Celine's reaction to her acting seemed pale.

Pearl sidled up and stared disapprovingly. Celine plucked at peeling paint on the banister. "She's my mother. The only one I have."

Alice made a small noise of acknowledgment, the wind hoovered out of her sails.

Celine sniffled. Pearl's long body formed a moat between them. "She lived to eighty-eight."

"That's a good, long life," Alice said, lightly touching Celine's shoulder. Celine felt warm, human.

"Forty-one years left for me," Celine said, glancing at Alice. Her face was like a bird after hitting glass. "From nothing into something and from something into nothing."

Celine's crass math in this moment, assessing her own longevity: She was really something. Then again, maybe it was something everyone did, past a certain age. In fact, Alice did a little crass calculation herself, imagining herself at age fifty piloting an ancient Celine in her wheelchair. She tried to blink away the ghastly thought.

"Maybe a few more. Funny how I already feel like a dinosaur," Celine said. "I don't feel like I could possibly be older than I am now."

The poured concrete stoop was glacially cold beneath them. Celine stared at her feet. She looked sunburned. The oversized Doc Martens on her skinny legs looked like a child had tried on someone else's shoes.

Celine clucked her tongue as if to say, "How sad." She looked resigned. The action struck Alice as insufficient. When a parent died, it wasn't supposed to be sad, it was supposed to be devastating.

"*Sadie*," Celine said. "I'll have to call her. I should call her now. She was the one they should have called."

"You're her next of kin," Alice pointed out.

Celine's lips blew a wet raspberry, discounting the significance of this. "I was a lousy child. Then again, she was a lousy mother." Celine picked a peel of house paint off the deck. She blew a chip off her fingernail. "Probably lead-based. Will probably give me seizures. Probably cancer."

A stocky beetle toddled across the porch. Celine set her phone onto a large stone, sheathed in lichen, cushioned with dried moss, and abandoned it. She took a few steps off the drive, down a marked walking trail, and stood dumbly, staring into the thicket of oaks that surrounded the cottage.

"It's just," she stammered, mournful and bewildered, stumped by death's thorny equation. "It's one of those things you can't make up for. There's no going back."

They fell into a deep silence, listening to the scrabble of ground squirrels in the dense trees. How strange to imagine that Celine had *parents*, that she had not descended onto earth fully formed.

* * *

The Thing was in sight. The thing itself. Celine had lost her appetite and developed a mild case of insomnia. She did not think she could face the funeral alone. "It just brings up a lot of stuff," she said. "This death thing. Stirs it all up."

When, without her blessing, Celine booked Alice a flight ticket to go along to Ohio as her personal, private grief counsel and moral support, Alice did not click the link for twenty-four-hour free cancellation.

Celine said she knew she should look with trepidation toward seeing Sadie. But mostly, she hoped she wouldn't be overtaken by a fit of the giggles. Church made her laugh. The absurdity of it, the proceedings, the solemnity—and now accompanied by the twin absurdity of death. What to do but laugh?

Of course, Celine's unkind words rang in Alice's mind. Of course, she had not forgotten them. The conflict had not yet reached its conclusion—quite feasibly a terminal one, given the direction in which they'd been heading—and hung like a rotten stench in the air. But truth be told, Alice had been dreading the weekend alone, the nonproximity. She surrendered, joining Celine on the trip. There was no point in resisting. Not when Celine was like this, weeping like a child.

"How can you just sit there?" Celine asked, from down in her well of grief.

"What can I do?" Alice asked, beside her in bed the evening before the scheduled flight.

"You're supposed to think of things. To make me feel better."

Alice offered a foot rub, but Celine said that was not the sort of thing to which she was referring. Alice was at a loss. In preparation for leaving, the early morning before the flight, she helped Celine refine her funeral outfit. "You can't wear your Converse," she said. She offered to loan Celine a pair of heels.

"Church shoes," Celine said resolutely, digging out a pair of clunky buckle shoes from the back of her closet. The last time she had worn them, she said, was her wedding day.

But she wanted to wear a T-shirt and wouldn't hear otherwise.

"You can't do that."

"I can and will."

Alice folded up the blouse she had offered to lend Celine. Wouldn't be Alice's fault. Sure was nice for Celine to have Alice—someone to play conservative, to put her in relief.

Together, they flew—well, not technically together; Celine had been upgraded to first class, the flight attendant acquiescing, albeit disapprovingly, to Celine's upgrade request on account of her dizziness caused by grief—and taxied to arrive at the franchise hotel. Alice had to provide the directions, as Celine's ears had become plugged on the plane.

They reached the Best Western. Alice had never stayed in a budget hotel. They were reminiscent to her of movies in which men drive down back roads, hating women: *Memento, Psycho, Fargo*. Alice was habituated to flawless facilities with rolling armchairs, rolling tea sets, rolling luggage racks, and no detail overlooked. Delicacies in lobby salons, petit fours, dusted with sneezy powdered sugar.

"I thought it over," Celine said. They had reached the room and she was fumbling with the key card with one hand. She still had her bag by the handle. Alice touched her key card to the door and the mechanism clunked to unlock. "I don't think it's such a good idea for you to come with me."

Celine held the door open, but Alice did not walk through. "What?"

Celine had worn her buckle shoes on the flight and clapped into the room. She wheeled her bag to the center of the room and abandoned it. She sank onto the paisley-zinnia-patterned bedspread. "I wouldn't be able to handle a scene. Not in my state of grief. These people are so conservative." Celine lifted the mattress and nosed up close to it, then closer.

Alice's heart sank. "Don't tell me there's bedbugs."

Celine did not seem to hear Alice. Replacing the mattress, seeming satisfied enough, she said she was petrified of her many cousins, people she had not seen since high school. "You have to remember, when I saw these people last I was *married*. They came to my *wedding*." Celine shook her head. "I can't take the drama."

"You had me come here," Alice stammered. "I came all this way."

Celine turned. Her eyes were black as river stones. "Sorry, are you talking? My ears."

Alice sat quietly, with her hands in her lap. But she knew what this was about. It was going to be easier for Celine to see Sadie without her; she was too chicken to face Sadie with her lover in tow. Maybe she'd even try to make a separate peace with her! Maybe mother and daughter would gallop off into the Ohio sunset, leaving Alice forlorn.

Celine busied herself around the room, trying to persuade her hair to flatten, inspecting the sheets once more for cleanliness, tapping the can's pedal with her toe to be sure the previous occupant's trash had been safely disposed of. She proceeded to the stucco bathroom, scrutinizing the hair dryer and lifting the lid off the wall-mounted dispenser to sniff the pink shampoo.

"What am I supposed to do here while you're gone?" Alice asked.

"Enjoy the amenities."

Alice was accustomed to spas and cocktail bars.

"Watch cartoons."

No matter how inauthentic and performative her bereavement seemed to be, the woman was leaving for her mother's funeral. So Alice swallowed it. Left marooned at a Best Western to kill time under the violet-tinged fluorescent lights, with a bucket of ice and an empty mini fridge with nothing to pour over it. She spent the afternoon sipping ice water and flipping channels between Judge Mathis and *Inside Edition*. She landed on local daytime news, thinking she might drop in on some antiquated and picturesque broadcast, teenagers broken into the local cemetery, cats run up a tree, minor theft at the taffy shop. Turned out nothing was quaint. Everything was awful everywhere.

Celine, taken off in the rental car, had not left any provisions. Alice checked Seamless: not operational in the township. Nibbling a cold strawberry Pop Tart from the vending machine, not entirely unpleasant, Alice lost the remote behind the headboard and didn't bother to retrieve it, leaving *Law and Order* running. She took her key card and wallet and trod the side of the long adjacent avenue, no sidewalk, in pursuit of anything edible, feeling like a teenage runaway.

The gray thoroughfare was checkered with skeletal billboard scaffolding and building facades with YOUR AD HERE signs in place of windows. Alice skirted a grassy patch between a Dunkin' Donuts and a Shell station, a heap of steel sheet piles outside a distribution center. She mounted a concrete staircase to a footbridge over an unlit tunnel, gaping. It exuded a lamenting, plaintive sound each time a car passed in the other direction, a kind of dirge.

Everything Alice wanted to tell Celine, that afternoon she had gone out to find her on the porch, sat heavy and unsaid like a lump in her throat. There were things she'd like to tell Sadie, too, given the chance. She'd like to say she was sorry. She'd like to say that it had not been worth the trade; that, given a do-over, she'd not have to think for a second, *she would take it all back.*

Chapter Twenty-One

SADIE

The Ohio chapter of the interfaith Pentecostal church was long and low, composed of a small, gloomy office, a bright children's ministry, the shuttered sanctuary, and, packed full today, the ill-equipped and unceremonious oblong meeting room, where services were being held while the sanctuary was under construction.

"Mamie never had great timing," Celine whispered, jittery and fidgeting beside Sadie, breath hot in her ear. Celine had barreled down the aisle—"Scoot," she'd insisted, with a flap of her hands—making herself comfortable beside Sadie before she could object. She was wearing the strangest shoes, Sadie noticed, shiny with buckles like a pilgrim's, somehow at once both pristinely new and out-of-date.

Even though Celine looked waterlogged, like she was sinking into a bottomless marsh, she couldn't resist snorting when the choir sang, "May we stroke the creatures there: ox, ass, or sheep?" Celine wiped her ash-gray eyes, leaky with mirth and, possibly, despondence. In the past, Celine would have jabbed Sadie. *Ass.* Today she only snuck her a look. Sadie did not flinch, though she herself couldn't help thinking of Cormac stroking *her* . . .

Celine appeared exasperated with Sadie, hoping she would hop into the ring, as usual. To *react*, as she had always reliably done. But Sadie was having a hard enough time keeping her focus on what she was there for—Mamie, handed off to the County Coroner's office by an RN, packed into a discount brass cremation urn, and placed atop a rented pedestal—without Celine poking at her.

Sadie leaned forward to listen. Today, she had a cushion of defense against her mother. And that was a blurred haze of endorphinal, hormonal protection. She had always thought that, in their relationship, Celine held the cards. She realized she had it upside down. Sadie had always taken Celine's bait. It was Sadie's *engaging* that had guaranteed Celine's supremacy. Without her participation, Celine had nothing. Sadie could imagine Alice and Celine's conversations: What a blow this will be to her, they must have imagined.

But Sadie was carrying her happiness, holding it like an egg. She wished Cormac had been able to come with her. It was the week when all the largest tech firms came around interviewing students at the university, scouting for the next Zuckerberg, throwing the entire young coding community into a fever of competition.

Sadie herself had gotten time off work for this errand of grieving and arranging. One day, when she had saved up enough cash, and not too far into the future, either, she would quit Blackbird and open her own interior design shop. Cormac thought this was a fantastic idea.

He was so great. Had even offered to bag the scouting weekend, but Sadie had said, "You can't do that," blow-jobbing his protests silent.

No, Sadie thought, do not think of blow jobs. Think of Mamie, in her urn. Desperately, Sadie forced herself to recall, fondly, the Rhubarb Period, when Mamie served the herbaceous perennial with every meal, as a ward against blood clots.

The hymn was "How Far Is It to Bethlehem?" according to the program.

Celine snorted a wad of oceanic mucus. To think, Alice *liked* this person. Liked and more. But then, when had Alice ever been a reliable judge of character? With wonderment, Sadie saw how flimsy the friendship had always been, made of bird bone, dandelion fluff. Alice was an ameba. This tandem-jump love affair was just something else she was trying on. But why waste time thinking about it? They were distant concerns. Sadie no longer had a mother. She did not have a friend. Their actions had nothing to do with her anymore.

But this was Mamie's party. The proof hung over the baptismal font as you entered the church: A recent photo, snapped by a Seven Oaks nurse on what must have been Saint Patrick's Day. Wearing green antennae, the pixelated Mamie was smiling, but looked less than happy. A course of steroids had left her face open, bloated, everything visible. In Sadie's mind, Mamie stubbornly refused to reveal herself. There were too few memories, also too many. All those hours together, and Sadie could recall a tiny fraction. Mamie, skin wrinkled as tinfoil, enclosed in her wax coat, boxy with tremendous orange buttons. Tipping her large-frame eyeglasses down her nose to read Frommer's or Fodor's in preparation for the trips she strategized extensively, but never booked.

The minister would conduct the funeral. Both Sadie and Celine had declined to give a eulogy. How about recite a poem? The minister had proposed. No, thank you. Lead the singing of a hymnal? No. Celine must have counted on Sadie giving one; Sadie felt the duty was squarely Celine's.

"We are here today to pay our tribute to a woman of God." The minister's prodigious hands rested on his belly. Mumbling into the air above him, praying, he looked like a braying penguin. He invited the congregation to please rise. Stand to worship, sit to learn, kneel to pray. He read out Romans 14:7–9, "Life and death are both in God's hands . . ."

The service had a meaningful effect on Celine. Every time Celine blubbed, hiccupping like an ornery drunk, Sadie became further unmoved. Sadie squirmed, pinned by the pastor's penetrating eyes as the congregation recited Corinthians 15, clocking her like he knew she didn't mean it.

Not Mamie's fault. Or was it? After all, hadn't she produced Celine?

Thoughts for later. Every time Sadie was called to stand, for song or Scripture, she winced. Her knees were sore, skinned from the rug where she had been splendidly gratified by Cormac minutes before she hastened off to the unwitting taxi driver, waiting to ferry her to the airport. Heaven, if there was one.

Sadie did not know if she believed in God but imagined she should spend some time thinking about it. Back when she was a child, just before the age when little girls learned to stop asking what everything was and how everything worked, Sadie wanted a share in the conviction that made her grandmother's pious eyes shine like plastic finish. Mamie, in a fever, had heard the voice of God.

"Was it a voice in your head or more like he was talking over a PA system?" Sadie had asked Mamie, still proudly fastened with the wings pin Southwest Airlines doled out to unaccompanied travelers under the age of twelve.

Mamie's weepy reply: that it was hard to describe. "All I know is it came from outside of me."

PA system, then. Sadie had spent hours staring into the radiant orange grate of Mamie's freestanding floor heater, imagining it was hell. She felt acutely and with a chill in her bones her attraction to this luminous glow, to the lustrous, untouchable coils behind the grate. She began to take the subject more seriously.

On speakerphone with Celine once, while Mamie looked on with hard eyes: round dismissal. Her voice, like a lash, said that Sadie was too smart to go Christian on her.

"You've always been Christian, Sadie," Mamie rectified, eyes shining obsidian. "You were born blessed in the Lord's eye."

"Be quiet, Mother. Sadie, speak into the receiver and tell me, no BS," Celine said. "Do you find it credible that Jesus Christ, the purported son of an unseen God, was sent to this earth to die in repentance for human sin? If so, then it's time to come home."

Mamie glared at the phone, wrathful as a plague.

Without recognizing it by name, Sadie felt a part of herself trampled. The part that had an attraction, even a *need*, for meaning. The part of herself that was not far from the magical-thinking phase of childhood.

"You don't believe in Cinderella, do you?" Celine continued her hectoring. Sadie's vision swam. She saw Cinderella in her ball gown, a sky-blue violet, almost white. She'd like to have believed. "Bibbidi-bobbidi? Tell Mamie I'm changing your flight home to tomorrow. Chagrin Falls is a cute town, they're *nice* people, but they're not critical. Can't you see why I don't want that for you?"

At home, Celine had a wooden statue of the Yoruba river deity Oshun and a mosaic tile of Minerva, the Roman goddess of wisdom and warfare. She had included, in one of her books, an epigraph to Aphrodite. It seemed that only Christian deities required renunciation. To this day, Sadie could still taste the anger and frustration about not being allowed to believe what she wanted to believe, about being mocked, especially when the authority mocking her was such a blinking hypocrite. Celine often bullied Sadie about things that attracted her. But Sadie knew what it was, in this case. Celine did not like her seeking solace in a big man, in a *father.* Celine was supposed to be enough.

Sadie understood now. God was nothing but a thought. Today, facing one of the more allegedly profound moments in life—an opportunity to contemplate God with a big G, the nature and meaning of existence, etc.—Celine had brought all her petulance and dramatics, as well as a sniveling fear of her own mortality. Sadie perceived all that, but it didn't carry the weight it once would have.

After Mamie's service, mourners were directed to the tree-shrouded lawn, specked with wilting dandelions. Celine and Sadie first, the others giving a respectful berth.

Sadie remembered the day Celine had called, in a panic. When it had finally happened: Mamie had not recognized Celine on FaceTime. She had gone into a fit of horror, crying, "You're not my daughter! My daughter is pretty!" She had clamped a hand on her caretaker and shouted, "Who is this ugly man pretending to be my daughter?"

Sadie had burst out laughing. "Sorry," she said, unable to stop. "Not funny at all."

"It's okay to laugh," Celine had said. "It *is* funny. Just is."

Nothing was funny now. It was a sunny, cloudless day, with quick streaks of breeze. On the road, the murmur of traffic headed to Eckel's Lake merged with the voices just inside the church, oldies feeling their way out into daylight. The lake water was green as the sun-soaked leaves; you could imagine you were looking at a pane of stained glass. Crosswise on Meridian Avenue, freighters stood frozen on their tracks. One thing prevented Sadie from fully enjoying the beauty of the day, and regretfully it was not Mamie's departure. Rather, she wished Cormac were there to partake of it with her.

On the plane ride over, Sadie had surprised herself. Just when she was tasked with elegizing the past, she had begun dreaming of the future. It was best to give birth in early spring, when the days lengthened and the birds returned; you could take the newborn out for crisp strolls, and new beginnings perfumed the air. While this involved having to buy a new winter coat to extend over the pregnant belly, it avoided a heavily laden, beefy-hot summer.

Sadie calculated. If she wanted to give birth in April, she would need to become pregnant in July. Late for that now. Even Sadie knew this was carrying it a little far. Still, she glanced covertly, making sure even her airplane seatmate was not snooping, toward the following year. She jotted a faint note in her diary, *bb?* Lightly, in pencil—she could always erase it. She had learned nothing this year if not that one could not count on one's own best-laid plans.

"Mother would have approved," Celine remarked now, in a melancholy voice she must have felt was appropriate. "The service honored her memory." Any other time, the hypocrisy of this supposed avowed atheist—her mother, the same old mocking hypocrite—being all institutional-religion-approving would have set Sadie spinning.

But the beauty of the day transfixed Sadie. She imagined a rural afternoon, she and Cormac racing bicycles away from a quaint village, down a steep hill leading to a field of poppies. He would chase her into the woods . . . there would be a reed-fringed pond, beside which they would lay out a picnic blanket on grass, soft as a new kitten . . . He would feed her strawberries. The juice would drip down her blouse and then he would trace a finger, leading to sex on the floating sun-soaked wooden dock . . .

"What are you thinking?" Celine's voice intruded, and with it her coffee breath. "Your face is telling me you're elsewhere."

Feeling a little guilty to be dreaming of a strawberry-scented fuck on clerical grounds, no matter how sanctified and love-soaked the vision, she came back to Celine, and to Mamie. "It's been what," Sadie tried to figure, "ten years since you saw her?"

Celine did not contest this. She shifted her weight and admitted uncomfortably, without needing to calculate, "It's been fourteen."

For over a decade, then, Sadie had gone to Ohio as Celine's surrogate. A decade of hours, she had listened carefully, trying to absorb the cluttered information, to Mamie—so happy to see Sadie that she always seemed to have tears in the corners of her eyes. Alice had always agreed that Celine's neglect of her old mom, her abdication of responsibility, was deplorable. Sadie wondered fleetingly what Alice would say now.

"It's easy to criticize," Celine snapped, mistaking Sadie's silence for condemnation. "I admit in some ways I neglected her, sure, fine, for reasons you wouldn't understand."

"Probably not," Sadie murmured.

"But my mother is dead," Celine sniveled. *"Dead."* As if it were Sadie's fault somehow.

But Sadie was admiring the scenery. A brief wind blew now, stirring the crowns of oak, sending leaves scattering over the church lawn. The swaying trees were supple; if they stooped down low enough, it seemed they'd have something to say. The air smelled sweet, like fertilizer. The lawn had been late-seeded. Grass would grow.

"I guess you're probably feeling your own mortality," Sadie observed, she thought, keenly.

"I'm not that old!"

Not that Sadie herself had not been thinking of human transience, of how long it had taken her to really *live,* how she could have been living all this time.

"I suppose I should be more like *you,*" Celine said with a sly, sober look. "Smiling at your grandmother's funeral? I saw you."

Sadie just kept smiling.

Celine stepped closer, as if to detect why. "What is this new la-di-da?"

"Sorry I'm not as devastated as you." Sadie's smile turned a little lazy.

"Oh my god," Celine said, backing away from Sadie with eyes narrowed. "You're having sex."

Sadie blinked.

"I know that look. You're getting laid!"

"Okay, be quiet."

"Admit it. You are getting bonked."

Sadie snuck a look at the closed doors leading to the rectory. "Shh."

Celine wagged her finger. "Not until you admit it."

Sadie shrugged.

Celine hooted, forgetting all about her mourning face. "When did this happen?"

"It's really nothing you need to know about."

"Do you like it?"

"Shut up."

"You did, you did, you did!"

The flock of mourners were trooping toward them.

Celine nudged Sadie with her elbow. "Do you like copulating?"

"Leave me alone." Sadie's face got the prickling sensation it always had when she was a child and Celine threatened to implode publicly. Thank god she hadn't let Cormac come.

A graying matron reached around Sadie with a wrinkled arm. They stood together stiffly. She had such a nice full head of hair, for an elderly woman, that Celine could not help requesting to know whether she wore a wig. To Sadie's astonishment, the woman was flattered. "You girls come over anytime," she said warmly. "I've got baskets of peaches sitting there that I don't know what to do with." Despite her squinty-eyed smile, it was evident her eyes had wept, unlike Sadie's, which were kiln-dry. "And they don't wait on you!"

"We'll be sure to arrange that," Celine assured the walnut-faced woman, ushering her along, back to her relatives. Sadie stared at her feet. "And how are you, Mister Willen?"

Leather lace-ups, and Mr. Willen presented himself: proprietor of the local antiques shop that sold wicker furniture, bruised baby shoes in faded silks, and teddy bears, thinned of stuffing, emptied by love and time. Mamie had liked to visit the shop. Mr. Willen jingling with his heavy ring of keys to his "specialty cases," stuffed with malachite pyramids and timeworn pewter goblets. "By the skin of my teeth, I'm managing." He tipped his Stetson and toggled down his tie. "Just trying to keep my sunflower out of my soybeans."

Celine asked if he was still cultivating his famous magnolias. Sadie looked hard at her when she made Mr. Willen rattle as he laughed, saying, "The only thing I ever want to hear at my funeral is 'Look, it's moving!' "

Seven Oaks had bare beige walls and smelled fresh, like newly picked tangerines. The hallways were stubby, abutted by nurses' stations. It had the distinct air of quarters struck frequently by death. Against her instinct, Sadie had assented to join Celine, to help dismantle Mamie's abandoned room, hoping sense memory might summon some untapped well of emotion.

Celine, meanwhile, had donned an NPR baseball cap, pulled down tight and low. Her face was shadowed under the exacting fluorescent light. "I salvaged a box from outside Albertsons, to ship home whatever I'm keeping," she told Sadie as they waited for the

CNA, in her white scrub smock and pants, to emerge from the back office and accompany them to Mamie's wing. "It looks like it was used to ship pineapples, which Mamie loved, so that's fitting." She sniffed one. "Still scented."

"You're not going to *buy* a box?" Sadie asked.

Just then, the perky CNA emerged."You must be Celine," she said. "A fellow contributor to listener-supported radio!"

"My mother," Sadie said, "an everyday hero."

Heroism seemed distant from Mamie's small unit, smelling like soap, but the everyday was fully in evidence. Sunlight bounced off the walls. An altogether cheery room except that the taupe, industrial wall-to-wall carpet had been blackened by a set of shoe tracks, as if the grim reaper had come, swung his scythe, and made a quick exit. "These medics cut across the lawn and don't bother to remove boots at the door," the nurse said, rueful. Her eyes were tiny, and it looked like she was struggling to widen them. "We'll be getting that taken care of."

Not for their benefit. A white sheet was laid on the bed, with a single rose in place of a pillow. Needlepoint-embroidered pillows littered every other plush surface. Mamie's hand-knitted sock monkeys huddled together in a basket with lopsided faces and ears so big they looked like elephants. The yarn had become coarser every year and Sadie had finally tossed the three she had accrued over her childhood—a series: see no, hear no, speak no evil—when redoing her teenage bedroom. The nurse provided each woman an extra-large black trash bag. "More at the front, if you need." With a last bracing look at Sadie, she turned away down that well-traveled hall.

Celine stared at the pattern on the carpet. Mamie had fastened

Post-it notes with the name of the bequeathed under every last lamp and vase, surmising that otherwise Sadie and Celine would rip each other to shreds. Sadie and Celine cased the room.

Finally, Sadie balled up the Post-its, knelt in front of the bookshelf—"I guess we just begin"—and began turning over the inventory, assembling piles on the unsteady card table where Mamie used to sit, adjusting her square eyeglasses to better clip senior discount coupons—noting the promotion run on six-packs of sodas, wondering where she could store them—and would sit at no point ever again. The last time Sadie visited, Mamie had assaulted the sun, banging on the window. "Close the lights," she had raved. "Close them now!" Sadie wondered whether Celine had this disease in store. Whether she did, too.

Celine, head down, cap fixed low, was slower to start, sifting through her father's illogical clutter, preserved by Mamie out of sentiment or respect. She salvaged a proportional scale, a geometry compass, a snail's coil of yellow tape from his bits and parts of drafting instruments. "A life's work," she murmured.

This was the second time, in fact, that Sadie had purged her grandmother's possessions. Sadie had moved Mamie into Seven Oaks. Sadie saw Celine clock how devastating the purge had been. Gone were Mamie's duct-taped garden hoses and Thermapen-fitted oven. All the extemporary repairs. The jerry-rigged appliances had been declined by the donation center receptionist. Who wanted a dryer drum manually fitted with a makeshift craft felt seal?

Mamie had saved Celine's press and reviews as clippings. When Sadie was moving her into Seven Oaks, she had asked Celine if she should move them. Celine had had too much pride to say more than "If there's room, and if she wants them." Sadie knew Celine had too much pride, now, to ask after them. "I don't know why she left you her songbooks," Celine said, frowning. "I was the one who took piano lessons."

Music often struck Sadie as inane and childish, a chorus daftly reproducing, with no variance, as if it were not a recreation for adults, but a nursery rhyme, a refrain like rope tying it all together. "Take it."

"I only half want it, anyway," Celine said.

With a troubled intensity, she fussed over Mamie's treasured salt and pepper shakers—flamingoes and toadstool mushrooms—in the glass vitrine, swiveling each to face outward. "These are kind of fantastic."

Like a worksite manager, Sadie plucked up a tiki head with no partner. "Trash."

Sadie stripped the bed, though it had been made neatly by the staff as a gesture, with hospital corners. Celine hunched over Mamie's papers, inscrutable under the bill of her cap. The ceiling fan ticked overhead. Working together was almost tranquil, until Celine stood up suddenly, like she'd gotten dizzy. "Do you feel you knew who she was? As a person?"

"No," Sadie admitted. "I never did."

Celine peeled the corners of the fitted sheet off one long side, then stopped. "This life that was wiped out. That I never felt I understood, no matter how hard I tried. And she felt the same. If a mother and daughter can't understand each other, who can?"

Sadie made a noise of agreement. "Do you want to talk about it?"

"We have so much to do here. Let's not." Celine groaned. She balled up the bedding. She tried to make sense of the mess, rolling the linens into a tube and folding in the ends.

"I've always wanted to know what it was like growing up with her," Sadie said, prying gently. It was strange to be talking like this with Celine, so nicely. "What she was like when you were a teenager."

"She adored your father. She never forgave me for leaving him.

The problem was, I was moving so fast through these stages and my mother couldn't keep up. But then again, she was the one propelling me. I had to break out. I had to move on. When I got pregnant, she probably thought it was the end of all that, that it would finally be the thing to tether me to her."

"You were younger than I am today."

"And I was so alone. I had inklings of an impending upheaval of my entire identity that I couldn't tell a soul about. And I had you inside me."

Sadie heard a glitch in Celine's voice. Was she crying?

"I see how that could have been hard."

"Anyway," Celine said. She cleared her throat, becoming pragmatic again. "I'll stay tomorrow to do the certificate, take care of the practicalities. Maybe it will be palliative, in some way, to have that closure. Or I might find out she was done in by a psycho nurse."

Celine busied herself with packaging Mamie's fine china teacups in quarter-page junker car ads. She carefully nested each cup into the Albertson's box in Styrofoam procured from the front desk. Sadie leaned over to admire how carefully she was working.

But, as if allowing herself a note of kindness required a balancing of scales, she reared back to ask, "What do you possibly plan to *do* with those?" Celine did not seem to know. "Somehow, I can't see you serving thimblefuls of Lady Grey. I'm telling you right now I'll never want them, if that's what you're thinking."

Mamie's small life, shrunken twice over, fit into all of eight boxes. The newspaper clippings about Celine, of course, were gone. When all was packed, taped, and twined, they stood back together and admired their undoing. "So," Celine said. Successfully, working side by side, they had disassembled an entire life.

"So," Sadie said. She pulled out her phone and, approving of her own remarkable efficiency, ordered the donation collectibles truck. She tucked the Albertson's box in among the rest.

Minutes later, beaten up, with a weak, watery voice, Celine assented. "I guess you're right about the thimblefuls."

After loading, Celine patted the truck's long face and watched it sally forth, indifferent to its cargo, for Ohio Ranch Thrift. Sadie watched too, as the truck turned the corner, spewing exhaust, and almost regretted lobbying for Celine to surrender the fragile last and final vestiges of her mother.

Chapter Twenty-Two

CELINE

Despite the rain, and the traffic clogging 77 North, Alice and Celine had reached their boarding gate with an hour to spare. The 10:48 p.m. CLE to OAK Flight 238 was listed on the display monitor, but, as there were no signs of boarding, they sat a little apart, watching planes touch down and taxi to gate. Rain clouds sifted sunlight.

Alice's thoughts appeared to be elsewhere today, not on Celine. She did not bother asking again about whether the scar on Celine's arm was a result of a harrowing airplane landing at Buchanan Field. Airplane landing? More like falling off the jungle gym at age three under her father's distracted care. These days, she'd have no scar; they'd have smoothed the tissue with lasers. *Contact, three miles, nine hundred knots, closure?* Any fool who'd seen *Top Gun* knew the landing scene.

Celine's mother was dead. One moment, the meaningfulness of it would wallop her sideways. The next, just as soon, like a dragonfly lifted off a leaf without leaving a tremor, the feeling was gone. Sadie had seemed to accept the loss. At the time, the death of young Celine's own grandmother had seemed unimportant, and had not meant more to her than one less well-wisher at her piano recitals.

She had not yet realized that the love allotted a person on earth was not boundless.

Neither Celine nor Alice had eaten. Celine was feeling faint. She had left the hotel cranky after waking late and missing the continental breakfast. Usually, Alice would try to reassure Celine, restore her good mood. But today, even Alice was sullen, removed.

Activity on the jet bridge had ceased, the plane's innards gutted of disembarking passengers. A voice crackled over the intercom. "Due to inclement weather conditions, we have been advised of flight delays. High winds are impacting flights from Dayton to Buffalo. We do apologize for the inconvenience." The gate agents vowed to keep everyone informed of updates.

"Hungry?"

"Badly."

Now they were seated at the terminal's only restaurant, Bubba Gump Shrimp, a tidy novelty sit-down adjacent to Boarding Section B advertising authentic Cajun cuisine. Alice had ordered barbecued jumbo shrimp; Celine filet sliders. Two slushie Crown Royals. Because what else was there to do? Over the doorway hung a nautical helm decoy and a twin pair of crossed oars.

The place was unexpectedly cheerful and raucous, heavy with the scent of fish and chips, thronging with servers dispensing liquorous pink slush into fishbowl-sized glasses and pale green slush into glasses shaped like chemical beakers. The walls were peppered with red-and-white-striped lifesaver rings. In fact, it was the sort of place Celine liked. Middling, lukewarm, with no pretensions to anything better.

Alice was wearing one of her T-shirts that she said her mother hated, so cluttered with holes that it wouldn't survive a wash. "You won't tell me anything. How can I support you if I don't know what happened?"

Typical Alice, needing her balloon inflated. "There's really nothing to tell." Celine said, not a lie. Sadie and Celine had reconnected, in their way.

Outside, it had started to pour. The rain fell in patterns that Celine's eye liked. Celine avoided Alice's expectant bug eyes. She knew she had instigated this, spending the bulk of the prior week petitioning Alice to accompany her, hell-bent on it in fact, insisting that Alice had a duty to provide support, going so far as to ask what the purpose of a romantic partnership was, if not for aid at such a time. She had laid it on thick as a truncheon. She could not now for the life of her imagine why she had thought the girl's presence would be mollifying.

Alice had rushed at Celine the moment she returned to the hotel and not let up since. "What did she do when she first saw you?"

Celine submitted to the cross-questioning. "Looked at me, then looked away."

"What did she do during the service?"

"Sat quietly."

"Did she cry?"

"No."

Alice, kneading Celine like dough, would not surrender her inquest for scraps of information. Celine did not know why, but she felt this was not the conversation they should be having. She had a feeling that something important was about to happen.

Alice responded with a starved look. A soccer team would be on board their flight, Midwestern girls with long legs and pale, blemished skin. Celine brooded. Why couldn't Alice be mild and sensible? Cooperate with Celine but also be capable of challenging her, training her off her worst impulses, calling her bullshit?

"Did she look pretty?" Alice persisted, with prying eyes. Though it had been something she herself had noticed distinctly—Sadie more beautiful than ever in her slim-fitting pencil skirt, long and thin as a cigarette, with careful pleating, radiant with some secret happiness—Celine gave Alice a look that said this was not an appropriate question, given the circumstances.

They watched their aircraft taxi in—short-haul regional—the jet bridge extended; bleary passengers flooded into the echoing terminal. It wouldn't be long before they left.

Celine decided to give Alice another crumb. She had to share the salacious bombshell with somebody. "You know, I feel we made some progress in our relationship. It went well. She's open . . ." Celine decided to offer the ultimate breadcrumb. "She's relaxed, and want to know why? Because she's finally discovered the joy of sex."

Alice seized on this. "What? She *told* you that?"

"I didn't need her to tell me," Celine said, with some pride. "We're closer than you might have been led to believe."

Alice looked badly hurt. "The last time she and I talked about it, she and Cormac had failed spectacularly . . ."

And it was in this moment that over Alice's shoulder—within the small, idled crowd of milling, displaced passengers loitering and chatting—Sadie appeared at the hostess stand and made her way toward them, advancing with each moment. Alice, brooding, did not see. Like a pileup, Sadie nearing, it was too late for them all.

"She made him change the lighting," Alice sallied on, without sensing the intrusion, Sadie in hearing distance, approaching close behind her seat now. "She had to take TUMS, for god's sake."

Sadie dropped her bag behind Alice's chair. Celine made a minute gesture, a cock of a finger directing Alice's attention. Alice looked over her shoulder and saw, finally, what she was up against.

Sadie smiled amiably at Alice. “Good to know my secrets are safe with you.”

“Hello,” Celine said.

Alice clapped her hand over her mouth. She flushed, florid mauve as the drink in her hand.

Sadie clocked Alice. A murmur as an adjacent boarding gate’s jet lifted off. “What are you doing here?”

“Hi, Sadie.” With a mild irritation, Celine saw that Alice, still inflamed but now with eyes beaming, actually looked radiantly *happy* to see Sadie. This incensed Celine and a violent feeling rose inside her. “She didn’t tell you that I came?” Alice looked to Celine for reassurance.

“She must have forgotten.” Sadie sat down heavily. Strangely enough, no fellow patrons stared. No onlooker would have known the first thing was wrong.

From two tables down, the hostess snuck a look back at their table. “Can you tell how she hates us?” Celine asked, smiling ominously. “She thinks we’re West Coast elites.”

Sadie glared. “Is it so unfathomable to you that someone might dislike you?”

The Crown Royal slushie anchored Celine, who observed the interaction tipping into confrontation. She felt better. She leaned coolly back against the booth, slurping the drink. She took a long slug, then contemplated the red plastic pebble tumbler.

“She just had you sitting in the hotel?” Sadie chuckled. “And you agreed to it? What did you do for three days while Jackie Kennedy was out flaunting her grief?”

Alice straightened, receiving this. “I was here to be supportive. In case Celine needed me.”

“I see. That’s beautiful.”

Alice smiled a little, feebly, and toggled her plastic straw.

"Turned out she didn't need me," she said, feeling more steady now. "Mostly, I was in an ambiguous hell of Dunkin' Donuts and highway on-ramps."

"That's not very friendly," Sadie said. Her phone vibrated on the table. She picked it up with a small smile, lit unnaturally by the screen.

"Sweetie," Celine said to Alice, "you are not the victim here." She scooted back in her chair. She swatted at an orange buoy, hung askew behind her. "In fact, she wasn't actually *all* that patient," she went on, feeling something brimming. The tussle was nascent, these wild swings between them customary, in fact almost cozy.

"Have I complained?" Alice swiveled to face Celine. "That's rich. I've been locked in a hotel room, shut out of the entire trip, and now I'm getting abused for it?"

Celine groaned. "You didn't need to complain. I could just *feel* you hanging around, moping."

"Shots fired," Sadie said, still texting into the phone.

"I didn't want to come!" Alice appealed to Sadie. Over her shoulder, a large yellow fish shivered across the aquarium. "She demanded I come, but when we got here . . ."

"And?" Sadie smiled thinly. "You expected her to be consistent?"

"You're right." Alice rolled her eyes for Sadie's benefit. "My mistake." In the restaurant kitchen, there was a crash of steam as a boiler was unlidded, and suddenly the air around them fell heavy and intimate.

Sadie took another text on her phone.

"But it's not like she had anything to do at home anyway," Celine said. "Hasn't booked a job in the last six months, that I know of."

Alice had a queer, unattractive look on her face. "You know, I never told you what Sadie actually said when I went to see her. She said that we deserve each other. I was so offended that she'd think I was as monstrous as you."

There. Alice had jumped at the chance, as if she'd only been waiting to finish to the hilt the fight they'd begun back home. Celine wanted to rip the smile off Alice's face.

Sadie dabbed her mouth with her paper napkin.

Celine turned her eyes to Alice. "You know what *else* she said? To me, over the years?" The cold of the Crown Royal squeezed Celine's brain, juicing it of her better impulses. "She said you're just a dilettante. All those flimsy hobbies—Brownie troop, soccer, photography, clown school? Didn't you take tai chi for five minutes?"

"Brownies?" Alice's smile turned cold. "I was supposed to become a career Girl Scout?"

Sadie was burrowed into her phone, tap, tap, tap. "Sorry." She smiled privately. And that was her daughter's primary relationship now, Celine thought. Her mother would never be the center of her universe again. This erasure burned Celine anew.

"Can you stop playing with that fucking phone for a minute?" she asked. She felt a rich and deep-seated deposit stir inside her. A biochemical reaction—a jet of rage spouted. The outburst had attracted, now, a few onlookers at the next table.

"I'm not a part of this," Sadie said, resisting the altercation. "I'm just a bystander. Wish I'd brought popcorn."

How would they get out of this one? What if they wouldn't? What if this was the last and final it? If so, Celine figured she might as well have the last word. "Now I'm a dancer, now I'm an equestrian, now I'm an actress, now I'm a *lesbian.*"

Outside, an employee in a neon-yellow reflective vest, wheeling a yellow mop kit and wet-floor sign, eddied his mop. At Auntie Anne's pretzels, the shopkeeper rolled the rattling steel security gate down to the terrazzo floor.

Alice stared at Celine. "You know, I was a happy person, before you. You people . . . are failed human beings."

Sadie smirked. "I thought you don't say anything bad about anyone."

Alice glared at Sadie. "That was last year." She dropped her napkin onto the table. She stood. "I'll find another flight."

"Good luck. This isn't JFK."

And Alice disappeared, leaving Celine and Sadie alone. No one tried to stop her.

Sadie shook her head in amazement. "You guys sure are great together."

On the monitor, flight status quietly shifted from a yellow DELAYED to a definitive red SEVERELY DELAYED. At the boarding kiosk, airline personnel began handing out compensation vouchers for "distressed passenger" rates at the Hilton Hotel, good while supplies lasted.

Chapter Twenty-Three

JANE

We've reached cruising altitude. When the seat belt sign dings, signifying freedom, I jump out of my seat, open the overhead storage bin to triple-check on the cardboard tube encasing the JD Beck and DOMi poster I peeled off a wall for Jacob, down in Hollywood. I've lucked out with a window seat, which means I have to disturb the person sitting next to me, in 19D, but I keep worrying it's going to get crushed in the overhead. Jacob's going to flip when he sees what I brought him. The two of us heard JD Beck and DOMi live at the Back Room Jazz Club—since we turned fourteen, we've been allowed to go alone—and haven't been able to get enough. JD Beck's a drummer with an almost-psychotic genius for rhythm, and DOMi is a prodigy keyboardist. Together, they make this swirling, oozing, buzzy sound. I wonder if the elderly man in 19D will ask about my poster, but he seems uninterested.

Jacob and I have been super close since we were old enough to know what a friend *was*. He was a weirdo and I was a weirdo and when he came over we had this whole little world. He's incredibly ordered, high-strung as a tightrope, and has a hard time relaxing. Even though he's almost a year older than me, he's just on the cusp, so we're in the same class. It's so crazy that he's my *uncle*. We call him our cousin. We decided calling him Uncle Jacob would be too weird.

He's super good at studying. I guess in some ways he's a lot like my mom. Mom and Jacob like to be indoors, studying or practicing, or playing chess together, while I read, and Dad and my brother Lex watch MMA, and my other brother, Noah, does whatever Noah does in his room. Dad often cooks dinner, Mom wincing when he goes off-recipe.

Mom, like Jacob, is very particular. If, up in Point Reyes, she doesn't get the seat next to the fireplace at the Olema House, we wait at the hostess stand until the occupying party finishes their meal. This drives Dad and Lex crazy, but Noah and I get it. She wants what she wants.

And Jacob's the same way, to a degree.

Growing up, I was always trying to get Jacob to relax and *play* the game; he meanwhile was fixated on getting the rules straight. While we three siblings competed to see who could cross the entire lawn by somersault the fastest, Jacob would sit braiding the long curtain of fringe that hung from Grandma's jacket.

"He's an adult in a kid's body," Lex said, smirking. Sometimes, Lex looks like a ferret. Slowly, I stopped somersaulting and began siding with Jacob. We laughed whenever Lex said anything ignorant or cruel, and resolutely ignored him.

Jacob and I spent hours pretending we were ducks, quacking through a pair of inverted Pringles, like platypus bills. Spent hours folding and unfolding Mom's Chinese fan, amazed at how each time the hidden image reappeared. It would be an unpopular opinion among our classmates, but we agreed it was better than television.

His favorite thing, in elementary school, was sitting together where we couldn't be seen, in the alcove behind the jungle gym, and ordering his markers. This suited me fine. To the faraway backdrop of the other kids' voices, I talked and he shuffled his colored markers into rainbow-ordered slots. He could never decide whether the browns should go with the pinks, or at the end with the grays. Black presented a special conundrum; at the top or the bottom? Every once in a while, he broke in to ruminate on something particular the teacher had done that day that bothered him, like forgetting to hand out snacks exactly as the clock struck noon or saying the word *binder* when she meant *folder*. I commiserated with him, though I didn't relate.

Now that we're a little older, Jacob and I walk around the city and ride bikes by Grizzly Peak. We leave the house with Dad and Lex—they ride in front and we in the back. Lex is Dad's favorite, which is okay because I'm my aunt's favorite. Every Christmas, a giant package would appear under the tree, addressed to me and me alone, always a new addition to my menagerie of jungle animals. For years, I was convinced they were life-sized. Turned out your average giraffe is taller than what, to me, had been a towering four feet tall.

I do worry about Noah. He does interpretive dance, threading his hands through his legs and making them into swan shapes, balancing a bowling pin on his nose like a circus seal. We're really proud of him. But, so far, no one relates to him very closely, not even Grandma.

Noah doesn't come cycling with us. All four of us unload our bikes together and then we break into our two groups. Dad and Lex take off on a route up El Toyonal through Wildcat Canyon to the top of Vollmer, cycling a hundred miles in one day. It's hilly and sometimes Dad has to put his hand on Lex's lower back, walk his own bike, and push him up the hill. Jacob and I prefer to take it slow, sticking to the Sourgrass Path, flying through the muddy trails and the tall grass, stopping for ice cream at the Station Burger.

Mom and Dad have their own thing going on. They have each

other's photo saved as their lock screens. They can never see how they're influencing each other's opinions. They come back from the symphony or a performance having both either loved or loathed it. They're so in sync that they even still have sex, we think, which is patently gross. Even if I guess it's better than Maya's parents, who sleep in separate bedrooms but stay together for the combined income.

Mom and Dad even work together. When I was a kid, Mom's career drifted. She had a fabric interiors store. She used to strap me to her chest and go every day to the shop. Her shop smelled of fresh linen and Styrofoam peanuts. No soggy diaper smells. No mother to drive her crazy. No husband to manage. Only seating cards and bamboo cutlery and guest-room soaps, tucked into boxes made of a fancy green stone with lots of curlicues. Malachite, she said. Picturesque things, half-unpacked on display stands with lockable wheels. She fed me between clients as she looked over a dossier of textile samples or a deck of PDFs, her logo stamped proudly on the front page. As I got older, I loved looking over the Pantones with Mom. She showed me all the nuances. "This pink has yellow in it," she'd explain.

"Yellow?"

"Undertones," Mom said, holding up the sample. "As opposed to gray. If you kind of squint?"

Mom had taken four years to open her little shop. She had wanted everything to be flawless and it dogged her that it wasn't. "It's not perfect," she'd said softly.

"But it's open," Dad said.

"But it could be better."

"But it exists."

My aunt, who's not my real aunt, was amazed at Mom's resourcefulness, how she could pull something from nothing.

But it turned out people didn't want exquisite little objects. Despite all Mom's precious selection of ornaments, the thing that ended up selling was altogether practical. The drapery fabric she'd designed and had produced was always flattening out, so she invented a provisional four-prong pinch pleat hook that would keep the pleats crisply in place. Every client who came in went, "Ooh, can I get one of those?" They weren't for sale, Mom said. But Dad said, Let's make a website. After all, Dad makes money by selling lucrative ideas. And Mom and Dad's hooks have supported the family.

Because it's a short-haul flight, there are no movies offered. I downloaded three episodes of *Ms. Marvel* onto my phone, but don't feel like watching.

I hope Grandma didn't torture Jacob while I was away this trip. Since she got married, she's happy, but she's still Grandma.

Jacob and I are no strangers to love. We both have crushes, which we shared with each other by counting down 3, 2, 1 and blurting out the names at the same time. Of course, we already knew exactly who they were. No surprises there. Neither of us are very slick operators. Still, it was fun to say the names out in the open, laying claim to the person. "Zach Streeter," I said. It felt a little like actually having him.

Once, my ex-friend Maya said Jacob was cute. I closed like an anemone and prayed it would never be mentioned again. I wasn't ready to share my best friend.

Every once in a while, I have to remind myself, *this is my mom's brother.*

Mom got pregnant with me and, six months later, Grandma shocked everyone by deciding to adopt a baby. Supposedly, she just showed up for her interview at the Alameda County Social Services Agency office, thinking she could walk out that day with a kid.

Actually, it was very difficult for someone like her to adopt, but she was fast-tracked after having agreed to foster Jacob first. The foster period was, apparently, a strange time, with no one knowing whether Jacob was Grandma's new son or just a much-loved guest. Jacob's was what was called a closed adoption; still, I know he and Grandma sometimes wonder if they're going to receive a portentous call, out of the blue, from an unknown area code.

Everyone talks about Grandma's mean, scary baby nurse everyone was afraid of, whom she used because she was too afraid not to. If Grandma questioned her medical expertise, she vowed to revoke her care, kick her to the curb, when it was far too late to secure care with anyone else.

"You couldn't even look at her wrong," Mom had said, "she'd turn you to stone."

"When she entered the room," Grandma said, "the candles went out, the flame evaporating into a wisp of smoke. That's a fact."

I wonder how weird it was for Mom to be preparing for a baby alongside her mother. Mom loves Jacob, but sometimes I feel a reservation in her. Like loving him might cost her something she couldn't spare.

I can imagine Grandma, unaware in her special way: "Isn't it fun, to have a baby shower together, like sisters?" Knowing Mom, she wouldn't have wanted a sibling so late in life. She'd wanted a mother, like she'd been promised.

Grandma has never been what I'd call grandmotherly. We never call her Grandma to her face; she insists on being called Celine. We're close, in our way, but there are certain things I don't expect of her. I just accept that we're not going to paste old photos into albums and have tea parties and bake cinnamon-apple pies. I've always had the feeling that she doesn't 100 percent want to be a grandmother. It sometimes even feels like she adopted Jacob as a way of cementing her not-going-to-be-grandma status. She would keep on being *Mom* instead.

She doesn't really do birthdays. She does Christmas, sort of. She'll bring a gift for one or two of us, not seeming to realize that it's an all-or-nothing affair. But we are used to it. She once gave me an iPhone case illustrated with cartoons of dogs doing yoga. "Do you love it?" she asked. Then she threw a tantrum because we kids had twice the number of presents under the tree as she did.

For whatever reason, she does Valentine's Day, stocking up on and making the circuit with a stack of peach-shaped gummies. The peach shape is suspiciously suggestive—I wondered privately whether she'd picked them up from Cupid's Closet, the gay sex shop off Alcatraz, the windows of which I'd stealthily peered into because it's in the same strip mall as Pet Food Express.

Jacob manages to stay unruffled, no matter what his mother does.

Sometimes, it was all a lot for Mom, she having been the longest rider on the roller coaster of life with Grandma. It was Mom who always left gatherings with Grandma the most emotionally exhausted. When we realize she needs a break, we let her take us for raspberry tartines at Le Grainne Café, where her favorite lemon cake is baked with so much butter that it is wet to the touch.

"I just wanted things to be normal for you kids," she told us once, blowing off a gust of powdered sugar before taking a careful bite.

"Normal is overrated," we rushed to say.

Even Lex chimed in: "Look at Raheem Mostert. What if he had had a normal childhood? Then this city wouldn't have a Lombardi trophy."

Lex can be sweet but it's rare. He and I get along only sometimes. He and Mom are still recovering their relationship; when he got caught smoking pot under the school bleachers, Mom went nuclear. Which was unusual for her—she rarely ever loses her composure. But Mom thinks that if she plans for something, it's airtight, a pact with Fate, guaranteed to turn out that way.

So a shift unsettles her, even if it's just a little glitch like that. Everyone knows Lex was just trying to fit in and thought puffing a little weed would make him look cool. It's not like he's a troubled teen. Still, it's not always easy scaling the Everest of Mom's expectations. Mom enrolled him in special counseling. Dad takes him twice a week to what he calls scared-straight meetings, where they trade tales with kids with actual problems—kids who have stolen a car, or three, or committed arson. Dad cries a little when he talks about it. Mom says, "There but for the Grace of God go . . ." And Lex flies from the table to his room.

Well, he wanted attention and he got it, though more than he bargained for. It wasn't the worst way to gain a bit of social standing at school, a reputation for disobedience. There's a certain level of social stature afforded to kids who have gone off the rails.

Mom thinks the rest of us are too used to having her around, and that we take her for granted. We don't, but it's hard to describe what I mean by that. We know that she'll be there when we wake up. And that's reassuring. I doubt Mom and Jacob would say the same of Grandma. I wonder what that was like for them, growing up. I check my phone. There are only thirty minutes left of the flight. The attendants come around collecting trash. Mom will already be waiting outside the pickup area, early so as not to be late. That's what I mean, things like that, that you can just count on.

This weekend, I got away from them all, visiting my Aunt Alice in L.A. I've been doing the short-haul flight, up and down from the Oakland Airport, by myself for years. I'm fourteen now, the age that my mom and my aunt first met and became best friends. Aunt Alice and I kept in touch over the years. We had long phone calls while she was in her trailer waiting to be called to set to shoot her scenes. Every so often, she would ask to speak to Mom and say the magic words: "Send Jane down to L.A. We'll have a weekend."

This time, Mom told me we could think about it. I asked *when* we would think about it. Mom said we would see. "Are you sure you want to go?" she asked. "You could stay here, we could order Golden Wok, and have a *Gilmore Girls* marathon."

"Are you crazy?" I asked. Sit here at home with the people I see every day when I could go to *Hollywood*? Mom had to be joking.

Mom always capitulated, relenting in the face of my enthusiasm. *Success!* My aunt sent a text with a shining star and palm tree emojis. Mom did not use emojis—prepared, prepackaged sentiment. She didn't even have the keyboard downloaded onto her phone.

I spent weeks preparing my outfits, swapping out glittery socks for polka dots and making Jacob give his opinion until he was blue in the face. As compensation, I let him update my college spreadsheet. Though college was still four years away, Jacob was already planning. He had compiled a document with factors to consider in ranked columns: tuition price, admission rates, campus size. Mom was so happy, if a little green-eyed she hadn't thought to make one for me herself.

Jacob was the best. But he wasn't cool. My aunt was the coolest person I'd ever met. The girls at my school were narrow and small-minded, staging popularity contests, caring what everyone else thought, pining for so-and-so to give them the time of day. I was never going to be like those girls. Because I had a secret weapon. I had my *aunt*. She taught me how to be free.

This past Friday, I boarded a plane after school and my aunt picked me up in the afternoon. We hugged like there was no tomorrow, so that the whole line of cars at LAX honked and a policeman berated us before realizing who Alice was and requesting she sign the top page of his spiral notepad for his nephew. We got shrimp tacos on Venice Boardwalk from a shop I'd read about in *Tacopedia*, a guide to all the tacos of L.A. After that, we had to go home because my aunt had an early call time.

The black car picked us up at 5, and we dozed in the heated backseats. The show is the spinoff of an NBC hit, a live-action Candyland, adapted to appeal to adults, to a quote-unquote Millennial nostalgia. It is set in the 1950s, with a complicated game element, all sorts of bizarre sexiness, and a touch of what the studio called soft horror.

Initially, Aunt Alice had had a bit part as Snowcone Girl, someone who was supposed to be a simple, happy person. But she brought so much depth and weird complexity to the character that people were always on the edge of their seat that she was going to melt, from all her inner demons.

Her few lines became a meme sensation among fans of the show. The line, "Make it rainbow, please," followed her everywhere—people shouted it at her on the street. The network could not deny the audience response. They fell in love with Snowcone Girl, and before long, it was a series regular role. And then it was a spinoff, all her own. I felt they'd cast her just to get to hang out with her, because she was so much fun to spend time with. I would have. Grandma picked this bone ceaselessly, calling all of us Pudding Boy and Mississippi Mud Girl and calling Dad the Jolly Rancher.

And now, every time I visit, we get to go to set. I've been going for years. This was my fifth trip. The hair-and-makeup trailer door groans every time it opens. I like it, it feels friendly. I like sitting like a doll as they restore Alice's cotton-candy-colored wig.

I sat quietly while they washed Alice's hair and tried to be unobtrusive. But soon, the girls' laughing rubbed off. They gave me pads for my tired eyes and a moisturizer with instructions to rub it in while my face was still damp. And suddenly I was leaning over Alice's chair, Mom-style, directing the cosmetologist in their job. "She needs more pink around the edges." They even agreed.

They did me up. Because my real hair would not hold a curl, they revamped me with the backup wigs, hung on mannequin heads on the counter, reserved for the extras. I'd always wondered what I'd look like as a spun-sugar blonde. Once, Alice had even gotten me a one-line part, but Mom wouldn't let me do it because she thought it would screw up my childhood. I'm still mad. But not surprised. That's Mom.

When it was time to shoot, a PA knocked on the trailer door. We rode in a leather-seat SUV to the studio lot. It used to be a golf cart, but now there was her hair to worry about. They were shooting day for night on a Gothic castle set with a green screen backing. The scene was physical. It had a gargoyle monster (a seven-foot tall guy in a prosthetic suit) chasing Alice as she scales the stone wall before barreling down a moonlit slushee slide. Alice set me up with a pair of headphones at Video Village. She gave me a wink each time before taking off, plunging down the blow-up slide, blouse flapping. Cotton candy CGI clouds would float over the scene, softly at first, then menacingly; they'd add that in later in post.

I don't know why Alice never had kids—and I suppose she still could—but I suspect it has something to do with not wanting to replicate the mother-daughter relationships she's seen. That, and wanting to live life on her own terms, as an independent, career-minded woman. Whatever the reason, I was secretly glad, feeling that a third member would have interfered. If Alice was provided a plus-one, I was always her first-choice guest. When I was little, I used to believe that she was afraid to go places without me.

PAs buzzed around set. The script supervisor; the horse wrangler, managing the candy-dyed ponies. The animal welfare supervisor, a plump Canadian in very thick glasses, huffed and puffed after the ponies, sometimes lifting their tails to check their vitals. Network executives, the series director, a few straggly writers. Day players—life-sized lollipops—ambled among gingerbread plum trees. The script supervisor and I shared a single-serving bag of cashews from craft services.

Between takes, Alice conferred closely with the producers in hushed voices. She had quibbles. She had seen dailies and objected to her lighting, which had not been gelled as promised. And where was the low soft light to smooth out her neck? They either make her look perfect now, or she'll make them pay more for CGI effects later. She'd have to phone her agent. A deal was a deal. They'd been giving her the runaround since she had lost out on a juicy role to Joanna Herrera. Probably, Alice said, because Joanna had flashed her panties to the press at the Golden Globes. Not much between the ears, Alice said, with uncharacteristic unkindness.

I like to slip off the Candyland stage and stroll the sprawling studio lot. Enormous sets, suburban lanes and cowboy saloons, all counterfeit. All this Hollywood glitz and imitation was cool, but also gave me a creepy feeling. Aunt Alice said she felt the same way, but she was more taken with it than I was. It was weird to have this awareness outside of her. I felt she was childlike in her tolerance for Hollywood's illusions and insincerity.

Even though all this was cool, I always prefer the days when Alice and I hang out off-set. We act silly and crazy, wrapping up in feather boas and winging around, riding the Ferris wheel, running up and down the esplanade overlooking the PCH, squawking and pretending we're pterodactyls. Mom would be mortified. Or going to an opening at a fancy art gallery and standing stock-still in the empty display window, pretending to be an artwork. Or maybe, by doing it, we actually *were* one. Lots of people stopped and took our picture. Hanging out with my aunt felt like that, like making art. Making it as we went along together, just existing.

All day, every day, she did exactly what she wanted. She had no expectations of how other people should be. She was so accepting. With Mom, life was always a little tense. I felt pigeonholed, like I had to be myself and Lex himself and Noah himself. And that if we tried to step out of our pigeonholes, we'd enter some kind of no-man's-land, unaccounted for. But with Aunt Alice, I never worried about contradicting myself. I felt like I had lots of selves who could all comfortably coexist.

Which is why it was strange that Alice and Grandma never got along. It seemed like they would. Instead, growing up, I had always sensed a bizarre, crackling energy between Aunt Alice and Grandma. They didn't spar like Mom and Grandma did. They were very polite, in a stilted way—then occasionally not. Grandma always became green-eyed when either Mom or I hung out with Aunt Alice. Once, I overheard her say to Mom, "I don't know what you all see in her."

And Mom replied, "Oh, *don't* you?" I wasn't sure how to read her tone.

Grandma would object to my visits down in L.A., as if believing that, somehow, my going to spend time with Alice would take something from her.

I needled Mom. "Does Grandma have an issue with Alice appropriating gay culture?" She had been accused of this, moderately, in the press—it had been mentioned—after her rainbow-dyed Snow-cone Girl had an unfulfilled love affair with the female Tourmaline Noir, the villain of Season 3. But I didn't think this was a fair assessment. Once, when I went down there, Alice was dating a fellow actor, a man. And the next time it was another fellow actor, only this time it was a woman.

"Yeah," Mom said, "there's that."

"That and? What's the rest?"

"That's it."

It *wasn't* it.

I even started to wonder if, somehow, Aunt Alice was my real mother. That would explain Mom's sensitivity to our bonding! But I ruled this out when I remembered that Lex, Noah, and I are carbon copies of one another, with Mom's ski-slope nose.

It was last year that I finally confronted Alice. I was in L.A., celebrating my thirteenth birthday, and we were lying together under a yellow umbrella, in twin deck chairs at her private beach club. I asked point-blank why Grandma seemed to dislike her. It was awkward to know how to word it, but somehow I got it out. "I asked Mom, but she gave me the runaround."

Alice's eyes were closed; she was lying back in her chair, magazine folded over her taut belly. She didn't sit up, didn't move a muscle. I wondered if she hadn't heard me, and was a little relieved. Maybe she was asleep. But she finally spoke, sounding uncomfortable. "It's complicated, but I crossed a boundary once with your mother, and I guess your grandmother is protective of her."

"Was it a fight?"

"Yes. Sort of. Not exactly." Without opening her eyes, Alice closed the magazine and dropped it into the sand at her side. I waved away an advancing cabana server, coming to see if we required refills on our banana smoothies. "It was a very complicated situation, and there were misunderstandings, but we got over it. Hard to imagine, but somehow it doesn't really matter much anymore."

This was like fertilizer in my mind. Crossed a boundary? Complicated misunderstandings? I turned this over and over. I flew home to Mom having developed a theory, one that felt it would burn a hole in me. I introduced it at breakfast.

"Mom, did Alice break your heart? Does Grandma dislike Alice because she tried to steal Dad from you?"

Mom smiled. "Where did you get that idea?"

A pile of heirloom tomatoes sat on the counter like pincushions, chunky and crabby-looking.

I told Mom what Aunt Alice had said. Or tried to, but it was just such a jumble.

The smile dropped from Mom's face. "Honey, I don't want you thinking that about Dad. Your dad is the most steadfast person I've ever known." She breathed a huge sigh and sat down. And that was when she decided to confide in me.

"So, I'm going to tell you something, and it's a little strange. You're just going to have to try to take it in. Your Aunt Alice, my best friend, had an affair, a love affair, with your grandmother."

Beneath me, the plane has a sudden jolt now, as it catches cross-wind.

I could barely look at Mom, after she said this. An affair? Grandma and *Alice*? None of it made any sense. I leaned forward, totally confused. "Oh my god." I didn't know what else to say. I looked at Mom, staring down at her lap.

It was bad enough to think of her and Dad. This was *Grandma*. I calmed down a little after realizing that I was picturing her the way she looked today. She hadn't been the age she was now. She was younger. But, *still*, it was my granny. And with Aunt Alice? It wasn't age or gender that bothered me. It was the familiarity of it all that was revolting.

"How did that happen?"

"I don't know exactly," Mom said. "I wasn't there."

"Was it at Grandma's house?"

"Some of it was."

"Were you *okay* with that?"

"It was weird for me."

"Did they ask first?"

"No." Mom said this so quietly that I knew the truth.

"They hurt you." I shook my head like it could shake loose the information. "I can't believe they did that!"

"Yeah," Mom said. "It was kind of hard to believe."

It was so weird to imagine. Still, the peacemaker in me was thinking, People do fucked-up things, right? Was it such a big deal? You still love each other, right? But another part of me saw how it was a major deal. Even unforgiveable. *Granny stole Mom's best friend.* Her best friend, Aunt Alice, had betrayed her in a terrible way. I'd hate if it happened to me.

"Probably not a good idea to share this with Lex and Noah," Mom cautioned. "They're a little young to grasp it."

I called Jacob, relating everything I knew. Breathless by the time I was finished, I waited for his reply.

"Yeah," he said, on the other end of the line, sounding strangely composed.

"What do you mean, *yeah*?"

"Honestly?" Jacob said, sounding a little tired. "I've known that for years."

"Oh my god. You were keeping a secret from me?"

"Your mom said she'd kill us if we ever told you."

I'd be angry with Mom later. In the meantime, something else had occurred to me. "And the affair took place the year before I was born. Which means that within six months afterwards—Mom decided to have me. She must have wanted to nest, to make her own new family. Do you think that, without the affair, I wouldn't exist?"

Jacob considered this. "Yeah, they might have waited to have a kid, and that would be some other sperm and some other egg, and you'd be someone else."

"Freaky."

"It is."

We sat in silence, then Jacob thought of something. "And what about me? Maybe *I'm* only in this family because Celine is competitive." Maybe it *wasn't* so generous, what Grandma did, adopting

Jacob. Maybe the adoption was just a screw-you to mom. Jacob's and my childhood days, rainbow-ordering markers, digging crystals out of concrete as a get-rich-quick scheme, suddenly seemed very far away.

"We're rebounds," I said, bewildered.

And, in my bewilderment, at the time, I began rethinking Mom and Aunt Alice. They had different colors now. I had always thought Mom was emotionally stingy, or something, and unforgiving. And Alice always seemed better, like a more openhearted person. Instead, I'd found out Mom forgave someone who had betrayed her. Alice, Miss Caring-Caring, wasn't so caring when she didn't care about stabbing Mom in the back. Grandma, meanwhile, had always been an immovable object. Her involvement didn't even surprise me.

Alice thought I was a silly kid, I realized, who couldn't handle the truth. I felt deeply misled. They hadn't trusted me with such an integral piece to our shared story.

I stopped taking Alice's calls last year after I learned the truth, refusing to visit her in L.A. for months, until one day—the first Friday of the month, which meant family dinner—I came home from school and found Aunt Alice and Mom sitting together in the kitchen. Mom was seated and Alice was leaning against the counter, both in sock feet. I don't know what gave me this sense, but I felt they'd been talking a long time. They both had glasses of wine. Mom had not turned on the lights, even though the afternoon was already darkening. Seeing Alice was like seeing a ghost. I had been giving Alice the cold shoulder since the news, and I was nowhere near ready to see her. I wanted to keep avoiding her for a bit longer. I felt this act of resistance was the least I could offer Mom.

But it was such an unusual scene that I couldn't help asking, "Where are Lex and Noah?" My brothers were usually camped out in the kitchen, feet on the table, with their homework spread out, pages buried beneath piles of snacks.

"Lex had a soccer game," Mom said.

They greeted me warmly, then Alice held my eyes. "I need to talk to you," she said. Outside, the wintry sky was muddy silver, the color of expended steel wool. Who did she think she was?

"I have a lot of homework," I stammered. "That paper . . ."

Mom changed tone, without warning. "Look, can you please sit down?"

Something in her voice let me know declining was not an option. I edged closer to the table but did not sit. It was weird; as soon as I did sit, Mom jumped up, moved to the sink, and began loading all Lex's and Noah's abandoned dishes into the dishwasher. I wondered if she actually wanted to have this conversation or not.

Alice coughed and Mom turned off the sink. She looked at me, then away. "That was pretty heavy stuff for you to hear."

"It was hard going through it," Alice said, "and it must be just as hard for you to hear it."

"I don't understand," I said, looking at the two of them, hunting for the flaw in the pattern. "You're sitting here together like everything is fine. Don't you think that was wrong?"

They looked at each other and sighed.

"It was a mistake."

"An error of judgment."

"What does *wrong* really mean?"

"Have you ever done something you suspected would hurt someone you loved, and done it anyway?"

I was angry with Alice for accepting Mom's kindness, her hospitality, her special-occasion chardonnay.

"Nothing like that." I scooted my chair closer to the table, away from Alice, closer to Mom. "Grandma told Jacob you didn't care because you were with Dad." Then again, I thought to myself, Grandma is not the most credible witness.

Mom was quiet a while, then laughed softly. "You know, that's actually true, up to a point."

I stared into the pantry, organized by Mom to perfection. The pasta shelf, the canned goods. The dried legumes. I felt so sad for her, trying to control everything in her world.

"Some level of my detachment was defensive, me protecting myself," Mom went on, "but I was also sheltered from the blow, by being in my own loving union. And over time, I began to see how I had a tiny hand in it."

"No, you didn't, but I was dying from the guilt," Alice replied.

"Perrier," Mom said, getting up and clinking down three bottles. As if that was the decisive need of the moment.

"How would you have a hand in it, Mom?" I asked.

Mom told me how she had sent Grandma to the play, skipping Alice's performance, so obsessed with her relationship with Dad that she cut off her best friend for months.

It just wasn't enough to add up. I felt there were pieces missing, parts to the story I still wasn't being told.

"But it all kind of turned out really well," Alice said. "We got our friendship back. And you know, all that shit-talking you did about me? About my lack of ambition?" Mom listened with raised eyebrows. "It totally motivated me to show you."

We sat silent a moment. Mom had not closed the windows over the sink, opened earlier, and a gust of wind blew in a few leaves from the broadleaf-poplar. We waited for Mom to get up to sweep them away, but she didn't. We were sitting in the atmosphere of all that had been said, when the front door burst open, with a trio of male voices. "Hell-o!"

"Anybody home?"

"We brought back lasagna."

I could hear Lex shedding his soccer gear, Velcro knee guards, and Noah pounding up the stairs to his room to check on his hermit crab. All this seemed to bring Mom back to some level of reality, because she checked the time. "My god, it's already seven-fifteen. *Where* is my mother? She probably hasn't even left the house."

Outside, Celine was trying to park. Sadie's clunker was obstructing the short driveway. Her hideous, oversized family car was unapologetically, even tauntingly, blocking Celine's way in. Did she and Cormac need *three* gas-guzzlers? And what was this additional car Celine didn't recognize, a rental, Enterprise agency frame encircling the license plate? Must belong to a neighbor.

Celine was late. On the way, she had had to stop briefly at Moe's Books for a colleague's chapbook launch. The poet was an online phenomenon, hired for their follower count, and it was the best-attended poetry reading since Homer recited in the Agora. Encouraged by the supportive crowd, the poet read out half of the book's contents. A relief: Celine heard enough that she'd not have to buy it. She had been unable to extricate herself—it would be considered rude. Of course, she'd not have minded that. It was that she literally could not shoulder her way through the dense crowd to the exit. Sadie would not give this fair justification any credence; she'd assume Celine hadn't tried.

Celine leaned on her horn with the heel of her palm, but no one came. Sadie must have been busy, occupied inside her dream home with her three kids. Celine could not believe this was her daughter's life. She hated this conventional, conformist suburban house, sitcom-perfect, with its trim garden, the basketball hoop. And here *she* was, Granny, G-rated, arriving for their monthly *family night.*

"Goddamnit," she said to Jacob, who, in her umbrage, she'd almost forgotten was beside her in the front seat. "I can't fucking park."

"Deep breaths," Jacob told her. Good kid. He could be useful.

The street was jammed with cars, other suburban dream chasers. There was a spot just across that Celine could maybe just squeeze into. Feeling terribly irritable now, she reversed, avoiding that ghastly fence Sadie had installed a few years ago, like a Stepford wife.

Celine dreaded these monthly dinners. She couldn't say why they grated on her exactly—after all (though Sadie had never said as much; she wouldn't), Celine understood she was the guest of honor—except that they never went the way she hoped they would, the way they *could* have gone. She was always happy to see her daughter, but also felt they were not really connecting.

"She's added a new fence," Jacob noticed.

"To keep out the wildlife."

In the life Celine had given Sadie, and Jacob, there were no fences. Sadie raised her children under rocks, safeguarding them clueless, sheltering them from racoons and rodents, the prairie dogs that the execrable Republicans were claiming as a justification for hoarding assault weapons, and anything she deemed personally unpalatable.

Despite all that, Jane had turned out pretty well.

Still, one day, Celine was going to get ahold of her and wake her up to some stuff. Things like what had really happened to their hamster, Harry. And give her an introduction to real culture, unsanitized—she'd already exposed Jane to her first R-rated movie. She was proud of that. No mind that, leaving the theater, Jane had asked her, "What's a blow job?" After a beat of thought, Celine had said she would tell Jane later. And she would! There remained a few things she might *not* expose Jane to. Like the fact that the only reason she existed was as a knee-jerk reaction. Celine had to congratulate herself for never having done so thus far. Still, it was sad for someone to go around not knowing *why* they were. Maybe it was only fair she knew.

It had made Celine crazy, ferocious, when Sadie had gotten pregnant, so early, age twenty-four, just to spite her. Like some rabid sorority girl, grabbing the first chance to sacrifice her life on a platter. No doubt she'd done it to mock Celine, everything she'd stood for and raised Sadie to believe mattered.

Not ideal to think of that now, while trying to fit the fucking car into the spot. Celine, frazzled, with blood pressure raised, stomped on the gas, promptly dinging the CR-V in front of her. Then, reversing hastily in response, she dinged the Fiesta behind her. She waited, alert, but no noisy disturbance followed. Thank god neither seemed to have a car alarm. She glanced at the house to see if anyone was watching. Nope. Safe there, too. Celine turned to Jacob: "They should have left a bigger space."

When he didn't say anything, Celine looked over her shoulder.

The adoption had followed naturally. It was not at all for the reasons Sadie had so shabbily suggested. Celine had done it because she wanted to. Because she wanted a baby, suddenly, and because no one could stop her. She had been accused, by her own daughter, of going through with the adoption in response to Sadie's pregnancy. Outrageous. Crazy stuff. Unbelievable that she would say that. Sadie strutting around through the long months of her pregnancy, preening like a peacock, sleeping through the afternoons, acting like she was the center of the universe.

Life with an infant had been an adjustment. She found herself surveying the child daily to see if he was, would be, beautiful or ugly. One moment, Celine would die for the baby. The next moment Celine had felt so estranged that she had the thought that if the feather-headed baby died she'd have had trouble being appropriately sad, given that she did not yet know the person, nor even be convinced he *had* a personality yet to begin with. It would be like losing a much-loved houseplant.

Not to mention a few years back, when Celine had finally finished her book. After months of struggling to get beneath the thoughts, like turning over a rock to find all the live organisms beneath, she had found the entry point. The book was about raising a baby at the same time as her daughter. What this meant in terms of time, generational gaps, industry, intention, the animal body. And what had Sadie gone and said at that week's family dinner, when Celine had shared the glad tidings that she had finally tackled her white whale? Intimated, *in front of the child,* that Celine had adopted Jacob *for material.* The girl could turn any miracle into a mockery.

Beside her, Jacob was timekeeping as usual. "Ready? The ice cream is melting."

Jacob was such a good kid. After everyone had bet against him. The thought made Celine sorry—then a little proud, feeling like Aphrodite looking down at the chessboard of life. She had made something good. She had made a lot of things good.

And he was not wrong. The ice cream was melting, the pint container beginning to sag as sticky rivulets ran down the seams. "Pick it up," Celine said. Jacob obliged, letting the ice cream pool in his hands. Celine reached across him and cracked open his door. "Go on in. See you in there."

Jacob gave her a pointed look.

"I'm right behind you! Just need a second to decompress."

Obediently, Jacob opened the car door and lolloped so the kid wasn't Baryshnikov—toward the porch steps with a bag of ice cream in each hand. He looked like a puppy. Her pup. But he couldn't cross into the house, not yet, the path impeded by the new teak gate. Celine watched as the front door was flung open: Jane. Who could have foreseen it, the two of them? Celine did not follow, yet, as if lingering in the car a few moments longer would sustain her on the safe side of a precarious force field. Jane admitted Jacob with a quick hug, then scanned, past him, for Celine. All right. Celine turned off the ignition. Time to go inside. Despite everything, Celine always turned up for these dinners, yet another of Sadie's fancies. Late, maybe, but even if Celine hated these evenings—the rush, the pretense, everyone crowded into a room, the ice cream always melted into an unappetizing splotch of wet paint, the flavors marbled together incomprehensibly, so that it was impossible to tell chocolate from vanilla—she never missed one.

ACKNOWLEDGMENTS

My deepest thanks to Ellen Levine and Martha Wydysh. This is the story of three women and ours is one, too. Thank you for being the engine that powered this novel into being. I am most grateful to my brilliant editor, Olivia Taylor Smith, who steered and sculpted with generosity and radiance across calls, houses, and countries. It was a joy.

I'd like to thank the team at Simon & Schuster, especially Brittany Adames, John McGee, Maggie Southard Gladstone, and Hannah Bishop, for their extraordinary support. My thanks and admiration to Chris Heiser at the great Unnamed Press, which raises the bar of literature and letters. To the Virginia Center for Creative Arts, the Kimmel Harding Nelson Center for the Arts, the Millay Colony, and Caryn Mandabach for their generosity and support. My teachers, Mary Gordon, Anne Lake Prescott, Julia Glass, Miriam Gershow, Cai Emmons, David Bradley, Jason Brown, Ehud Havazelet, for their inspiration and insight. To Audrey Wollen, for the iconic *No dads, no boyfriends*. To my dear colleagues, for a decade, at *A Public Space*: Brigid Hughes, Brett Fletcher-Lauer, Yiyun Li, Elizabeth Gaffney, Bob Sullivan, Laura Prescott, Sidik Fofana.

I am very grateful for my early readers. Megan Cummins,

Samantha Kassay, Aaron Fai, Maria Thomas, Constance Hoag, Georgie Nichols, Topper Lilien, Alex Bower, Stefan Merrill Block, Libby Flores, Ira Silverberg, Catherine Hardwicke. For Willa, Lara, Molly, Zondie, Katie, Erin, Cassie, Chloë, Laurie. For my mother. For the Andes community, of which I'm lucky to be a part.

For Nicolas Party, my love and my foundation. And for Swan, who is my home.

ABOUT THE AUTHOR

Sarah Blakley-Cartwright is the author of *Red Riding Hood* (Little, Brown Books for Young Readers), a *New York Times* #1 bestseller that was published worldwide in thirty-eight editions and fifteen languages. She is the editor of Hauser & Wirth's The Artist's Library for *Ursula* magazine. She is publishing director of the *Chicago Review of Books*, and associate editor of *A Public Space*.